S*avage* RUN

**Center Point
Large Print**

ॐ श्री गणेशाय नमः

C. J. Box

Savage
RUN

CENTER POINT PUBLISHING

THORNDIKE, MAINE

To Jack and Faye Box,
my parents

This Center Point Large Print edition
is published in the year 2003 by arrangement with
G. P. Putnam's Sons, a division of Penguin Putnam Inc.

The text of this Large Print edition is unabridged. In other
aspects, this book may vary from the original edition. Printed in
Thailand. Set in 16-point Times New Roman type by
Bill Coskrey and Gary Socquet.

ISBN 1-58547-249-2

Library of Congress Cataloging-in-Publication Data.

Box, C. J.
    Savage run / C.J. Box.--Center Point large print ed.
        p. cm.
    ISBN 1-58547-249-2 (lib. bdg. : alk. paper)
    1. Game wardens--Fiction. 2. Environmentalists--Fiction. 3. Conspiracies--Fiction.
4. Wyoming--Fiction. 5. Large type books. I. Title.

PS3552.O87658 S38 2003
813'.54--dc21

                                                                    2002067630

Acknowledgments

I would like to acknowledge the Wyoming Game and Fish Department for providing the opportunity to "ride along" and provide a glimpse into the day-to-day duties of a game warden. Specifically, thanks to Game Warden Mark Nelson, who is a credit to his profession.

Special thanks as well to Sergeant Mitch Maxwell of the Cheyenne Police Department, who assisted with expertise on ballistics, weaponry, and law enforcement procedure.

Much of the background for actual ecoterrorist groups came from Bruce Barcott's article "Stalking the Ecoterrorists: The Secret Life and Prying Times of Barry Clausen," which appeared in the October 2000 issue of *Outside*.

My huge thanks to design genius Don Hajicek, the creator of www.cjbox.net.

A wealth of appreciation for Martha Bushko, my editor extraordinaire; Ken Siman, publicist extraordinaire; and G. P. Putnam's Sons for its encouragement and support. And, of course, for Andy Whelchel, my agent and fishing partner.

A place called Saddlestring does exist, but it is a tiny post office located on a historic ranch, not a real Wyoming community. The fictional Saddlestring, Wyoming, is an amalgam of at least three different towns.

Part One

No compromise in defense of Mother Earth.
EARTH FIRST!

1

TARGHEE NATIONAL FOREST, IDAHO
June 10

ON THE THIRD DAY OF THEIR HONEYMOON, infamous environmental activist Stewie Woods and his new bride, Annabel Bellotti, were spiking trees in the forest when a cow exploded and blew them up. Until then, their marriage had been happy.

They met by chance. Stewie Woods had been busy pouring bag after bag of sugar and sand into the gasoline tanks of a fleet of pickups in a newly graded parking lot that belonged to a natural gas exploration crew. The crew had left for the afternoon for the bars and hotel rooms of nearby Henry's Fork. One of the crew had returned unexpectedly and caught Stewie as he was ripping the top off a bag of sugar with his teeth. The crew member pulled a 9mm semiautomatic from beneath the dashboard of his truck and fired several wild shots in Stewie's direction. Stewie dropped the bag and ran away, crashing through the timber like a bull elk.

Stewie had outrun and outjuked the man with the pistol when he literally tripped over Annabel as she sunbathed nude on the grass in an orange pool of late afternoon sun, who was unaware of his approach because she was lis-

6

tening to Melissa Etheridge on her Walkman. She looked good, he thought, strawberry blonde hair with a two-day Rocky Mountain fire-engine tan (two hours in the sun at 8,000 feet created a sunburn like a whole day at the beach), small ripe breasts, and a trimmed vector of pubic hair.

He had gathered her up and pulled her along through the timber, where they hid together in a dry spring wash until the man with the pistol gave up and went home. She had giggled while he held her—*This was real adventure,* she said—and he had used the opportunity to run his hands tentatively over her naked shoulders and hips and had found out, happily, that she did not object. They made their way back to where she had been sunbathing and, while she dressed, they introduced themselves.

She told him she liked the idea of meeting a famous environmental outlaw in the woods while she was naked, and he appreciated that. She said she had seen his picture before, maybe in *Outside* magazine, and admired his looks—tall and rawboned, with round rimless glasses, a short-cropped full beard, wearing his famous red bandana on his head.

Her story was that she had been camping alone in a dome tent, taking a few days off from a freewheeling cross-continent trip that had begun with her divorce from an anal-retentive investment banker named Nathan in her hometown of Pawtucket, Rhode Island. She was bound, eventually, for Seattle.

"I'm falling in love with your mind," he lied.

"Already?" she asked.

He encouraged her to travel with him, and they took her vehicle since the lone crew member had disabled Stewie's

Subaru with three bullets into the engine block. Stewie was astonished by his good fortune. Every time he looked over at her and she smiled back, he was poleaxed with exuberance.

Keeping to dirt roads, they crossed into Montana. The next afternoon, in the backseat of her SUV during a thunderstorm that rocked the car and blew shroudlike sheets of rain through the mountain passes, he asked her to marry him. Given the circumstances and the supercharged atmosphere, she accepted. When the rain stopped, they drove to Ennis, Montana, and asked around about who could marry them, fast. Stewie did not want to take the chance of letting her get away. She kept saying she couldn't believe she was doing this. He couldn't believe she was doing this either, and he loved her even more for it.

At the Sportsman Inn in Ennis, Montana, which was bustling with fly fishermen bound for the trout-rich waters of the Madison River, the desk clerk gave them a name and they looked up Judge Ace Cooper (Ret.) in the telephone book.

JUDGE COOPER WAS A TIRED and rotund man who wore a stained white cowboy shirt and elk horn bolo tie with his collar open. He performed the wedding ceremony in a room adjacent to his living room that was bare except for a single filing cabinet, a desk and three chairs, and two framed photographs—one of the judge and President George H. W. Bush, who had once been up there fishing, and the other of the judge on a horse before the Cooper family lost their ranch in the 1980s.

The ceremony had taken eleven minutes, which was just

about average for Judge Cooper, although he had once per-formed it in eight minutes for two American Indians.

"Do you, Allan Stewart Woods, take thee Annabeth to be your lawful wedded wife?" Judge Cooper asked, reading from the marriage application form.

"Anna*bel*," Annabel corrected in her biting Rhode Island accent.

"I do," Stewie said. He was beside himself with pure joy.

Stewie twisted the ring off his finger and placed it on hers. It was unique; handmade gold mounted with sterling silver monkey wrenches. It was also three sizes too large. The Judge studied the ring.

"Monkey wrenches?" the Judge asked.

"It's symbolic," Stewie had said.

"I'm aware of the symbolism," the Judge said darkly, before finishing the passage.

Annabel and Stewie beamed at each other. Annabel said that this was, like, the *wildest* vacation ever. They were Mr. and Mrs. Outlaw Couple. He was now *her* famous outlaw, as yet untamed. She said her father would be scandalized, and her mother would have to wear dark glasses at New-port. Only her Aunt Tildie, the one with the wild streak who had corresponded with, but never met, a Texas serial killer until he died from lethal injection, would understand.

Stewie had to borrow a hundred dollars from her to pay the judge, and she signed over a traveler's check.

After the couple left in the SUV with Rhode Island plates, Judge Ace Cooper went to his lone filing cabinet and found the file with the information he needed. He pulled a single piece of paper out and read it as he dialed the telephone. While he waited for the right man to come to the telephone, he stared at the framed photo of himself on his former ranch. The ranch, north of Yellowstone Park, had been subdivided by a Bozeman real estate company into over thirty fifty-acre "ranchettes." Famous Hollywood celebrities, including the one whose early career photos he had recently seen in *Penthouse*, now lived there. Movies had been filmed there. There was even a crackhouse, but it was rumored that the owner wintered in L.A. The only cattle that existed were purely for visual effect, like land-scaping that moved and crapped and looked good when the sun threatened to drop below the mountains.

The man he was waiting for came to the telephone.

"Stewie Woods was here," he said. "The man himself. I recognized him right off, and his ID proved it." There was a pause as the man on the other end of the telephone asked Cooper something. "Yeah, I heard him say that just before they left. They're headed for the Bighorns in Wyoming. Somewhere near Saddlestring."

ANNABEL TOLD STEWIE that their honeymoon was quite unlike what she had imagined a honeymoon would be, and she contrasted it with her first one with Nathan. Nathan had been about sailing boats, champagne, and Barbados. Stewie was about spiking trees in stifling heat in a national forest in Wyoming. He even asked her to carry his pack.

Neither of them noticed the late-model black Ford pickup that trailed them up the mountain road and continued on when Stewie pulled over to park.

Deep into the forest, Annabel watched as Stewie removed his shirt and tied the sleeves around his waist. A heavy bag of nails hung from his tool belt and tinkled as he strode through the undergrowth. There was a sheen of sweat on his bare chest as he straddled a three-foot-thick Douglas fir and drove in spikes. He was obviously well practiced, and he got into a rhythm where he could bury the six-inch spikes into the soft wood with three blows from his sledgehammer, one tap to set the spike and two heavy blows to bury it beyond the nail head in the bark.

Stewie moved from tree to tree, but didn't spike all of them. He approached each tree using the same method: The first of the spikes went in at eye level. A quarter-turn around the trunk, he pounded in another a foot lower than the first. He continued pounding in spikes, spiraling them down the trunk nearly to the grass.

"Won't it hurt the trees?" Annabel asked, as she unloaded his pack and leaned it against a tree.

"Of course not," he said, moving as he spoke across the pine needle floor to another target. "I wouldn't be doing this if it hurt the trees. You've got a lot to learn about me, Annabel."

"Why do you put so many in?" she asked.

"Good question," he said, burying a spike deep in the tree as he spoke. "It used to be we could put in four right at knee level, at the compass points, where the trees are usually cut. But the lumber companies got wise to that and told their loggers to either go higher or lower. So now we fill up a four-foot radius."

"And what will happen if they try to cut it down?"

Stewie smiled, resting for a moment. "When a chainsaw blade hits a steel spike, the blade can snap and whip back. Busts the sawteeth. That can take an eye or a nose right off."

"That's horrible," she said, wincing, wondering what she

was getting into.

"I've never been responsible for any injuries," Stewie said quickly, looking hard at her. "The purpose isn't to hurt anyone. The purpose is to save trees. After we're finished here, I'll call the local ranger station and tell them what we've done—although I won't say exactly where or how many trees we spiked. It should be enough to keep them out of here for decades, and that's the point."

"Have you ever been caught?" she asked.

"Once," Stewie said, and his face clouded. "A forest ranger caught me by Jackson Hole. He marched me into downtown Jackson at gunpoint during tourist season. Half of the tourists in town cheered and the other half started chanting, 'Hang him high! Hang him high!' I was sent to the Wyoming State Penitentiary in Rawlins for seven months."

"Now that you mention it, I think I read about that," she mused.

"You probably did. The wire services picked it up. I was interviewed on 'Nightline' and '60 Minutes.' *Outside* magazine put me on the cover. Hayden Powell, who I've known since we were kids, wrote the cover story for them, and he coined the word 'ecoterrorist.' " This memory made Stewie feel bold. "There were reporters from all over the country at that trial," he said. "Even the *New York Times*. It was the first time most people had ever heard of One Globe, or knew I was the founder of it. After that, memberships started pouring in from all over the world."

Annabel nodded her head. *One Globe*. The ecological action group that used the logo of crossed monkey wrenches, in deference to late author Edward Abbey's *The*

12

Monkey Wrench Gang. She recalled that One Globe had once dropped a shroud over Mount Rushmore right before the president was about to give a speech there. It had been on the nightly news.

"Stewie," she said happily, "you are the real thing." Her eyes stayed on him as he drove in the spiral of spikes and moved to the next tree.

"When you are done with that tree, I want you," she said, her voice husky. "Right here and right now, my sweet sweaty . . . *husband.*"

Stewie turned and smiled at her. His face glistened and his muscles were bulging from swinging the sledge-hammer. She slid her T-shirt over her head and stood waiting for him, her lips parted and her legs tense.

STEWIE SLUNG HIS OWN PACK NOW and stopped spiking trees. Fat black thunderheads, pregnant with rain, nosed across the late-afternoon sky. They were hiking at a fast pace toward the peak, holding hands, with the hope of getting there and pitching camp before the rain started. Stewie said that after they hiked out of the forest tomorrow, they would get in the SUV and head southeast, toward the Bridger-Teton Forest.

When they walked into the herd of grazing cattle, Stewie felt a dark cloud of anger envelop him.

"Range maggots!" Stewie said, spitting. "If they're not letting the logging companies in to cut all the trees at taxpayer's expense, they're letting the local ranchers run their cows in here so they can eat all the grass and shit in all the streams."

"Can't we just go around them?" Annabel asked.

"It's not that, Annabel," he said patiently. "Of course we can go around them. It's just the principle of the thing. Cows don't belong in the trees in the Bighorn Mountains—they're fouling up what is left of the natural ecosystem. You have so much to *learn,* darling."

"I know," she said, determined.

"These ranchers out here run their cows on public land—our land—at the expense of not only us taxpayers but of the wildlife as well. They pay something like four dollars an acre when they should be paying ten times that, even though it would be best if they were completely gone."

"But we need meat, don't we?" she asked. "You're not a vegetarian, are you?"

"Did you forget that cheeseburger I had for lunch in Cameron?" he said. "No, I'm not a vegetarian, although sometimes I wish I had the will to be one."

"I tried it once and it made me lethargic," Annabel confessed.

"All these western cows produce only about five percent of the beef we eat in this whole country," Stewie said. "All the rest comes from down South, from Texas, Florida, and Louisiana, where there's plenty of grass and plenty of private land to graze them on."

Stewie picked up a pinecone, threw it accurately through the trees, and struck a black baldy heifer on the snout. The cow bellowed in protest then turned and lumbered away. The rest of the small herd, about a dozen head, followed it. They moved loudly, clumsily cracking branches and throwing up fist-sized pieces of black earth from their hooves.

"I wish I could chase them right back to the ranch they

belong on," Stewie said, watching. "Right up the ass of the rancher who has lease rights for this part of the Bighorns."

One cow had not moved. It stood broadside and looked at them.

"What's wrong with that cow?" Stewie asked.

"Shoo!" Annabel shouted. "Shoo!"

Stewie stifled a smile at his new wife's shooing and slid out of his pack. The temperature had dropped about twenty degrees in the last ten minutes and rain was inevitable. The sky had darkened and black roiling clouds enveloped the peak. The sudden low pressure had made the forest quieter, the sounds muffled and the smell of the cows stronger.

Stewie Woods walked straight toward the heifer, with Annabel several steps behind.

"Something's wrong with that cow," Stewie said, trying to figure out what about it seemed amiss.

When Stewie was close enough he saw everything at once: the cow trying to run with the others but straining at the end of a tight nylon line; the heifer's wild white eyes; the misshapen profile of something strapped on its back that was large and square and didn't belong; the thin reed of an antenna that quivered from the package on the heifer's back.

"Annabel!" Stewie yelled, turning to reach out to her— but she had walked around him and was now squarely between Stewie and the cow.

She absorbed the full, frontal blast when the heifer detonated, the explosion shattering the mountain stillness with the subtlety of a sledgehammer bludgeoning bone.

FOUR MILES AWAY, a fire lookout heard the guttural boom

and ran to the railing of the lookout tower with binoculars. Over a red-rimmed plume of smoke and dirt, he could see a Douglas fir launch into the air like a rocket, where it turned, hung suspended for a moment, then crashed into the forest below.

Shaking, he reached for his radio.

2

EIGHT MILES OUT OF SADDLESTRING, Wyoming, Game Warden Joe Pickett was watching his wife, Marybeth, work their new Tobiano paint horse, Toby, when the call came from the Twelve Sleep County Sheriff's office.

It was early evening, the time when the setting sun ballooned and softened, defining the deep velvet folds and piercing tree-greens of Wolf Mountain. The normally dull and pastel colors of the weathered barn and the red-rock canyon behind the house suddenly looked as if they had been repainted in rich acrylics. Toby, who was a big dark bay gelding swirled with brilliant white that ran over his haunches like thick paint that spilled upward, shone deep red in the evening light and looked especially striking. So did Marybeth, in Joe's opinion, in her worn Wranglers, sleeveless cotton shirt, her blonde hair in a ponytail. There was no wind, and the only sound was the rhythmic thumping of Toby's hooves in the round pen as Marybeth waved the whip and encouraged the gelding to shift from a trot into a slow lope.

The Game and Fish Department considered the Saddlestring District a "two-horse district," meaning that the department would provide feed and tack for two mounts to be used for patrolling. Toby was their second horse.

Joe stood with his boot on the bottom rail of the fence and his arms folded over the top, his chin nestled between his forearms. He was still wearing his red cotton Game and Fish uniform shirt with the pronghorn antelope patch on the sleeve and his sweat-stained gray Stetson. He could feel the pounding of the earth as Toby passed in front of him, making a circle. He watched Marybeth stay in position in the center of the pen, shuffling her feet so she stayed on Toby's back flank. She talked to the horse in a soothing voice, urging him to gallop—something he clearly didn't want to do.

Marybeth stepped closer to Toby and commanded him to run. Marybeth still had a slight limp from when she had been shot nearly two years before, but she was nimble and quick. Toby pinned his ears back and twitched his tail but finally broke into a full-fledged gallop, raising the dust in the pen, his mane and tail snapping behind him like a flag in a stiff wind. After several rotations, Marybeth called "Whoa!" and Toby hit the brakes, skidding to a quick stop where he stood breathing hard, his muscles swelled, his back shiny with sweat, smacking and licking his lips as if he were eating peanut butter. Marybeth approached him and patted him down, telling him what a good boy he was, and blowing gently into his nostrils to soothe him.

"He's a stubborn guy. A lazy guy," she told Joe over her shoulder as she continued to pat Toby down. "He did *not* want to lope fast. Did you notice how he pinned his ears back and threw his head around?"

Joe said yup.

"That's how he was telling me he was mad about it. When he does that it means he's either going to break out of the circle and do whatever he wants or he's going to do what I'm asking him to do. In this case he did what he was supposed to and went into the fast lope. He's finally learning that things will go a lot easier on him when he does what I ask him."

Joe smiled. "I know it works for me."

Marybeth crinkled her nose at Joe, then turned her attention back to Toby. "See how he licks his lips? That's a sign of obedience. He's conceding that I am the boss."

Joe fought the urge to theatrically lick his lips when she looked over at him.

"Why did you blow in his nose like that?" he asked.

"Horses in the herd do that to each other to show affection. It's another way they bond with each other." Marybeth paused. "I know it sounds hokey, but blowing in his nose is kind of like giving him a hug. A horse hug."

Joe was fascinated by what Marybeth was doing. He had been around horses most of his life, and by now he had taken his buckskin mare Lizzie over most of the mountains in the Twelve Sleep Range of the Bighorns. But what Marybeth was doing with Toby, what she was getting out of him, was a different kind of thing. Joe was duly impressed.

A shout behind him pulled Joe from his thoughts. He turned toward the sound, and saw ten-year-old Sheridan, five-year-old Lucy, and their eight-year-old foster daughter April stream through the backyard gate and across the field toward Joe and Marybeth. Sheridan held the cordless phone out in front of her like an Olympic torch, and the other two girls followed.

"Dad, it's for you," Sheridan yelled. "A man says it's

very important."

Joe and Marybeth exchanged looks and Joe took the telephone. It was County Sheriff O. R. "Bud" Barnum.

There had been a big explosion in the Bighorn National Forest, Barnum told Joe. A fire lookout had called it in, and reported that through his binoculars he could see fat dark forms littered on the ground throughout the trees. They suspected a "shitload" of animals were dead, which was why he was calling Joe. Dead game animals were Joe's concern. They assumed at this point that they were game animals, Barnum said, but they might be cows. A couple of local ranchers had grazing leases up there. Barnum asked if Joe could meet him at the Winchester exit off of the interstate in twenty minutes. That way, they could get to the scene before it was completely dark.

Joe handed the telephone back to Sheridan and looked over his shoulder at Marybeth.

"When will you be back?" she asked.

"Late," Joe told her. "There was an explosion in the mountains."

"You mean like a plane crash?"

"He didn't say that. The explosion was a few miles off of the Hazelton Road in the mountains, in elk country. Barnum thinks there may be some game animals down."

She looked at Joe for further explanation. He shrugged to indicate that was all he knew.

"I'll save you some dinner."

JOE MET THE SHERIFF and Deputy McLanahan at the exit to Winchester and followed them through the small town. The three-vehicle fleet—two county GMC Blazers and Joe's dark green Game and Fish pickup—entered and exited the tiny town within minutes. Even though it was still early in the evening, the only establishments open were two bars with identical red neon Coors signs in their windows and a convenience store. Winchester's lone public artwork, located on the front lawn of the branch bank, was an outsized and gruesome metal sculpture of a wounded grizzly bear straining at the end of a thick chain, its metal leg encased in a massive sawtoothed bear trap. Joe did not find the sculpture lovely, but it captured the mood, style, and inbred frontier culture of the area as well as anything else could have.

DEPUTY MCLANAHAN LED THE WAY through the timber in the direction where the explosion had been reported and Joe walked behind him alongside Sheriff Barnum. Joe and McLanahan had acknowledged each other with curt nods and said nothing. Their relationship had been rocky ever since McLanahan had sprayed an outfitter's camp with shotgun blasts two years before and Joe had received a wayward pellet under his eye. He still had a scar to show for it.

Barnum's hangdog face grimaced as he limped alongside Joe through the underbrush. He complained about his hip. He complained about the distance from the road to the crime scene. He complained about McLanahan, and said to Joe, sotto voce, that he should have fired the deputy years before and would have if he weren't his nephew. Joe suspected, however, that Barnum also kept McLanahan around because the deputy's quick-draw reputation had added—however untrue and unlikely—an air of toughness to the Sheriff's Department that didn't hurt at election time.

While they had been walking, the sun had dropped below the top of the mountains, the peaks now no more than craggy black silhouettes. The light dimmed in the forest, fusing treetops and branches that had been discernible just moments before into a shadowy muddle. Joe reached back on his belt to make sure he had his flashlight. As he did so, he let his arm brush his .357 Smith & Wesson revolver to confirm it was there. He didn't want Barnum to notice the movement since Barnum still chided Joe about the time he lost his gun to a poacher he was arresting.

There was an unnatural silence in the woods, with the exception of Barnum's grumbling. The absence of normal woodland sounds—the chattering of squirrels sending a warning up the line, the panicked scrambling of deer, the airy winged drumbeat of flushed Spruce grouse—confirmed that something big had happened here. Something so big it either cleared the wildlife out of the area or frightened them mute. Joe could feel that they were getting closer before he could see anything to confirm it. Whatever it was, it was just ahead.

McLanahan suddenly stopped and Joe heard the sharp intake of his breath.

"Holy shit," McLanahan whispered in awe. *"Holy shit."*

The still-smoking crater was fifteen yards across. It was three feet deep at its center. A half-dozen trees had been blown out of the ground, and their shallow rootpans were exposed like black outstretched hands. Eight or nine black baldy cattle were dead and still, strewn among the trunks of trees. The earth below the thick turf rim of the crater was dark and wet. Several large white roots, the size of leg bones, were pulled up from the ground by the explosion and now pointed at the sky. Cordite from the explosives, pine from broken branches, and upturned mulch had combined in the air to produce a sickeningly sweet and heavy smell.

What little daylight was left was quickly disappearing, and Joe clicked on his flashlight as they slowly circled the crater. Barnum and McLanahan followed suit, and the pools of light illuminated the twisted roots and lacy pale yellow undergrowth in the crater.

The rest of the herd, apparently unhurt, stood as silent shadows just beyond Joe's flashlight. He could see dark heavy shapes and hear the sound of chewing, and a pair of eyes reflected back blue as a cow raised its head to look at him. He approached the nearest cow and shined the flashlight on its haunch to see the brand. It was the letter V with a U underneath, divided by a single line—the Vee Bar U Ranch. These were Jim Finotta's cows.

McLanahan suddenly yelped in alarm, and Joe raised his flashlight to see the deputy in a wild, self-slapping panic, dancing away from the rim of the crater and ripping off his jacket as quickly as he could. He threw it violently to the ground in a heap and stood over it, staring.

"What in the hell is wrong with you?" Barnum barked, annoyed.

"Something landed on my shoulder. Something heavy and wet," McLanahan said, his face contorted. "I thought it was somebody's hand grabbing me. It scared me half to death."

McLanahan had dropped his flashlight, so from across the crater, Joe lowered his light and focused a tight beam on the deputy's jacket. McLanahan bent down into the light and gingerly unfolded the jacket, poised to jump back if whatever had fallen on him was still in his clothing. He threw back a fold and cursed. Joe couldn't see for sure what McLanahan was looking at, but he could make out that the object was dark and moist.

"What is it?" Barnum asked.

"It looks like . . . well . . . it looks like a *piece of meat.*" McLanahan looked up at Joe vacantly. The flashlight reflected in his eyes.

Slowly, Joe raised his flashlight, sweeping upward over McLanahan and then up the trunk of a lodgepole pine and into the branches. What Joe saw, he knew he would never forget.

Part of it was simply the initial shock. Part of it was seeing it in the harsh beam of a flashlight that lit up the texture, colors, and shapes and threw misshapen shadows about in unnatural and unsettling ways. He was not expecting—and could never have imagined—what it would look like to see the whole of a half-ton creature exploded into a thousand shards of different lengths, hanging down from branches like icicles, as high as his flashlight's beam would reach. Entrails looped across the branches like popcorn strings on a Christmas tree.

He gagged as he swept the flashlight from tree to tree on McLanahan's side of the crater. McLanahan retrieved his own flashlight and started sweeping the trees with the beam as well.

"I want to go home and take a shower," McLanahan said. "The trees are covered with this shit."

"How about you go back to the Blazer and get the crime-

23

scene tape and your camera instead," Barnum barked. Barnum's voice startled Joe. The sheriff had been so quiet that Joe had almost forgotten he was there. He looked over to where Barnum stood, several yards away, his flashlight pointed down near his feet. "There's a pair of big-ass hiking boots sitting right here. The laces are popped open."

The sheriff paused and looked at Joe. "I think the poor dumb son-of-a-bitch who was wearing these got blown right out of them."

THEY WEREN'T FINISHED TAPING OFF the area until well after ten. The clouds that had covered the mountains and kept the sky closed like a lid on a kettle had dissipated, leaving a gauze of brilliant blue-white stars, like a million pinpricks in a dark cloth. The moon was barely more than a thin slash in the sky, providing a scant amount of light to see, so McLanahan and Joe, their flashlights clamped under their arms, fumbled clumsily through and around trees with rolls of the plastic band reading CRIME SCENE CRIME SCENE CRIME SCENE while Barnum tried in vain to maintain radio contact. Joe wondered how much evidence they were crushing or disturbing as they wound the plastic through the timber. He mentioned this to Barnum, but Barnum was busy trying to contact the Sheriff's Department dispatcher via his radio and just waved him off.

"We started with an explosion called in by the fire lookout and now we've got us a full-fledged murder investigation," Barnum growled into his handheld between ferocious bouts of static. "We need state forensics as fast as they can get here and we'll need the coroner and a photographer out here at dawn. We can't see a goddamn thing."

"Come again?" the dispatcher asked through more static.

"She can't hear a word I'm saying," Barnum declared angrily.

"Why don't you wait and try her again from the radio in the Blazer?" McLanahan asked. Joe was thinking the same thing.

Barnum cursed and holstered his radio. "I need to take a leak and then let's get out of here." Barnum turned and limped away into the dark brush.

Joe tied off the tape on a tree trunk sticky with pine sap and took his flashlight from where he had been holding it steady under his arm. He shined it on his boots. They were slick with blood.

"Jesus Christ!" Barnum yelled from the darkness. "We've got a body. Or at least half of one. It's a girl. A woman, I mean."

"Which half?" McLanahan asked stupidly.

"Shut the fuck up," Barnum answered bluntly.

Joe didn't want to look. He had seen enough for one night. The fact that Barnum was coming toward him, limping as quickly as he could around the crime scene tape, didn't even register with Joe until Barnum stopped two feet in front of him and waved his finger in Joe's face. Joe couldn't tell if the sheriff was really angry or he was watching another display of Barnum's famous bluster. Either way, being this close reminded Joe of how formidable Barnum still was, even after twenty-six years as Twelve Sleep County sheriff.

"Why is it, Game Warden Pickett, that we rarely if ever have any trouble in my county," the sheriff's voice rising as he spoke, "but every goddamned time we find dead bodies strewn about you *seem to be standing there in the middle of them?*"

Joe was taken aback by Barnum's sudden outrage. It was now obvious to Joe that Barnum had been harboring resentment for quite some time because Joe had solved the outfitter murders. Joe could not come up with a good response. He felt his cheeks flush red in the dark.

"Sheriff, you called me to the scene, remember?"

Barnum sneered. "But I thought we had a bunch of dead elk."

Abruptly, Barnum turned and began to limp in the direction of his Blazer. McLanahan dutifully fell in behind him after giving Joe a look of superior satisfaction. Joe wondered just what it was he had done to arouse Barnum. He guessed it was exactly what Barnum had said: that he was *there* was enough. The new game warden, two years in the Saddlestring District, still wet behind the ears, who was now right square in the middle of another homicide. Or suicide. Or something.

There had been few violent deaths in Twelve Sleep County in the past two years aside from the outfitter murders. The only one of note was the rancher's wife who killed her husband by burying a hay hook into his skull, straight through his Stetson, pinning his hat to his head. In one version of the story that Joe had heard, the wife had gone home after the incident, mixed herself a pitcher of vodka martinis, and then called the sheriff to turn herself in. The pitcher was nearly empty when they arrived a short time later.

Before following the sheriff and his deputy, Joe stood quietly in the dark. He could hear the rest of the herd of cows grazing closer to the crater. In the distance, a squirrel chirred a message. The wildlife was cautiously moving back in. But there was something else.

A tremor quickly ran the length of his spine, and he felt the hairs prick on his forearms and neck. He looked straight up at the cold stars, then swept his eyes through the black pine branches. He knew that the fire lookout station was out of range. The black humps of the Bighorn Mountains did not show a single twinkling light of a cabin or a head-light. So why did he feel like someone or something was there with him, watching him?

DRIVING BACK ON THE INTERSTATE toward Saddlestring, Joe watched the little screen on his cell phone until it indicated he was finally receiving a signal. As he had guessed, Mary-beth was still awake and waiting to hear from him. He gave her a quick summary of what they had found.

She asked if the victim was someone local.

"We have no idea," Joe said. "At this point we don't even know if we've got one body or two. Or more."

She was silent for a long time.

"A *cow* exploded?" she finally asked, incredulous.

"That's what it looks like."

"So now we've got exploding *cows* to worry about?"

"Yup," Joe said, his voice gently teasing. "As if there weren't enough things to worry about with three little girls, now we need to keep them away from cows. And they're everywhere, those cows. In all of the fields and in all of the pastures. It's like there are ten thousand ticking time bombs all around us just waiting to explode."

She told him he was not very funny.

"It's been a bad night," he said. "Barnum asked me to notify the rancher who owns the cows tomorrow, which I'll do. He said that beyond that, he really doesn't need my help on the investigation. Hell, he was upset with me just because I was *there*. He's calling in the state crime boys tonight."

"Barnum just wants everything to go smoothly until he retires," Marybeth said. "He just wants to cruise on out of here without a ripple. And he especially doesn't want you to steal his thunder in the meantime."

"Maybe," Joe said, knowing she was probably right.

"Who's the rancher?" Marybeth asked.

"Jim Finotta. All the cattle had his Vee Bar U brand."

Marybeth paused. "Jim Finotta, the trial lawyer?" she asked warily. Joe knew her antennae were up.

"Yup."

"I haven't heard many good things about him," she said.

"Maybe so," Joe said. "But you know how people like to talk. I've never met the man."

It was almost as if Joe could hear Marybeth thinking. Then she abruptly changed the subject. "I saved some dinner for you," Marybeth said as the highway straightened out and Saddlestring came into view. The town at night looked like a handful of jewels scattered through a river valley.

"What did you have?" Joe asked.

Marybeth paused. "Hamburgers."

Joe forced a bitter smile. "I'll have to pass. I'll grab some chicken at the Burg-O-Pardner."

"I understand. Please hose yourself off in the front yard before you come in."

28

3

AN HOUR AFTER THE TAILLIGHTS of the law enforcement vehicles vanished down Hazelton Road to return to Saddlestring, two men emerged from the darkness of the forest on the other side of the mountain. In silence, they approached a sleek black pickup that was parked deep in the trees, away from the rough logging road they had used to access the area. Using mini-Mag lights with the beams choked down to dim, they repacked their equipment and electronics gear—optics, radios, the long-range transmitter, and unused packages of C-4 explosives—into brushed aluminum cases in the bed of the truck.

"Too bad about that woman," the Old Man said.

"Collateral damage," Charlie grunted.

"Except for her, everything worked perfectly."

Charlie snapped the fasteners shut on the optics case and looked up at the Old Man.

"Yup."

THE OLD MAN had been stunned by the force of the explosion, even from the distance from which they had observed it. In rapid succession, he saw the flash as Charlie toggled the transmitter, felt a tremor surge through the ground, and heard the detonation as the sound rolled across the mountains. The booming rumble washed over them several times as it echoed like distant thunder.

The Old Man had lowered his binoculars and whistled. Charlie, who had been watching through his spotting scope as Stewie Woods and the woman worked their way up the mountain, clucked his tongue.

THEY HAD TRACKED Stewie Woods across three states, and Stewie had never known they were there. Even when he took up with the woman and switched vehicles, they had stayed close. He had been sloppy, and more than a little preoccupied. When the judge in Ennis reported that they were headed to "somewhere near Saddlestring" in the Bighorn Mountains, Charlie had demonstrated to the Old Man, for the first time, why he was so good at what he did. When it came to hunting men, Charlie Tibbs was the best.

The national forest was huge, with dozens of access points. But Charlie anticipated exactly where Stewie Woods would end up, and they had beaten him there. From Charlie the Old Man learned that this part of the forest had been the subject of a dispute involving environmental groups, the U.S. Forest Service, and the local ranchers and loggers who had been leasing the area for years. The dispute had been used by the environmentalists as a test case, and they had thrown their best lawyers into it. They had wanted to end what they saw as sweetheart deals made to ranchers on public land. But, as Charlie explained to the Old Man, the ranchers and loggers won when the judge—once a rancher himself—ruled to continue the leases.

One Globe, Stewie Woods's organization, had been the most vocal in the dispute. Woods himself had been forcibly removed from the courtroom for acting out when the verdict was read. On the courthouse steps, in front of television cameras, Woods had proclaimed, "If we can't save the planet through the courts, we'll do it in the forests."

The tract that would lure Stewie Woods, Charlie guessed

correctly, was the one most recently opened to both logging and grazing. The best access to the parcel was from a trail-head near Hazelton Road. From there, Charlie had determined, Woods would hike toward the peak where the trees to be logged would soon be marked. On the way, Woods would undoubtedly run into the herd of cattle that had recently been moved into the high country. The Old Man wasn't sure what they would have done if Woods had skirted the herd of cows, especially with the tethered heifer that had been strapped with the explosives and the detonation receiver. But even if Woods had taken another route and evaded their trap, the Old Man had no doubt that Charlie would have quickly come up with another plan. The man was relentless.

As THEY OPENED THE DOORS of the pickup, the interior light came on. The Old Man looked at Charlie, and Charlie looked back. The harsh light emphasized their facial characteristics. They were both weathered, and aging. They shared a smile.

"Step one in winning back the west," the Old Man said.

Charlie drove while the Old Man stared through the windshield. Their tires ground on the gravel road.

When they hit the pavement, Charlie turned the pickup northwest. They were headed to Washington state.

4

MORNING SUNLIGHT POURED over the jagged horizon as Joe Pickett turned his pickup off of the state highway onto the Vee Bar U Ranch's gravel road, which led to Jim Finotta's house. Maxine, the Pickett's yellow Labrador, sat in the passenger seat looking alert, as if helping Joe to navigate the turns. Joe drove the truck beneath the ancient elk antler arches and wound through hundred-year-old cottonwoods. This was the first time Joe had ever had a reason to visit. He wished the reason for the call wasn't to tell Mr. Finotta that ten of his cattle had been found dead and at least one of them had been blown up.

Finotta's ranch, the Vee Bar U, was, by all standards, huge. Counting both deeded and leased land, it stretched from the highway all the way to the top of the distant Bighorn Mountains. The ranch held the second water right on the Twelve Sleep River, and leased more than forty thousand acres of spectacularly scenic and remote national forest land, including a geological wonder of a canyon known as Savage Run.

Joe had heard a couple of stories about how local lawyer Jim Finotta acquired the ranch, and he wasn't certain which one was true. One version was that Mac "Rowdy" McBride, a fourth generation McBride, was a notorious drinker and carouser and had simply run the ranch into the ground. McBride could still be found from noon on perched on his corner stool at the Stockman Bar, or the booth closest to the bar at the Rustic Tavern. Finotta, fresh off of a string of personal injury cases with multimillion-dollar settlements, had purchased the ranch at a time when cattle prices were low and Rowdy McBride was too. But there was another theory on how Finotta had come to own and control the Vee Bar U.

The other version, which Joe had had whispered to him by an inebriated fishing guide at the Stockman Bar, was much more sinister. According to the fishing guide, Finotta had represented Rowdy McBride in a dispute when environmentalists were trying to persuade the federal government to proclaim the rugged, spectacular, and remote Savage Run canyon as a national monument. McBride, of course, was against it. Finotta persuaded McBride to take his claim all the way to the U.S. Supreme Court, even though virtually all legal scholars who studied the case opined that he had no case, and Rowdy McBride had already lost on state and district levels. The Supreme Court refused to hear the case, which left McBride with hundreds of thousands of dollars in legal bills at a time when beef prices had plummeted to record lows.

Finotta settled for the ranch in payment, and the suspicion of the fishing guide and his friends was that obtaining the historic ranch was Finotta's plan all along—that Finotta had fueled McBride's anger at the Feds and confidently assured the rancher of an eventual win or settlement, knowing all along that it was virtually impossible. Once he had taken over the ranch, Finotta had used his personal political contacts (of which he had many) to stall the canyon's national monument designation, which was finally forgotten by a new administration.

Ranching to Finotta, according to the fishing guide, was a hobby and a means of dispensing power and influence in a state where ranchers occupied an exalted status. When moneyed entrepreneurs sought the ultimate cocktail-party aside, they now talked about their ranches in Wyoming, Montana, or Idaho.

Joe didn't know Finotta well, although they nodded at each other when they happened to see each other, usually at the courthouse or occasionally at the post office. Finotta was a man known for his personal and political connections and for not being humble about them. He was a personal friend of the governor and was listed among the largest in-state contributors to the U.S. senators and the lone congressman for Wyoming. He treated local law enforcement officials well, and had half and quarter beefs sent to their homes at Christmas. Sheriff Barnum often had morning coffee with Finotta, as did the county attorney and chief of police.

So when Jim Finotta decided to create a subdivision—officially renamed Elkhorn Ranches—he had no trouble financing it or having it approved by the county. Elkhorn Ranches was a topic of conversation among the local coffee drinkers in the morning and the beer drinkers at night—a land scheme involving three-acre lots on three hundred acres of Finotta's property nearest to the highway. The streets, curbs, gutters, and cul-de-sacs were already surveyed and poured in concrete. The sales effort was international. Three-hundred-and-fifty-thousand-dollar homes were being constructed on the prime lots, usually on the top of every hill. Only a few homes had been completed and purchased.

THE TREES PARTED, and the huge gabled stone house came into view, and so did a ranch hand on a four-wheel ATV who was racing up the road as if intent on having a head-on collision with Joe's pickup.

Joe braked to a stop and the ranch hand swung around the grill of the pickup and slammed on his brakes adjacent to Joe's door, a roll of dust following and settling over them both.

The ranch hand was wiry and dark with a pockmarked and deeply tanned face. He wore a T-shirt that said "I Know Jack Shit" and a feed store cap turned backward. He squinted against the roll of dust and the bright morning sun and rose in his seat with his fists on the handlebars until he could look Joe square in the eye.

"Name's Buster," the ranch hand said. "State your business." Only then did Joe notice the holster and sidearm that was tucked into Buster's jeans.

"I'm Joe Pickett. I'm here on business to see Mr. Finotta. I'm with the Wyoming Game and Fish Department."

"I can see that from your truck and your shirt," Buster said, raising himself a little more so he could see into the cab of Joe's truck. Maxine, always kind to strangers, lolled out her tongue and panted.

"What do you need to see Mr. Finotta about?"

Joe masked his irritation. No need to antagonize a hand. He said simply, "Ten dead cows."

This concerned the ranch hand. "Were they ours?"

"Yup," Joe said, and offered no more.

Buster was puzzled in thought for a moment. Then he told Joe to wait in his truck while he went to tell Mr. Finotta.

Joe winced at the racketing sound of the ATV as Buster revved it and spun around the back of Joe's pickup and on to the house. Disobeying Buster, Joe drove toward the house and parked against a hitching rack next to Finotta's black Suburban.

The house was impressive and daunting. It looked to be constructed at a time when ranchers thought of themselves as feudal lords of a wild new land, and built accordingly.

There were three sharp gables on the red slate roof and a two-story stone turret on the front corner. The building was constructed of massive rounded stones, probably from the bottom of the river, in the days when dredging didn't require a permit. Huge windows made up of hundreds of tiny panes looked out over the ranch yard and beyond to the mountains.

When Buster opened the front door, Joe half expected the hand to bow and say something like "Mr. Finotta will see you now." Instead, Buster nodded toward the interior of the house and told Joe to go inside. Which he did.

The foyer was decorated in pure mid-fifties ranch gothic. The chairs and couches were upholstered with dark Hereford red-and-white hides. The chandelier, suspended from the high ceiling by a thick logging chain, was a wagon wheel with 50-watt bulbs on each spoke. The dominating wall was covered with the brands of local ranches burned into the barnwood paneling, with tiny brass plaques under each brand naming the ranch.

Joe stopped here. He was taken aback by the fact that he had surveyed the room without taking notice of a small seated figure in the corner of it, shaded from the window by a bushy Asian evergreen tree.

"Can I get you something?" Her voice was scratchy and high. Now Joe could see her clearly. He was embarrassed by the fact that he had missed her when he entered because she was so still and he was so unobservant. She was bent and small and still, seated in a wheelchair. Her back was curved so that it thrust her head forward, chin out. She held her face at a forty-five degree angle, her eyes large but blank, her airy light-brown hair molded into a helmet shape by spray. One stunted arm lay along the armrest of her chair like a strand of rope and the other was curled on her lap out of view. He guessed her age as at least seventy, but it was hard to tell.

"I'm sorry I didn't see you there," Joe said, removing his hat. "Thanks for the offer but I'm fine."

"You thought I was a piece of furniture, didn't you?" she asked in a high voice.

Joe knew he flushed red. That's exactly what he was thinking.

"Don't deny it," she chided, letting out a bubble of laughter like a hiccup. "If I were a snake I could have bitten you."

Joe introduced himself. She said her name was Ginger. Joe had hoped for more than a name. He couldn't be sure whether Ginger was Jim Finotta's wife or mother. Or someone else. And he didn't know how to ask.

Jim Finotta, a small man, appeared in the foyer. Finotta wore casual pleated slacks and a short-sleeved polo shirt. Finotta was slight and dark; his full head of hair moussed back from his high forehead. His face was dour and pinched, foreshadowing the tendency of his mouth to curl downward into an expression that said "no." Finotta carried himself with an air of impatient self-importance.

His $800 ostrich-skin boots glided over the hardwood flooring, but he stopped at the opposite wall under what appeared to be an original Charles Russell painting and spoke without meeting Joe's eye. He nodded kindly to Ginger and asked her if she minded if he met with the "local game warden" for a minute in his office. Ginger hummed her assent, and Finotta smiled at her. With a nod of his head he indicated for Joe to follow him.

Finotta's office was a manly classic English den with floor-to-ceiling bookshelves filled primarily with legal volumes. A framed fox hunting print hung behind the massive mahogany desk and a green-shaded lamp provided most of the light. A massive bull elk head was mounted on the wall in the shadows above the door. Finotta walked briskly around the desk and sat in his chair, clasped his small hands together, and looked up expectantly at Joe. He did not offer Joe a seat.

"You run cattle in the Bighorns near Hazelton Road?" Joe asked, feeling awkward and out of place in Finotta's study.

"I run two thousand head practically the entire length of the Bighorns in both Twelve Sleep and Johnson County," Finotta answered crisply. "We also feed another eleven hundred on our pastures for the summer months. Now how can I help you?" Finotta made no attempt to hide the impatience that colored his voice.

"Well," Joe said his voice sounding weak even to himself, "there are at least ten of them dead. And there may be a human victim as well."

Finotta showed no reaction except to arch his eyebrows in a "tell me more" look. Joe quickly explained what they had found the evening before.

When he was done, Finotta spoke with a forced smile. "The cows are mine but we aren't missing any employees, so I can't help you there. As for the cattle, those are— were—first generation baldy heifers worth at least $1,200 each. So I guess someone owes me $12,000. Would that be the Wyoming Game and Fish Department?"

Finotta's question caught Joe by complete surprise. He hadn't known how Finotta would react to the news that ten of his cows exploded—anger, confusion maybe—but Joe would never have guessed he'd respond this way. The state did pay ranchers for damages to property and livestock if those losses were the result of wild game, such as elk herds eating haystacks meant for cattle or moose crashing through fences. But he could not see how the department would be liable for the loss of ten cows in a freak explosion.

As Joe stood there, trying to think of a way to explain this, Finotta was drumming his fingers on his desk. The sound both irritated and distracted Joe.

"Joe Pickett . . ." Finotta said, as if searching his mind for more information. "I've heard your name. Aren't you the same fellow who arrested the governor a couple of years ago for fishing without a license?"

Joe flushed red again.

"The same warden who had his gun taken off of him by a local outfitter and was suspended for it? The same game warden who shot my good friend Vern Dunnegan in the hip with a shotgun?"

Joe glared at Finotta but said nothing. He admitted to himself that he was not handling the situation well. He was off balance and defensive.

"I came here to tell you about your cows," Joe said, his voice cracking. "The sheriff asked me to come here because he was busy at the crime scene. This doesn't involve me or the department."

"Doesn't it?" Finotta asked facetiously, sitting back in his leather chair. "It seems to me that a case could be made that because of the policies of both the U.S. Forest Service and the Wyoming Game and Fish Department we have in our state an overabundance of game animals. And because of that overabundance, there is an exaggerated sense that the 'wild' and 'natural' creatures are being crowded out of their rightful forage by cattle. Therefore, environmentalists are targeting cattle and ranchers, and poachers are targeting wild game. Which creates a state of affairs where this kind of violence can happen.

"I think we could win that one before a jury of my peers," Finotta said, smiling. Finotta's peers would be local ranchers. This kind of jury stacking had happened before in the county. "And we would be talking about the loss of my cows plus legal expenses plus punitive damages." He let this sink in. "Or Game and Fish could save the taxpayers hundreds of thousands and simply pay the damage claim. That could happen very cleanly if the local warden made the argument in his report."

Joe was flummoxed, angry, and completely off his stride. Joe could see himself taking three quick steps and knocking the smirk off of Finotta's face. It would give him immediate satisfaction, but would also result in termination and, given Finotta's obvious penchant for going to court, prosecution.

It was obvious that Jim Finotta enjoyed this, Joe thought. Finotta reveled in humiliating people he considered below his station. He was good at it. He knew the tricks. Finotta compensated for Joe's advantage of youth by making him stand there foolishly. He addressed their height difference—Joe was at least six inches taller—by sitting behind his massive desk.

"Joe, I think you know who I am," Finotta said, now

40

charming. "I know how much the state pays its employees. Your family would probably appreciate a half a beef come Christmastime. We're talking about prime steaks, roasts, and hamburger. This is good beef that will never exceed seven percent fat. I'll need to add you to our gift list."

Rather than continue to look at Finotta in a growing rage, Joe focused on the reflection of the mounted elk head in the glass of the hunting print above the lawyer's head. As Joe stared at it, he realized that there was something about the elk mount that bothered him.

"Do you have any questions, Warden?" Finotta asked gently.

Joe nodded yes.

"That elk on your wall . . ." Joe asked, turning and looking at the impressive bull over his shoulder. The antler rack was thick and wide. It was a rare, exceedingly large bull. The kind of bull, and mount, that trophy hunters would pay $15,000 to $20,000 for a chance to get. "That's quite a prize, isn't it?"

Now Finotta was caught off guard. But he recovered very quickly. "Yes it is. He came off of my ranch, in fact."

"Seven points one side and nine on the other, that right?"

"Yes."

"You know, I think I'm familiar with this bull elk," Joe said, rubbing his chin. "I never saw it, but I heard of him. A guide I talked to about a year ago had scouted him out. He said he counted seven tines on one side and nine on the other. He said it was the biggest elk he had ever seen in his life."

Finotta studied Joe, clearly wondering where this was going.

"He had put the word out to some clients that this bull elk existed and would probably be the biggest one taken in the Bighorns in the last twenty years. That guide scouted that bull for an entire year. He knew where the bull grazed, where it slept, even where it drank water in the evening.

"Then that bull just went away," Joe said. "Broke that guide's heart. He reported it to me, and said maybe the big bull got poached since it was still four months until hunting season."

Finotta responded evenly. "Maybe it just died. Or maybe it moved. Wild animals will do that, you know." He paused. "Or maybe it exploded like ten of my cows."

Joe grabbed a hardback chair, slid it under the mount and stepped up before Finotta could stop him. He examined the head, then rubbed his hand along the antler. "There's still some velvet on these antlers," Joe declared.

Velvet is the soft feltlike layer that encases antlers of deer, moose, and elk as they grow back each year. Normally, the animals shed their antlers in winter and grow them back— usually larger—in the spring. By fall and hunting season, the velvet has been rubbed off completely and the antler takes on a hardened sheen and strength like polished bone. Joe had seen instances where patches of velvet remained on the antlers through October, but it was rare. Velvet on Finotta's elk might be suspicious but it was proof of nothing.

Joe stepped down. "When exactly did you shoot this elk?" he asked.

Finotta quickly stood up, slapping his palms down on the top of the desk. "Are you accusing me of *poaching?*"

Joe shrugged in innocence. "I'm just wondering when

and where you shot the elk."

Finotta took a deep intake of breath and his eyes became hard. "I got him during hunting season. Last fall. *On my ranch.*" He hissed the last words out.

"Okay," Joe agreed. "That being the case, I'm sure you won't mind me checking. We found a huge bull carcass up on the forestland last May with the head cut off. We took a DNA sample of the carcass and it's in my freezer. The poachers hadn't even taken any of the meat, which personally, to me, is a crime of the first order because it means a headhunter did it. I *hate* trophy hunters who just take the antlers and leave the rest. Not to mention that it's illegal as all hell."

The room was absolutely silent. Finotta glared at Joe under a bushy frown.

"So I would like your permission to take a small sample from this trophy."

"Forget it," Finotta cried, appearing offended. "I paid a lot of money for that mount in Jackson Hole. You don't have my permission to damage it."

Joe shrugged. "I won't damage anything. I'm just talking about a few shavings from the base of the horn, from the back side of it, where no one could ever even see it."

"You'll need a court order," Finotta said, back on firm footing. "And I don't think you can get that in Twelve Sleep County." What Finotta didn't say was what was well known—that Judge Hardy Pennock was one of Finotta's closest friends and had a financial interest in Elkhorn Ranches.

"You might have me there," Joe conceded. But Finotta was clearly still angry. Veins pulsed on his temples, although his eyes and expression remained serious and steady.

"This meeting is over," Finotta declared. "You should be aware that I plan to contact your immediate supervisor as well as the governor you once arrested."

Joe shrugged with resignation. That was to be expected. He knew something like this would likely happen if he mentioned the elk, but he hadn't been able to stop himself.

"Or," Finotta said, this kind of negotiating as natural to him as breathing, "you can consider making the case for damage reimbursement for my dead cattle."

Joe was being given one more chance. He knew that the governor was known to micromanage state agencies and also knew of state employees who had been drummed out of a job. He and Marybeth were still literally a paycheck away from poverty, and the house they lived in was state-owned. Joe had gained some political capital since he started out in the Twelve Sleep District following his run-in with Assistant Director Les Etbauer while he was investigating the murder of three local outfitters, but not enough for comfort. Grievance procedures were in place, of course, but the state bureaucracy had time-tested methods of making conditions so miserable that employees, even game wardens, eventually left on their own accord. Sometimes, game wardens who were out of favor were reassigned to areas that no one wanted, like Baggs or Lusk. These locations had become the Wyoming equivalent of the back-water, hellhole location that FBI agents were once sent—Butte, Montana.

"Let me get back to you on that," Joe heard himself say, and left the room.

Ginger had not moved from her place near the tree in the living room. Joe told her good-bye. She said again that if she was a snake that she could have bitten him.

HE LEFT VIA THE SUBDIVISION, angrily negotiating wide and empty paved roads, one time screeching his tires when he took a wrong turn into a cul-de-sac, shooting bitter passing looks at new foundations and huge fresh dirt piles, nearly decapitating a hydrant, and wondering what kind of people would choose to buy a three-acre lot and live in Elkhorn Ranches.

And wondering what he would say when he got back to Jim Finotta.

JOE PULLED OFF of the highway into a hilly BLM tract hazy with new spring grass. He found a familiar hill, parked on top of it, and for an hour watched three- and four-month-old pronghorn antelope with their herd. He knew that watching the wild herd would soothe him, calm him down, help him, he hoped, put things into perspective. Related biologically to goats, not antelope (despite their name), pronghorn were uniquely evolved to survive and prosper in the arid and mountainous Rocky Mountain west. Yearling pronghorns, often produced as twins, were amazing wild animals, and becoming Joe's favorites. Young pronghorns didn't have the soft features, big eyes, and the bumbling cuddliness of most baby animals. Within a few weeks of their birth, they became tiny versions of their parents, with perfectly proportional but miniature long legs, brown and white camouflage coloring, and the ability to accelerate from zero to sixty when they sensed danger, leaving only a rooster tail of dust.

He watched the antelope, but in his head he replayed his conversation with Jim Finotta. The conversation and the situation had gotten off track quickly and gone in directions Joe hadn't anticipated. He hadn't reacted well, either.

When he thought about the exchange, it wasn't so much what Finotta had said, or implied. It was what he *didn't* ask that unsettled Joe.

Joe had no experience with notifying a rancher that his cows had exploded, as ridiculous as that sounded when he thought about it. Nevertheless, it wasn't like notifying the next of kin about a highway accident, or even a hunter's wife about a terrible accident, which Joe had done and which resulted in several nights of lost sleep afterward. With Finotta, there had been no questions about possible human victims—how they came to die, no queries about whether the dead were local, or even the status of the investigation. Wouldn't a lawyer, litigious by trade, be at least somewhat interested in whether or not anyone could establish liability?

Something didn't sit right.

Joe's gaze slowly rose from the antelope in the sagebrush hills toward the blue-gray mountains that dominated the horizon. The Vee Bar U stretched as far as he could see, counting Forest Service leases. The ranch was one of the crown jewels of Twelve Sleep County, sweeping from the highway to up and over those mountains. And somewhere up there, practically inaccessible, was the place called Savage Run.

THE CANYON CALLED SAVAGE RUN cut a brutal slash through

46

the center of incredibly rugged and almost impenetrable Wyoming mountain wilderness. The Middle Fork of the Twelve Sleep River, which created the canyon over millions of years of relentless shaving and slicing, was now a trickle due to upstream irrigation. But the results—knife-sharp walls, a terrifying distance from the rim to the narrow canyon floor, virtually no breaks or cracks through the rocks to assure a crossing—was geologically stunning. The canyon was so steep and narrow that sunlight rarely shone on the stream. The canyon cut through eight different geological strata. While the rim was twenty-first century Wyoming in drought, the floor was pre-Jurassic rain forest. The last time the floor was exposed, *Tyrannosaurus rex* peered through gaping eyes at prey.

The legend of Savage Run came from the story of a band of a hundred Cheyenne Indians—mainly the elderly, women, and children—who were camped near the eastern rim of the canyon while their men were on an extended buffalo hunt in the Powder River country. The band was unaware of the Pawnee warriors who had been following them for days, and unaware that the Pawnees stayed hidden while the hunting party rode away.

The Pawnee had planned to attack fast and hard, both to claim their special reward from the U.S. Army of $10 per scalp as well as to gain access to prime Rocky Mountain foothills hunting land when the Indian Wars were finally over. They were also after the large herd of Cheyenne horses.

Somehow, the band of Cheyenne learned of the impending attack before nightfall. The Pawnees had no idea they had been discovered, and they dry-camped and prepared for a vicious dawn attack.

Before first light, with weapons drawn and already painted black and white for war, the Pawnees swooped up the draws and flowed toward the Cheyenne camp. When the Pawnees moved in on the camp they found only the tipi rings, still-warm campfire embers from the previous night, and more than a hundred dead horses, their throats slashed. It appeared to the Pawnee that the Cheyenne had literally flown away. The Pawnee knew the logistics of moving all of those people out, and they knew that it should have been impossible for the Cheyenne to get by them at night. There was no way the band of Cheyenne had flown through them, the Pawnees thought, and the only escape had been away from them, toward a canyon that could not be crossed. Furious, they pursued.

What the Pawnee found when they reached the rim of the canyon was evidence of an otherworldly occurrence. The band of Cheyenne was gone, but there was visible evidence of their flight. Somehow, remarkably, the entire band had descended the sheer cliffs to the bottom and climbed back out on the other side. The evidence, hundreds of feet below, was the number of telltale discarded tipi poles and bits of hair and clothing clinging to spiny brush. The entire Cheyenne band—the aged men and women, their grand-children and daughters, the few able men in the camp, as the story went—had somehow, one by one, climbed down the canyon side to the Middle Fork, forded the river, and climbed up the other side to their escape. The tipi poles had been discarded sometime during the night, and they now stood, to the Pawnee, as awful proof that the incomprehensible had happened: The Pawnee had lost their advantage of surprise, lost the horses, and lost the Cheyenne.

The Pawnee chose not to even try to pursue the Cheyenne. They admired the escape and were somewhat awed by the pure determination of the people who had managed such an escape. That the Cheyenne would leave in the middle of the night, risking the lives of all, kill their horses, and succeed was beyond anything the Pawnee had ever encountered. It was that respect, as the story went, that caused the Pawnee to turn their horses around and go home to Fort Laramie. In Pawnee, the roughly translated name they gave the canyon was "Place Where the Cheyenne Ran Away from Us." Soldiers who heard the story, and who were at war at the time with the Cheyenne (who they regarded as barely human), renamed the geological anomaly "Savage Run," although none of them ever found the place or really knew where it was. The legend of Savage Run was passed on. Eventually, several white elk hunters claimed they had found the passage. A national historian wrote about it well enough to create interest; thus the move for National Monument designation. But outside of a few American Indian hunting guides and the original elk hunters, few were exactly sure where the passage across the canyon was located.

JOE LOOKED AT MAXINE, and the Labrador looked back with her big brown eyes. Labradors forgave everything. Joe wished he could.

He wished he could get a handle on the uncharacteristic hatred he felt toward hobby rancher/lawyer Jim Finotta. But he sure wanted to get that son of a bitch.

5

THREE DAYS LATER, Joe Pickett sat idly sipping coffee and waiting for Marybeth to return with the newspaper from her morning walk. She walked every day, even through horizontal snowstorms in the winter, and was strong enough now that she could pitch fifty-pound bales of hay from the stack in her barn. The exercise, she said, had helped her recover her balance and strength after her shooting injury, and she never missed a morning. She was proud of the fact that she could now handle all of the duties at the stables, where she worked part-time, including tacking up fifteen-hand horses and working them in the round pen. Marybeth often went to her other part-time job at the Twelve Sleep County Municipal Library smelling of horses. It was a good smell, Joe thought, and was pleased that Marybeth wasn't ashamed of it. The two jobs offered enough flexibility that she was able to see her children off to school in the morning and be there when they returned.

"Why didn't you tell me that the man killed in the mountains was *Stewie Woods?*" Marybeth fired at Joe as she came into the kitchen. The *Saddlestring Roundup* was clutched in her fist.

Joe was raising a mug of coffee to his mouth. Sheridan, Lucy, and April were still bleary-eyed, in their pajamas, and were distractedly eating bowls of breakfast cereal. Everyone's eyes were on Marybeth; Joe thought the girls all looked as if they had been caught in the act of committing a crime.

"How could you not tell me, Joe Pickett?" she asked angrily, her voice getting louder with each word. Joe had not moved. The coffee cup was still poised for a sip. He knew that whatever he said now would not be the right thing to say.

"Barnum called and said the victim was named Allan Stewart Woods," Joe said lamely. "I didn't make the connection at the time to Stewie Woods."

She glared at him with eyes that could melt ice.

"Besides," Joe said, "why is it so important?"

Suddenly, Marybeth gave an angry little cry, threw the newspaper onto a chair, and stormed up the stairs to the bedroom, where she slammed the door and noisily threw the lock.

Joe and the girls stared dumbly at the space Marybeth had just occupied.

"What's wrong with mom?" Sheridan asked.

"She's just upset," Joe answered. "Everything's fine."

"Who is Stewie Woods?" Lucy asked Sheridan.

Sheridan shrugged, and turned back to her breakfast, giving Lucy a "please be quiet" glare.

"You girls need to finish up and get dressed for school," Joe said gruffly.

HE WALKED THEM to the bus, kissed them good-bye, and said hello and good morning to the driver, and then went back in to read the newspaper. Joe knew from experience that when Marybeth was upset she would need some time, and he would give her that time.

The front-page story was more accurate than usual and Sheriff Barnum was quoted throughout. While the woman who was killed at the scene was yet to be officially identified (although Joe knew that they had found her Rhode

Island driver's license in a fanny pack at the scene and had been as yet unable to connect with relatives), the man was tentatively identified as environmental activist Stewie Woods. A wallet with his driver's license, credit cards, and One Globe membership card (he was Member number 1) had been found in an abandoned Subaru near the trailhead. Woods's shoes, backpack, and famous red bandana had been found at the crime scene. A carpenter's pouch, filled with sixty-penny spikes, was recovered as well as a small sledgehammer covered with fingerprints. Forest Service officials confirmed that trees had been spiked near the crime scene and that there was a discernible "trail" of spiked trees leading from the road to the crater. Forensics results had not yet come back from Cheyenne as yet, but all of the circumstantial evidence suggested the vaporized dead man was Woods.

Joe had talked with Sheriff Barnum the day before, when they had met on the same two-track gravel road. Each had eased to the shoulder so that their vehicles were parallel, and they rolled down their windows and had a "cowboy conference" in the middle of the sagebrush prairie. Barnum divulged his theory that Woods was attaching explosives to a heifer as a spectacular publicity stunt. Stewie Woods and One Globe were known, after all, for this kind of thing. Blowing up cows that were grazing on public land was just a short step up from spiking trees, disabling the machinery and heavy equipment used for forest road building, or other "direct actions" that One Globe claimed credit for. Blowing up cows would be an escalation in ecoterrorism.

Barnum doubted that Woods or his cronies had the training or expertise required to use C-4 explosives in a safe manner. Barnum's guess was that Woods and his companion were in the process of attaching the explosive to the animal when it went off.

Afterward, Joe had followed Barnum to his office. "I like my investigations the way I like my women and my eggs," Barnum said to Joe, "I like 'em over easy."

Joe had heard Barnum say that more than once in the past two years and he still thought it was ridiculous.

Barnum showed Joe a sheaf of faxes that had come into the Twelve Sleep County Sheriff's Department over the past two days, most filled with newspaper clippings of Stewie Woods's and One Globe's past monkey-wrenching activities. Joe read several of them. Woods and his colleagues had attracted a good deal of attention just a few years ago when they unfurled a massive canvas banner from the catwalk of a Colorado dam that made it look like the $800 million structure had a huge crack in it. They had done this behind the U.S. Secretary of Interior as the secretary gave a speech about hydroelectric power. The stunt was caught on videotape and broadcast throughout the country and around the world.

"Blowing up cows is just another form of monkey wrenching," Barnum said. "Some dead writer made up the term to promote sabotage in the name of the environment."

"Edward Abbey," Joe said, "it was Edward Abbey. He wrote a book called *The Monkeywrench Gang*."

Barnum looked blankly at Joe. "Whatever," he said dismissively.

Then Joe paused. "Any chance somebody tipped off Finotta about the explosion before I talked to him?

Barnum's eyes narrowed. "Why? What did he say?"

"It wasn't what he said . . . it's what he didn't say," Joe continued. "It's what he didn't ask. About the victims, for example. When I thought about it later, I realized he hadn't shown much interest in who died. Like he might have already known."

"Did you ask him about it?"

"No."

Barnum sighed, then shrugged. "Finotta has lots of contacts, so it's possible. Maybe he heard about it over a scanner or something. I don't see where it much matters, to be honest with you. The death of an environmental whacko probably wasn't very high on his priority list. Or mine."

Joe put the newspaper down and drained the last of his coffee. He hadn't had a chance to tell Marybeth about the conversation when he got home the night before, other than to say that the victims had been identified and that they weren't local. Joe wondered why the name of the dead man had affected Marybeth the way it had. Or was it the fact that he had forgotten to tell her?

Joe was aware that within the town of Saddlestring, Stewie Woods's death was already turning into something of a joke. He guessed that it was the same throughout the west in the logging communities, the mining towns, and the farm and ranch centers, where Stewie Woods and One Globe were known and despised. One Globe was one of the most extreme of the environmental groups, a media darling, and one of the few organizations that openly advocated direct action. They hated cattle, they hated the practice of grazing on public land, they hated the ranchers who had or applied for leases, and they hated the politicians and bureaucrats who continued to allow the practice.

Barnum had speculated that Woods was hoping for head-lines like "Cow Explodes In National Forest"—something that would focus attention on the grazing debate—when something went horribly wrong.

An interesting angle raised in the newspaper, and previously unknown to Joe, was the fact that Stewie Woods was a local boy, born and reared in Winchester. He had attended high school in Saddlestring and had played middle line-backer for the football team with a recklessness that made him All-State. Then, according to his coaches and neighbors, he had gone to the University of Colorado in Boulder and instead of playing football for the Golden Buffaloes, he hooked up with the wrong people and went crazy.

Joe wondered about the embarrassing legacy Woods's death would leave. Like an overweight Mama Cass, who died from choking on a sandwich, or Elvis Presley, who died on the toilet, or fitness author Jim Fixx, who died while running, Stewie Woods would forever be remembered as the environmental activist blown up by a cow. Despite the stunts, the publicity, the best-selling biography written by Hayden Powell, and the attention Woods had garnered through the years, Stewie Woods would always be linked with a cow explosion. Joe knew there were ranchers, loggers, and politicians who would find this all very amusing.

Joe raked a hand through his hair. What he still didn't know was why Marybeth was so upset by the news. But he knew she would tell him when she felt she was ready. Since her shooting injury and the loss of their baby, Marybeth readily admitted that she was more prone to quick mood swings and tremendous bouts of strong emotion—mostly sentimental ones. Sometimes she couldn't identify exactly what it was that triggered the tears. He had learned not to press her, not to make her give him a definitive answer right away because sometimes she simply didn't have one. It bothered her more than it bothered Joe, for she was a woman who had no room or time for baseless theatrics.

So whatever it was, Joe knew he would find out what was bothering her when Marybeth was good and ready to tell him.

He waited half an hour and finished his coffee. When she didn't come downstairs, he pulled on his hat, called Maxine, and walked outside to his pickup to go to work.

6

JOE CALLED IT "PERCHING." Perching was patrolling in the break lands in the foothills of the Bighorns, where the sagebrush gave way to pines, driving his truck up rough two-tracks to promontories and buttes where, with his Redfield spotting scope mounted to the driver's-side window, he could scope flats, meadows, and timber blowdowns for game, hunters, hikers, and fishers. After two years on the job, he was still locating new adequate perches throughout his district, which consisted of 1,500 square miles of high plains steppe, sagebrush flats, craggy break lands, and mountains. These raised vantage points, where he could "sit and glass," generally had some kind of road to the top that had been established over the years by ranchers, surveyors, or hunters.

Perching is what Joe had done for the past few days, since Marybeth's outburst. He had left early, stayed late, and filled the hours between with routine patrolling of his district in the strange season between hunting and fishing activity. Even if he patrolled every working hour, Joe knew he could never adequately cover his 1,500-square-mile district. But it was an important part of his job.

At night, he had worked late in his small office near the mudroom at home, updating logs and reports, writing out a comprehensive purchase request from headquarters for the goods and equipment he would need in the coming fiscal year (saddles, tack, new tires, roof repair, etc.) and waiting for Marybeth to come to him and explain what had happened that morning. They still needed to talk and clear the air. Every time he heard her walk by his door, he paused, hoping she would enter and close the door behind her and say "About the other morning . . ." He didn't push her, either, although the incident hung around the house like an unwelcome relative. Several times, he wanted to go to her, but he talked himself out of it. The guilt he felt about her injury, and the subsequent loss of their child, was like a blade, ever poised, near his heart.

That morning, after the girls had left for school and the silence between them seemed to approach white noise, he told her about his encounter with Jim Finotta. She listened, and seemed grateful to be discussing anything except what he wanted to discuss. Her eyes probed his while he talked.

"Joe, are you sure this is something you want to pursue?" she asked.

"He poached an elk. He's no better than any other criminal. In fact, he's worse."

"But you can't prove it, can you?"

"Not yet."

She stared at a spot behind Joe's head. "Joe, we're within

sight of getting our debts paid for the first time since we've been married. I'm working two jobs. Is this the time you want to go after a man like Jim Finotta?"

Her question surprised him, although it shouldn't have, and it momentarily put him off balance. Marybeth was nothing if not a pragmatist, especially when it came to her family.

"I've got to check it out," Joe said, his resolve weakened. "You know that."

A slow, resigned smile formed on her face. "I know you do, Joe. I just don't want you to get in trouble again."

"Me neither."

And for a moment, he could see in her expression that she wanted to add more. But she didn't.

IT WAS RARE to find many people about in the mountains in the late spring and early summer, when unpredictable squalls could sweep down from the Continental Divide in buffeting waves of wet snow, and when the snowmelt runoff was still too foamy, cloudy, and violent to fish or swim in. Crusty drifts of snow still lay in draws and swales, but had retreated and regrouped from the grass and sagebrush into the safe harbor of thick wooded stands.

Maxine slept on the passenger seat, her head resting on her forepaws, her brow crinkled with concern from whatever peril she was dreaming about.

Hazelton Road, the route to the site of the cow explosion, cut upward through the timber to the west and there was a small streamside campground, empty except for a single vehicle that was partially obscured by trees. Near the vehicle was a light green dome tent. Joe zoomed in on the tent and the campsite with the spotting scope, feeling like a voyeur. Through a shimmer caused by the distance and warmth, he could see people sitting at a picnic table. Two stout women, one with a mass of thick brown hair and the other with short straight hair, sat on opposite sides of the table. Between them, on the tabletop, were pieces of equipment Joe couldn't identify from this distance. Their heads were bent over whatever they were doing, so Joe could not see the face of either woman.

Joe zoomed out and moved the scope through the rest of the campground. Empty.

Upstream, though, a reed-thin man with a straggly beard and baggy trousers cast a spinning lure into the boiling creek. The man stood bolt upright, with one shoe on shore and the other on a rock in the stream. Joe smiled to himself. No fishing vest, no tackle box, no creel, no waders, no stoop to his back as he sneaked up on a promising pool. This man did not look like a fisherman any more than Joe looked like a cricketer. The stream was wild and would calm down, clear, and become fishable in about six weeks, in mid-July. Now, it was swelled past the banks with spring runoff, and lures cast into it would rocket down the stream with the fast flow and hang up in streamside willows.

Nevertheless, fishers were required to have both licenses and state habitat stamps, even if it was unlikely that a fish could be caught, as was the case here. Joe's job was to make sure fishermen had licenses. He zipped the spotting scope in its case, rolled up the window, and started the truck, which woke Maxine from her worrisome adventure.

ONE OF THE STOUT WOMEN at the picnic table turned out to

be a man wearing thick dreadlocks that cascaded across his shoulders and down his back, but the woman looked vaguely familiar. Both turned to him as he stepped out of his pickup in the campground. They had been reassembling a well-worn white gas camping stove on the table, and the man seemed frustrated by it.

Joe left Maxine in the truck in case the campers had dogs of their own and approached them on a moist, pine-needled path. Their vehicle was a twenty-year-old conversion van with California plates. He introduced himself, and the couple exchanged a furtive glance.

The two were purposely ragged looking. He wore khaki zip-off trousers that were fashionably blousey and stained, and an extra-large open shirt over a T-shirt.

"Raga," the man said, wiping his hands on his pants and standing. "This is Britney. We can't get our stove to work."

"You could use the fire ring instead," Joe offered, pointing to the circle of fire-blackened rocks. "It's real early in the year and there are no fire restrictions as yet."

"We don't do fires." The man called Raga snorted. "We don't do charred flesh. We're low-impact." It was said as a kind of challenge, and Joe had no desire to follow it up.

"Raga?" Joe asked.

"It's short for Ragamuffin," the woman said abruptly. Her voice was grating and whiney. Joe turned to her, and the sense of familiarity was stronger.

Raga shook his hair and tilted his head back, and looked down his long nose at Joe. "This is Britney Earthshare. It's not her real name, of course, but it's the name she goes by. You might have seen her in the press a couple of years ago. She lived in a tree in Northern California to protest the log-

60

ging of an old-growth forest."

Yes, Joe thought. She was familiar. He had seen her on television, being interviewed by reporters who raised their microphones into the air alongside the trunk of the tree she had named Duomo. She would answer their questions by shouting down from her platform, which was equipped with thousands of dollars of high-tech equipment and state-of-the-art outdoor gear.

Britney Earthshare glanced at Joe from her place at the table and then looked quickly away. She was already bored with him, he surmised.

"You may not do charred flesh," Joe said, "but do you know the guy who's fishing upstream?"

"Tonk?" Raga asked.

"Is he with you?"

Raga nodded yes. "Is he doing something wrong?"

"Probably not. I need to check his license, though."

Raga crossed his arms and Britney, at the table, rolled her eyes.

"A driver's license?" Raga asked.

"Fishing license."

Raga said "Hmmm."

As he did, Tonk walked into the camp from the stream, pushing his way through the brush. He was talking as he entered, and had obviously not yet seen Joe.

". . . Fucking fast water threw my lures all over the place," he was saying. "Lost two good Mepps and a Rooster Tail and now I got—" Tonk saw Joe and froze in mid-sentence. Joe finished for him: "Now you've got a treble hook in your arm."

Tonk held his arm out and winced painfully and almost

comically, like a child will do when an adult points out an injury the child has forgotten. The No. 12 Mepps spinner had bitten deeply into Tonk's sinewy bicep. All four sets of eyes moved to it.

"It got hung up in a bush and when I pulled it back—look what happened. It came flying straight back at me," Tonk said, looking a little sheepish. "It hurts."

Joe advised Tonk to drive into Saddlestring and get the lure removed at the clinic. "If Doc Johnson isn't in you can get it taken out at the veterinary clinic," Joe explained. "The vet removes fish hooks from fishermen and their dogs all the time, and it'll cost you about half of what Doc Johnson charges."

Tonk nodded dully. He was fascinated by the lure embedded in his flesh. Britney and Raga seemed to be fascinated with it as well.

Sharply, Britney turned. "You said you were the game warden, right?"

Joe nodded.

"I read somewhere that there was a game warden present when the exploding cow was discovered a week ago," she said. "And that the place where the explosion happened is close to here."

Raga was suddenly more interested in Joe than in Tonk's mishap.

"That was me," Joe said. "I was one of the first on the scene."

The campsite seemed to have quieted, and Joe was being examined by all three campers with a different level of intensity than just a moment before.

"That's why we're here," Raga declared. "To find the

place where they claim Stewie was murdered."

It took Joe a moment to respond. "Who says he was murdered?"

Raga displayed a self-satisfied smirk. He shook his head as if to say, *I'll never tell you.*

"Did you find his body?" Tonk asked, forgetting his own injury for a moment.

"All we found were his shoes," Joe said. "There wasn't a body to find."

"I fucking knew it," Tonk said, stepping forward to stand abreast of Raga. He spoke with the loopy intensity patented by generations of the drugged and dispossessed: "I fucking *knew* it, Raga!"

Joe stared back at Britney, who was performing surgery on him with her eyes.

"You found her body, but you didn't find his, right?" she asked.

"The state investigator's report concluded that he had an accident with explosives," Joe said. "The sheriff agreed with that. Accident, not suicide. And definitely not murder."

Raga laughed derisively. "Yeah, like President Kennedy's little 'accident.' " Tonk agreed by nodding his head vigorously.

"Stewie Woods is not dead," Britney Earthshare stated. Joe felt a chill crawl up his spine. Then: "Stewie will never be dead. They can't kill a man like Stewie."

Oh, Joe thought. *That's* what she meant.

"Just like they couldn't kill Kurt Cobain, or Martin Luther King, man," Tonk chimed in.

"I understand," Joe mumbled, not understanding. These three campers were not much younger than he was, but were so entirely different.

They asked for directions to the crater. Joe saw no reason not to give them. He pointed back toward the Hazelton Road, told them it was about six miles up, and where there was a turnout where they could park.

"I knew we were close," Britney said to Raga, "I could just feel it, how close we were."

"That's why you're here?" Joe asked.

"Partly," Raga said. "We're on our way to Toronto to an antiglobalism rally. Britney's speaking."

She nodded.

Joe turned to go.

"The people who did this will be back," Britney said quite clearly as he walked away. He stopped, and looked over his shoulder.

"They can't kill Stewie Woods that easily," she sang.

JOE WAS BACK UP on his perch before he realized he had forgotten to ask Tonk to show him his fishing license. But he stayed in his truck.

Things were certainly more interesting since Stewie Woods had died in *his* mountains. Although the official investigation was already all but closed, and obituaries and tributes to Stewie had faded from the news, unofficial speculation continued unabated. That there was a strange, disconnected underground made up of people like Raga, Tonk, and Britney who now came to see the crater was disconcerting. They seemed to know something—or thought they knew something—that the public did not.

He hoped this had been an isolated incident. But he doubted it.

7

BREMERTON, WASHINGTON
June 14

OUTSIDE A HUGE tree-shrouded home in a driving rain, the Old Man waited. Next to him, in the cab of the black Ford pickup, in the dark, was Charlie Tibbs.

The Old Man stole glances at Charlie, careful not to turn his head and stare directly at him. Charlie's face was barely discernible in the dark of the cab, lit only by the light from a distant fluorescent streetlight that threw a weak shaft through the waving branches of an evergreen tree. The rivulets of rainwater that ran down the windshield cast wormlike shadows on Charlie, making his face look splotched and mottled.

They were here to kill someone named Hayden Powell, the owner of the house. But Powell had not yet come home.

The Old Man and Charlie Tibbs had driven up the fern-shrouded driveway two hours before, just as the storm clouds had closed the lid on the sky above Puget Sound. They had backed their black pickup into a tangled thicket so that it couldn't be seen from the road unless someone was really looking for it. Then the rain had started. It was relentless. The rain came down so hard and the vegetation was so thick that the wide leaves, outstretched toward the sky like cartoon hands, jerked and undulated all around them as if the forest floor was dancing. The liquid drumbeat of the storm intimidated the Old Man into complete silence and made the atmosphere otherworldly. Not that

Charlie was the kind of guy to have a long—or short—discussion with anyway.

The Old Man was in awe of Charlie Tibbs. Charlie's stillness and quiet resolve was something from another era. Charlie had never raised his voice since they had been together, and the Old Man often had to strain to even hear him. Despite his age (the Old Man guessed sixty-five, like him) and bone-white hair, Charlie was a powerful presence. Men who didn't know Charlie Tibbs, and who had never heard of his reputation, still seemed to tense up in Charlie's presence. The Old Man had seen that happen just this morning, as they neared Bremerton, Washington, from the east. When they entered a small café and Charlie walked down the aisle toward an empty booth, The Old Man had noticed how the rough crowd of construction workers and salmon fishermen paused over their chicken-fried steak and eggs and sat up straight as Charlie passed by them. There was just something about the man. And none of those workers or fishermen had any idea that this was Charlie Tibbs, the legendary stock detective, a man known for his skill at manhunting for over forty years throughout the Rocky Mountains, the Southwest, South America, and Western Canada.

Since the days of the open range in the 1870s, stock detectives had played a unique role in cattle country. Hired by individual ranchers or landowner consortiums, stock detectives hunted down rustlers, nesters, and vandals in an effort to bring those offenders to justice. Or, in some cases, to remove them from the earth. Few stock detectives still existed. Of those who did, Charlie Tibbs was considered the best. All these locals knew was that this tall man with white hair and a Stetson was someone out of the ordinary, somebody special. Someone who made them sit up straight as he passed by.

"I don't like this rain," the Old Man said, raising his voice over the drumming on the top of the cab. "And I don't think I like this part of the country. I'm not used to this. If you died out there tonight you'd be covered by weeds before morning."

The Old Man waited for a response or a reaction but all there was from Charlie was the twitch of a smile.

"I just don't think you can trust a place where they have leaves bigger than a man's head," the Old Man offered.

The Old Man watched as Charlie raised his hands—he had huge, powerful hands—and rested them on top of the steering wheel. Charlie's index finger flicked out, pointing through the windshield. The Old Man's eyes followed the gesture.

"There he is," Charlie said flatly. "He's home and it looks like he's by himself."

"Did he see us?" the Old Man asked.

"He didn't even look. He drove up without his head-lights. He must be drunk."

The Old Man raised a heavy pair of night vision binoculars. Through the rain-streaked windshield, he could clearly see Hayden Powell's car cruise up the drive slowly, as if anticipating that the garage door would open, which it didn't. Powell applied the brake inches from the door and his taillights flashed a burst of light that temporarily blinded the Old Man through the binoculars—and he cursed.

All the Old Man could see was a green and white orb

similar to the aftereffect of a flashbulb. While the Old Man waited for his eyes to readjust, Charlie gently took the binoculars from him to look.

"He's drunk," Charlie declared. "Just as we thought he would be. He couldn't figure out how to open his garage and now he's trying to figure out which key to use to open the door. He dropped his keys in the grass. Now he's on his hands and knees looking for them. We could get him now."

The Old Man looked to Charlie for guidance. What weapons would they use? What was the plan here? The Old Man fought back panic.

The Old Man didn't know a lot about Hayden Powell but he knew enough. He knew that Powell was a well-known environmental writer who had originally come to fame by writing many articles about and later the biography of his boyhood friend, Stewie Woods. Powell had struck it rich, not in publishing but through an early investment in a Seattle-based software company. As the company took off, professional management was brought in to run it and Powell was eased out. With his huge home, bulging stock portfolio, and free time, he had returned to the two things he loved most: drinking tequila and writing provocative pieces on the environment.

The rumor was that his next book would be titled *Screwing Up the West* and was a vicious indictment of corporations, landowners, and politicians. Excerpts had been published in magazines and journals. Powell was in big trouble, though. The SEC was investigating the software company and investors who Powell had recruited—many of whom had sunk millions into the company—were furious. There had been death threats made against Powell, which he duly reported to the SEC and the FBI. Powell had even been quoted as saying that he looked forward to going to jail, where he would feel safer.

And now the Old Man and Charlie were here to kill him—but not because of the failing software company. Charlie had said it needed to look as if an angry investor had done it or had it done. There should be absolutely no link to the upcoming book.

The Old Man had not been told what the details of the plan would be. He was uncomfortable, and scared. He wasn't like Charlie—these things didn't come naturally to him. He did not want to disappoint either Charlie or his employers, but this thing was getting bigger and more complicated than he had thought it would be. What was he supposed to do, run across the grass and hit Powell in the back of the head with a hammer? Shoot the guy in the dark? What?

"He's up and he's in," Charlie said, lowering the binoculars.

The Old Man watched as the porch light went on. They followed Powell's drunken progress through his house as he switched on lights. First the kitchen, then the bathroom, then the living room. They waited.

"He's probably passed out on his couch," Charlie whispered after nearly an hour.

"What is the plan?" the Old Man asked, trying to suppress the panic he felt rising up in him.

Oddly, Charlie Tibbs smiled, showing his perfect teeth, and turned in his seat. The smile made the Old Man feel better, but it also disturbed him in a way he couldn't put his finger on.

"Later . . . ," Charlie began, the word drowned out by the rain. "I'll tell you later when you need to know."

WEARING A RAIN SUIT with a hood that slipped over his clothes and covered his face, the Old Man waited in the soaking undergrowth until Charlie Tibbs reached the front door. When Charlie signaled him, the Old Man raised his scoped and silenced .22 rifle and shot out the back porch light with a sound no louder than a cough. The Old Man had shot from an angle so the bullet would pass cleanly through the lamp and lightbulb and off into the night. It would not be wise to leave a bullet lodged in the siding that might be found by investigators. Now the outside of the expensive home of Hayden Powell was once again dark. With a tiny flashlight in his mouth, the Old Man located the spent brass casing that had been ejected from the rifle into the mud. He pocketed it while he walked across the lawn toward the darkened back door. While the tire tracks and footprints would be washed away in the driving rain, bullet casings could be recovered.

Careful to not lose his footing on the rain-slick steps, the Old Man entered the house. Charlie had been right about Powell not locking the back door after him.

Inside it was warm and dry. The Old Man stood in the kitchen by the back door and concentrated on regulating his breathing. He did not want to be heard. The pounding of the rain was muffled inside the house. As he stood, a puddle formed near his boots from the wet rain suit.

The Old Man surveyed the room and then positioned himself behind the kitchen island with his back to the door he had entered. The kitchen island was built so that the end of it pointed to the living room. His job was to block the back door while Charlie entered the front. From where the Old Man stood he could see down a hallway into a sunken living room sparsely filled with leather furniture. A television set was on and the channel tuned to what looked like the local news. He could see half of the front doorway, and clearly heard Charlie knock on it.

The Old Man swallowed and readied his rifle. He was instructed not to use it unless absolutely necessary. According to Charlie, Powell would never even make it out of the living room, much less into the kitchen.

Charlie knocked again, this time louder. The Old Man heard a couch squeak and the back of Hayden Powell came into view. Powell was younger and more powerfully built than the Old Man had guessed. Powell's hair was awry and he shuffled to the front door in his socks. He had been sleeping on the couch. Once again, Charlie had been exactly right.

Powell asked who was at the door. The Old Man couldn't hear what Charlie shouted back. Powell squinted into the peephole and the Old Man could only imagine what Powell was thinking: There is an old cowboy standing on my front porch.

The front door was not open three inches before Charlie's fist, wrapped in thick brass knuckles beaded with rain, smashed through the opening, flush into Hayden Powell's face. The power of the blow threw Powell straight back and he slid along the hardwood floor. The Old Man tensed and raised his rifle, keeping the barrel pointed at the hallway. Charlie entered the house and closed the front door behind him; his frighteningly intense eyes fixed on the crumpled form of Hayden Powell.

The Old Man let out a deep breath. It was already over.

But suddenly it wasn't, as Powell scrambled to his hands and knees with sudden sobriety and shot away from Charlie, straight toward the kitchen. The Old Man caught a glimpse of Powell's wide, bloodied face and frightened eyes and he raised his rifle just as Powell ducked below the kitchen island out of sight. Charlie yelled, "Get him!" and the Old Man kicked the back door shut a second before Powell slammed into it.

Powell was thrown backward again and was writhing on the kitchen floor between the island and a huge walk-in freezer. What the Old Man saw next reminded him much more of a hunter dispatching a wounded animal than a man killing another man. Charlie Tibbs mounted the three steps from the living room and pinned Powell to the floor with his knees. Powell struggled and tried to throw Charlie off, but after taking a half-dozen powerful and methodic blows with the brass knuckles, Powell was still.

Charlie Tibbs slowly got to his feet. The Old Man could hear Charlie's knees creak and his back pop. Charlie's face was flushed from the exertion and his right arm, from the elbow down, was soaked in blood.

"You almost let him go," Charlie barked, glaring at the Old Man.

"You did, too," the Old Man countered, instantly regretting that he said it. For the first time, the Old Man saw the chilling, ice-blue stare directed at *him*. But like a storm cloud passing, Charlie's eyes softened and the Old Man found that he could breathe again.

"It's done now," Charlie said softly. "Grab a foot and

help me drag him back out into the living room."

The Old Man put the rifle down on the counter and rounded the island. He turned his head so he wouldn't see the mess that Charlie had made of Powell's face and head. He caught Charlie looking at him, sizing him up, as they dragged the body through the kitchen and down the stairs.

THEY TOOK THE MICROCASSETTE TAPE from Powell's answering machine because Charlie had called the house earlier in the afternoon to hear Hayden Powell's recorded voice and confirm they had the right address. Although no message was left, the ambient traffic sounds in the background might provide a clue for investigators that someone had called to check an occupancy. The Old Man pocketed the microcassette. They found Powell's Macintosh computer in the home office and ripped it from the wall. The computer, files, and a box of disks and zip drives were all thrown into the back of the pickup. Charlie placed incendiary bombs in all four corners of the first floor of the house and splashed five gallons of gasoline through the kitchen and living room. As they left, the Old Man lit a traffic flare and tossed it through the back door. The mighty *whoosh* of the fire sucked the air out of the Old Man's lungs and left him gasping for the cold, moist air.

As they drove through Bremerton toward the highway, Charlie dutifully pulled over as each fire truck passed them, their sirens whooping and flashing lights reflecting back from rain-slicked streets and buildings.

At the scene the firefighters would find a $1.7 million home burned to the ground. Later, tomorrow, a charred body would be found. An autopsy would show that the skull was crushed, probably by huge vaulted beams that crashed down from the second floor during the fire. The autopsy would also show that Powell's blood-alcohol level was far past the legal limit. Why and how the fire got started would be subject to debate. Speculation about whether one of his declared investor enemies had something to do with it or whether Hayden Powell lit the fire himself in a drunken fit of rage and depression would probably go on for months.

"I'm not sure I like this close-in work," the Old Man said as they approached the egress to the highway. "And I sure as hell don't like all this rain and jungle out here."

Charlie ignored the Old Man and asked him if he had picked up his shell casing. The Old Man sighed and showed it to him. Charlie was nothing if not thorough. And, in the Old Man's opinion, thoroughly efficient and coolly heartless.

"Where is the next project?" the Old Man asked.

"Montana."

"I was kind of hoping we'd get some time off. We've been going nonstop. I've seen the Rocky Mountains and the Pacific Ocean in the last four days. That's more miles than I want to think about."

This was the first time the Old Man had complained about their work. The result of his complaint was a pained squint from Charlie Tibbs as he drove.

"We took a job and we're going to finish it," Charlie said with finality. His voice was so low that it could barely be heard over the rain-sizzle of the tires.

The Old Man let it drop. He watched walls of dark wet trees strobe by in the headlights. The rain never stopped.

The sky was close, seemingly at treetop level. It was as if they were going through a tunnel. He briefly closed his eyes to rest them.

When he opened them again his hands were still shaking. The big black pickup, like a land shark, was speeding east devouring miles of wet shining road.

Heading east to Go West, the Old Man thought.

8

MARYBETH SLAMMED DOWN the telephone receiver and, wide-eyed, looked around her house to see if anyone was watching her. Of course, no one was. But she was shaking, scared, and angry nonetheless. And very self-conscious.

It was the same voice on the telephone from the day before. He had called at the same time: after the kids had left for school and Joe had gone to work, but before Marybeth left for the stables. He had either guessed very well when he could talk to her alone or knew her schedule. Either way, it was disconcerting.

"Is this Mary?" the man had asked. "Maiden name Harris?"

That was as far as it went yesterday before she hung up. When the telephone rang again this morning, she knew intuitively that it was him. This time, she wanted more information about why he was calling, although she was afraid she already knew.

"Who is this?" she asked.

He identified himself as a writer for *Outside* magazine. He said he was doing research for a story he was writing about deceased ecoterrorist Stewie Woods.

"Why are you calling me?" she asked. "You should be

talking instead to our sheriff or my husband. Would you like the sheriff's telephone number?"

The reporter paused. "You're Mary, aren't you?"

"Mary*beth*," she corrected. "Marybeth Pickett."

"Formerly known as Mary Harris?" he asked.

"My name has always been Marybeth," she insisted. This was not completely a lie. Only two people had ever called her Mary.

The reporter's voice was more tentative. "Maybe I've got the wrong person here, and if so, I apologize for wasting your time. But my research led me to you," he said. "Did you know Stewie Woods when you were growing up?"

She hung up on him.

IT HAD BEEN a wonderful summer. That summer, the one between high school and college, had been tucked away in her memory but still came back to her from time to time. She had fought it back successfully and never let it bloom. She had tamped that flower back into the earth with her heel. But when she read in the newspaper that Stewie Woods was dead it all came back. Even now, fifteen years later, the memory of it was still vibrant.

Back then, Stewie Woods was terribly homely but very charismatic, a gawky teenager turning into a fine but unpredictable athlete, who was already envisioning the building of an environmental terrorist organization that would rock the world. Hayden Powell was handsome, sardonic, and talented and vowed to make Stewie and their joint mission to Save the West famous. Although she never shared their radical passion for environmental causes, Marybeth's attraction to both rogues was exciting in the same way that it was exciting for other girls her age to hook up with rock stars or rodeo cowboys. Stewie and Hayden were bad boys, smart boys, wild boys, but they had good hearts. They were already wreaking havoc with environmental vandalism. An evening out with them generally involved pulling up survey stakes for a planned pipeline or letting the air out of bulldozer tires. Although there were several close calls, the three of them never got caught.

And they loved her. Stewie, especially. He was so in love with her that it was as embarrassing as it was flattering. Once, after intercepting a pass for the Winchester Badgers and taking it into the end zone for a touchdown, Stewie had turned to the partisan Saddlestring crowd and spelled out "M-A-R-Y" with his long arms because he knew she was watching the game with her friends.

During the summer, the three of them spent nearly every evening together. They fished, they went to movies, they committed sabotage.

Hayden Powell went on to Iowa State for the writing program. Stewie got a football scholarship to Colorado. Marybeth went south to the University of Wyoming, intending to become a corporate lawyer. Instead, she met Joe Pickett, a gangly, soft-spoken sophomore majoring in wildlife biology.

She had not kept in touch with Stewie Woods or Hayden Powell because they were dangerous. With Joe's job as a fledgling game warden, they had moved six times in the first nine years and so it had been relatively easy for her to miss the telephone calls, letters, or Christmas cards they might have sent. With her name change and the fact that her mother remarried and moved to Arizona, she knew she would be difficult to track down. But she had read about Stewie's exploits and seen him on television. The biography had been published six years before, and had garnered minor critical attention but instant cult status. At the time, Joe and Marybeth were in Buffalo, Wyoming, with Joe's first full-fledged district as game warden. Marybeth was pregnant with Lucy, Joe worked insanely long hours, and Sheridan was a four-year-old. Marybeth couldn't have been further removed from the environmental derring-do of Stewie Woods or the literary escapades of Hayden Powell if she lived on the moon.

Finally, a year ago, during her breaks while working in the county library, she had read the biography. She had not checked the book out or brought it home. Stewie had mentioned "his first love, Mary Harris" but, thank God, he didn't know her married name. But she was in there. And she had to admit to herself that when she found the volume the first thing she looked for was her name and what Stewie had said about her.

Marybeth assumed that the reporter had read the same biography, but unlike Stewie, the reporter had located her. And the reporter wanted some comments from her for his story.

She had never told Joe about this short period in her life. It hadn't seemed necessary; it would have complicated things that didn't need complicating.

But now, she thought, she needed to talk to her husband. She would do so when he got home that evening. He deserved to know why she was upset at breakfast the week before and he needed to know about the telephone calls from the reporter. It was better she tell him than that he find out when a story was published in a magazine or he heard it some other way. It was time.

Marybeth checked her watch and realized it was time for her to leave for her job at the stables.

As she grabbed her purse and headed out the front door, she could hear the telephone ringing in the kitchen.

9

BECAUSE THE SNOW HAD FINALLY MELTED and backwoods mountain roads were opening up to four-wheel-drive vehicles, fishermen were starting to work the streams and spring creeks in the Bighorns and Joe Pickett needed to check licenses and limits. Most of the streams were still high and muddy and wouldn't clear and level out for another month, but local flyfishing guides were already placing clients at deep pools and beaver ponds. Mayfly hatches, the first sign of summer for flyfishermen, had begun. And if there were fishermen and -women, that meant there were licenses to check. Fishers used the Hazelton Road for access to the streams, which is how Joe found himself once again near the site of the exploding cow. He wanted to see the crater again, for reasons he wasn't quite sure of.

Joe approached the crater along the same path he had taken two weeks earlier with Sheriff Barnum and Deputy McLanahan. Because of the heavy foot and gurney traffic of the EMTs, forensics teams, state Department of Criminal Investigation (DCI) agents, curiosity seekers, and dozens of locals trooping back and forth from the road to the crime scene, the path had become a trail. It was churned up and easy to follow.

He wanted to visit the site again in the daylight and, possibly, resolve the impression he had that night of being watched. As he approached the crater he hoped that something would put that lingering suspicion to rest.

This kind of thing had happened to him before. There had been a turn on the road near the foothills of the mountains that had, for months, given him an uneasy feeling whenever he drove by. There had been something in an aspen grove that troubled him. The evening hours as the sunset lengthened shadows and a certain stillness set in unsettled him. Finally, he had stopped his truck and walked up the grassy draw. As he neared the trees he drew his weapon because the ill feeling, whatever it was, got stronger. Then he saw it and for a brief, terrifying moment, he was face to face with the Devil himself. Within the thick stand of trees stood the gnarled, twisted, coiled black figure of . . . a single burned tree stump.

The distance to the crater through the trees seemed shorter than it had that night, and he was surprised how quickly he was upon it. Within and around the crater, Joe knew there would be nothing to be found that hadn't already been examined, tested, or photographed. The official conclusion of the joint report filed by both the Sheriff's Office and DCI bore out Barnum's original theory—that Stewie Woods had accidentally set off explosives because he was unfamiliar with them. They also found out that the woman who was with him was actually his wife of three days. A Justice of the Peace in Ennis, Montana, had come forth with the marriage certificate.

He slowly circled the crater. The dead cattle had long been removed. Fallen pine needles had begun to carpet the exposed earth of the hole. A few pale blades of grass were the first soldiers to reclaim the ground. The exposed roots that had looked so white and tender that night had hardened or thrust themselves back into the earth.

If he looked at the trees and branches in the right light Joe could still see dried blood, but rain, insects, birds, and rodents had cleaned nearly all of the bark. Years from now, Joe thought, passing hikers or hunters might remark on the depression in the trail, bypass it when it filled with rain. But there would be nothing remarkable about it.

So far he hadn't seen anything that could make him forget or explain that feeling he'd had of being watched.

Squinting, Joe tipped his head back. The explosion had cleared a passage in the spruce trees through which he could see the sky and two lone clouds. High in the tree above him was a stout branch that had been stripped of bark. Joe stepped into the crater for a better look. Something about the color of the dead branch didn't look right. Exposed dead pine turned a cream color. This branch, angled up from the trunk in the shape of a fishhook, was coffee brown. The branch was thick enough to support a big man. Especially if the man were skewered to the tree by the force of an explosion.

Joe crossed his arms and shook his head. There was no way what he was thinking could be possible. Even if it was, he thought, there was no way that all of the people who had been there since the explosion would not have seen it. Someone, at some point, *had to look up.*

He left his daypack and holster at the base of the tree and started to climb. Dime-sized scales of bark snagged at his shirt and jeans, but there were enough sappy branches to

81

provide footholds and handholds. He climbed until he was just below the dead branch and found a protruding knot he was able to rest a boot on. Hugging the trunk, he raised himself up until he was eye-level with the dead branch. His other foot was suspended in the air, so he wouldn't be able to maintain his position long. Already, the quad muscles in his thigh were beginning to burn.

The branch, close up, was certainly dark enough to have been stained with blood. But what he hoped to see was proof—dried rivulets or strands of fiber from clothing. He saw neither. Pulling himself even tighter to the tree with one arm, he reached out with his free hand and tried to break the branch, to no avail. Using his fingernails, he tried to chip off some of the stained wood so he could have it tested. But the branch was hard and he had no leverage to splinter it. His leg began to quiver and his calf and thigh muscles screamed. To relieve the pressure, Joe grasped the dead branch to balance himself. He pressed his cheek to the trunk of the tree.

Suddenly, there was percussive flapping above him. The sound frightened him and nearly made him lose his grip. He looked up at a huge black raven that had just landed inches from his hand. The raven looked down at him with sharp ebony eyes and sidestepped along the branch until one clawed black foot touched Joe's hand. The bird stared at Joe and Joe stared back. He had never seen a raven this close, and it was remarkable how inert and shiny the bird's eyes were. Its beak was slightly hooked on the end and was the color of dull black matte. Its feathers were so black that they reflected blue, like Superman's hair in the comics.

Then the raven struck, burying its beak into the back of

Joe's hand. Reflexively, Joe let go, which shifted his balance, and his boot slipped off of the knot. He clearly heard the hum of his shirt on the bark as he dropped and he felt his trouser cuffs gather up beneath his knees. A live branch that had been welcoming on the way up hit him under the arm on the way down and knocked him backward where he fell cleanly for a moment, then crashed through another branch, then landed hard on his back at the base of the tree with his knees wrapped around the trunk like a lover.

WHEN HE WAS ABLE to breathe normally, Joe opened his eyes. Small orange spangles floated through the sky along with the clouds. He did an inventory of his limbs and found that nothing was broken. His back ached, his hand was punctured and bloody near the knuckles from the raven, and his shirt and pants were disheveled and torn. The insides of his legs were rubbed raw and his shins were scraped. But he was all right.

He rolled to his feet and stood up warily. He had landed on his hat so he retrieved it and tried to restore the smashed-in crown. Painfully, he looked back at the dead branch. The raven was still there, and stared coldly back at him.

"You okay?" someone asked from the other side of the crater. The voice startled Joe, and he turned toward it. "You really made a lot of noise coming down out of that tree. We thought a tree was falling over or something."

It was Raga and Tonk, the two campers he had met the week before. They had just emerged from the pathway in the trees. Both wore daypacks.

"I'm fine. You're still here?" Joe asked. "Weren't you

going to Canada or somewhere?"

Raga leaned forward on a walking stick. "Been there and back."

"Where's the woman who was with you?" Joe asked.

Raga and Tonk shared a conspiratorial glance, but didn't answer Joe's question.

"Did you hear about Hayden Powell? The writer? His house burned down in Washington state," Raga said, his eyes cold. "This time, they found the body."

Joe had heard the name Hayden Powell somewhere, but was not familiar with him or Tonk's story.

"Charred beyond recognition," Tonk added for emphasis.

"So first there was Stewie, then Hayden," Raga continued, his tone fused with deliberate irony. "I wonder who will be next?"

Joe clamped his misshapen hat on his head. "You folks like conspiracies, don't you?"

Raga sneered and gestured toward the crater. "The people who did this will come back. I hope you're ready for them when they do."

Joe tried to read the faces of the two men. Raga was still sneering, Tonk nodding in agreement with what Raga had just said.

"Do you know something you should tell me?" Joe asked.

Raga slowly shook his head no. "They'll be back here," he said simply.

1 0

RETURNING HOME, Joe crossed the bridge that spanned the Twelve Sleep River and drove through the three-block length of Saddlestring's sleepy downtown. The insides of his thighs and the palms of his hands still stung from the fall. There was a dull ache in the back of his neck. Worst of all, his hat was crushed. It was just after five o'clock and most of the shops were already closed and the street virtually empty of traffic. Knots of cars and pickups were parked in front of the two bars on Main Street.

Saddlestring, once on the verge of a natural gas pipeline boom two years before that Joe inadvertently helped stymie, had once again settled into being a place considered "unchanging and rustic" in the view of some or "nearly dead" in the view of others. The discovery of species thought extinct—Miller's weasels—had created a tourism surge at the same time the town was seeing a brief cessation of traditional industries such as logging, mining, and outfitting in the remote area of the Bighorns, now known, sort of, as the Miller's Weasel Ecosystem. Interagency squabbling was still delaying the official unique designation of the ecosystem. In the meanwhile, the last known colony of Miller's weasels, the Cold Springs Group, had died out. Although Joe knew of another colony, the location remained a cherished secret between Sheridan and him, and neither ever talked about it. Scientists, biologists, and ecotourists no longer came for the purpose of seeing where the creatures that "captured a nation" once were, but the town, and the valley, continued to limp along. Saddlestring, as a place of interest to most outsiders, had once again dropped out of view.

Joe stopped at the corner before he turned toward Bighorn Road. Across the street were two buildings with ancient western storefronts, Bryan's Western Wear and

Wolf Mountain Taxidermy. The taxidermy studio was a rarity in that it was so well known in the state and throughout the Northern Rockies that it stayed open the entire year. Most studios closed for three or four months until hunting seasons opened again. The taxidermist, Matt Sandvick, had won dozens of awards for his work and was sought out by wealthy hunters. In addition to moose, deer, pronghorn antelope, and other Wyoming big game and fowl, Sandvick often did tigers, Alaskan brown bears, and other exotic species from around the world. He was the taxidermist of choice for wealthy, status-conscious men.

Which is why Joe canceled his turn signal and proceeded through the intersection and parked his pickup on the curb. He had been thinking of Matt Sandvick's work for several days. He was the best Joe had ever seen. A Sandvick mount had a certain clean, natural simplicity that brought the animal back to life. His work was subtle but regal, and left an impression on the admirer. Joe was just such an admirer. And it made him wonder about something.

As usual, there was no one in the outer office when Joe entered Wolf Mountain Taxidermy. Dozens of photos of mounts were beneath a sheet of glass on the counter, and a huge moose head dominated the wall above a door that led to the studio. Joe rang a bell next to a brochure rack full of price lists and waited.

Matt Sandvick was a short, powerful man with close-cropped red hair and thick horn-rimmed glasses. He emerged from his studio cleaning his hands with a stained towel. Joe had met him several times and had been in the shop during hunting season to confirm that hunters had properly tagged all of the game animals turned over to

Sandvick. Sandvick took a good deal of pride in his work. They got along well.

"What happened to you?" Sandvick asked, his eyes widening as he looked at Joe's torn shirt, bloody hand, and crushed hat.

Joe tried to think of something snappy to say, but couldn't think of anything.

"Fell out of a tree," Joe said, smiling with a hint of embarrassment.

Sandvick stifled a laugh. "Okay," he said, drawing the word out to indicate disbelief.

"Getting ready for hunting season?" Joe asked in a neighborly way.

"Always," Sandvick nodded. "Things are slowing down around here. A few fish is all. A nice twenty-two-inch cutthroat trout back there. You want to look at it?"

Joe shook his head no. He agreed that 22 inches was big for a cutthroat. *Matt,* Joe thought, *I'm sorry for what I'm about to do.*

Then: "You know that big bull elk you did for Jim Finotta last year? Was that an eight-by-eight?"

"Nine-by-seven," Sandvick corrected. "The only one I've ever seen."

"I would have sworn it had eight on each side," Joe said, looking quizzically at Sandvick. "I saw it just a few weeks ago in his office."

"Nope," Sandvick countered, "I'll prove it to you." Sandvick pushed his glasses up on his nose and studied the photos under the glass on the counter. He settled his index finger on a shot of Finotta's bull elk mount while it was still in the studio. Joe bent, a little stiffly, to get a better look.

"You okay?" Sandvick asked.

"My back hurts from that fall," Joe said, distracted. He studied the photo. There were nine tines on one antler and seven on the other, just like Sandvick said. There was also a very small LCD date stamp on the bottom right of the photograph that read "9-21."

"That's it, all right," Joe conceded. "You were absolutely right."

"That was a damned big elk," Sandvick said, but there was something different about his voice. Joe looked up to see that Sandvick was studying him intently, practically squinting. There was fear in Sandvick's eyes.

"You had this mount finished by the twenty-first of September," Joe said. "And rifle hunting season doesn't open until the fifteenth of October. You say in your brochure that it takes about six to eight weeks to finish a mount. So when did he bring it in? June or July?"

Sandvick's face drained of color and his eyes widened. He was caught. A taxidermist who worked on a game animal that wasn't accompanied by paperwork to prove it was properly taken could not only get his license revoked and be put out of business, but he could be jailed or fined. Matt Sandvick was well aware of that. So was Joe Pickett.

"June or July?" Joe asked, not unkindly.

"Maybe I ought to call my lawyer or something," Sandvick said weakly, then swallowed. "Except I don't have a lawyer."

"I'll tell you what, Matt," Joe said, feeling ashamed of his trick but pleased with his discovery, "if you agree to sign an affidavit stating that Jim Finotta brought that animal in to you out of season I won't ask the County Attorney to prosecute you. I'll even argue against it if he brings it up. But I can't promise that he won't do it anyway."

Sandvick brought both of his hands to his face and rubbed his eyes. "Finotta didn't bring it in himself. His ranch hand brought it in."

"When?"

"I think it was June," Sandvick said. "I could check my records for the exact date. I talked to him on the phone. Finotta offered me one of his new lots for it. That was kind of hard to pass up. Plus I didn't want to piss the man off."

Sandvick continued to rub his eyes, then his face. It was painful for Joe to watch.

"You do good work," Joe said. "Finotta told me he had that mount done in Jackson Hole, but everybody knows you're the best around and you're right here in town. So it makes sense he would come to you."

"He said he had it done in *Jackson?*" Sandvick asked, clearly hurt by that.

Joe nodded. "I'll leave you alone now. But I'll be in touch about that affidavit, okay?"

"That's really an insult. *Jackson?*"

Before Joe left the studio, he reached across the counter and patted Sandvick on the shoulder. "You're a good guy, Matt, but don't ever do that again."

Sandvick didn't need to be told. He was still trembling.

"The thing was," Joe explained, "they *left the meat.* Finotta shot it, probably got his flunky to cape it and take the head off, and they left the body to rot."

Sandvick said nothing. He lowered his hands to grip the counter and steady himself.

"That just makes me mad," Joe explained. Then he

tipped his bent hat brim at Sandvick and left the shop.

I THINK I GOT HIM," Joe told Marybeth when he entered the house, tossing his misshapen hat through his office doorway.

She looked him over carefully, her eyes widening in alarm at his appearance.

"I'm fine," Joe said. "I think I've nailed Jim Finotta."

"I heard you," she said, approaching him and fingering a tear in his shirtsleeve.

In his excited state, he blurted: "Marybeth, we have to talk."

She probed his eyes with hers, then patted his cheek.

"Soon," she said.

11

MARYBETH PICKETT WAS REPLACING videotapes in the shelves behind the check-in desk when she heard the door to the library open and close. It was weekend procedure to try to keep count of the people in the library because of the early afternoon closing. Several months before, one of the other volunteers had inadvertently locked a patron who was in the bathroom inside the building. The man locked inside had to call the sheriff and wait for someone with a key to be tracked down.

Marybeth glanced around the video shelf at a shrunken woman in a wheelchair being pushed by a dark man who had a toothpick in his mouth. The man saw her, tipped the brim of his dirty ball cap, and looked Marybeth over as he walked past. Marybeth nodded cryptically and continued to replace the videos. Since the Twelve Sleep County Library had started renting movies for $2 each a year ago, the librarians fretted over the fact that books would become an afterthought in the community. That had happened, to some degree.

When she was done with the videos, she returned to the front counter to find the man there. He was leaning forward on the counter resting on his elbows, and chewing his toothpick. He had dark eyes and rough skin, and the expression on his face was a self-satisfied leer.

"May I help you find something?" she asked coolly.

He grinned at that, showing a mouthful of broken yellow teeth, and when he did the toothpick danced.

"I just love it when pretty ladies ask me that question."

Marybeth shook her head. It wasn't often that a man was so pathetically transparent. She had no desire to engage in any kind of banter with him.

"Was that your mother you brought in here?"

He chortled. "Shit, no. That's Miss Ginger."

"Should I know her?"

"I'm surprised you don't. I bring her to the library once or twice a week. She's doing some kind of research for a book she claims she's writing."

Marybeth looked beyond the man. The woman in the wheelchair, Miss Ginger, was parked in an aisle in the western history section. She had pulled a book from the shelf that was now on her lap. It was obvious to Marybeth that the woman wanted to go to one of the tables to read it, but didn't have the strength to push herself there.

"I think she needs your help."

"She can wait," the man snorted. "My name's Buster, by the by. I work out on the Vee Bar U for the boss. But instead of workin', I have to bring *her* into town and sit around on my ass in this place while she does research for a book she's never going to finish. I guess we've never been in here before when you were working."

Marybeth nodded, ignoring the opening provided to reveal her schedule to Buster. She did her best to keep her reaction in check. "You work for Jim Finotta, then?"

"Yup," Buster said proudly.

"Then she's Jim Finotta's mother?"

"She's his *wife*, for Christ's sake." Buster laughed. "Not his ma."

Marybeth recalled Joe telling her about an old woman at the house, as well as about the stupid ranch hand who she now knew as Buster.

"What is wrong with her?" Marybeth asked gently.

"You mean besides the fact that she's a crabby old bitch?" Buster asked, raising his eyebrows. He actually seemed to think he was charming her, Marybeth thought in amazement. "She's got Lou Gehrig's disease. ALS or ACS or something like that. She's getting worse all of the time. Pretty soon, she'll be flat on her back and her speech will go away completely."

"Are you going to help her?" Marybeth asked archly.

Buster rolled his eyes. "Eventually, yeah. When we're done here."

Marybeth looked at him coldly. "We *are* done here," she said, and left him leaning on the counter while she approached Ginger Finotta.

Ginger Finotta's face was contorted and her lips were pressed together in a kind of sour pucker. Her eyes were rheumy with fluid, but they welcomed Marybeth as she approached. Marybeth removed one of the straight-backed chairs at the nearest table and wheeled Ginger into the empty space.

"Did you find everything you need?" Marybeth asked over Ginger Finotta's shoulder. Marybeth noted the stiff helmet of hair and the woman's skeletal neck and shoulders, which couldn't be hidden by her high-necked print dress.

"Isn't Buster an awful man?" Ginger Finotta asked in a scratchy voice.

"Yes, he is," Marybeth agreed.

"He is an *awful* man."

Marybeth said "Mmmmhmmm" and walked around to the other side of the table so they could see each other. It took a moment for Ginger Finotta's eyes to catch up. When they did, Marybeth sensed the immediate pain that the woman was in.

"I'm doing research for my book."

"That's what I understand from Buster."

"How much do you know about the history of Wyoming?" Ginger asked. Her voice was not well modulated, and questions sounded like statements.

Marybeth said she knew a little from school, but wasn't a scholar or historian by any means.

"Do you know about Tom Horn?" Ginger Finotta asked.

"A little, I guess," Marybeth said. "He was a so-called stock detective and he was hanged in Cheyenne for killing a fourteen-year-old boy."

Ginger Finotta nodded almost imperceptibly. "But he didn't do it. He did so many other bad things, though, that it doesn't matter if he shot that boy or not."

Buster had finally left the counter and was approaching the table.

"Mrs. Finotta, do you need anything?" he asked, and shot Marybeth a conspiratorial wink that she ignored.

"I need you to go to some other part of this building. I'll call you when I want to go home."

Buster raised his palms and said "Whoa!" before departing with a smirk on his face.

Ginger Finotta's attention remained on Marybeth. Marybeth wondered if the woman knew anything about the situation between Jim Finotta and Joe. It was hard to guess how lucid she was. She was a prisoner of her twisted and contorted frame.

"You need to know about Tom Horn," Ginger Finotta said, tapping the book on the table. It was called *The Life and Times of Tom Horn, Stock Detective.*

"Why is that?"

The question hung in the air while Ginger's eyes closed, slowly at first and then so tightly that her face trembled. She seemed to be battling through something. When her eyes reopened they were almost blank.

"Because if you know about history, it's easier to understand the present. You know, why we do the things we're doing now."

"What do you mean?" Marybeth asked softly.

Ginger's eyes searched Marybeth's face. She clearly wanted to answer, but suddenly couldn't. Her face trembled, tiny muscles and tendons dancing under waxed-paper skin. She seemed to be concentrating on conquering the tics, trying to get her own body under some kind of control. But when she opened her mouth there was a bubble of spit, and the only sound she made was an angry hiss. Her eyes betrayed her immense disappointment.

Marybeth could not discern where this was headed, or if the woman truly needed help, but she did have to get back to the front counter. A woman with two children was waiting with an arm full of books to check out.

"Are you okay, Miss Finotta?"

The woman nodded that she was.

"I'll read about Tom Horn when you're done with the book," Marybeth said with a forced smile. "I promise. But now I've got to get back. Please let me know if you need anything else while you're here."

As Marybeth started to turn there was a slight movement of Ginger Finotta's thin hands on the table. She was trying unsuccessfully to raise her hand and stop Marybeth from leaving.

"You don't understand!" Ginger Finotta squawked, finding her voice again.

Her voice made Marybeth freeze. It carried throughout the library. Newspaper readers in the small lounge area lowered their papers. The woman at the counter and her children turned and stared at the trembling woman. Buster emerged from the periodical aisle with a sour look on his face.

"Are you all right?" Marybeth asked.

"Do I look all right to you?"

Marybeth was confused. "What don't I understand?"

Ginger Finotta's moist eyes swept the ceiling before once again settling on Marybeth. "I know who you are and I know who your husband is."

Marybeth felt a chill crawl up her spine and pull on the

roots of her hair.

"That's why you need to know about Tom Horn," Ginger Finotta said, her voice shrill.

"Let's go," Buster spat, suddenly appearing behind Ginger Finotta's wheelchair. Roughly, he pulled the chair out from under the table and started for the front door. Ginger clutched the book to her shrunken breast, as if saving it from a fire.

"Sorry, ladies," Buster called over his shoulder, his toothpick dancing. "Mrs. Finotta is having some trouble here and she needs her rest. *Bye-bye!*"

Marybeth stood stock still, wondering what exactly had just happened. She watched as Buster pushed Mrs. Finotta down the sidewalk, much too fast, toward the handicapped-accessible van he had parked near the front door. Marybeth slowly unclenched her fists, and took a deep breath.

THAT EVENING, Marybeth told Joe about her experience at the library with Ginger Finotta.

"His wife?" Joe asked, surprised. "That woman was his *wife?*"

Joe said he had heard of Tom Horn before, had read a book a long time ago, about the infamous stock detective.

"I don't get it," he said, confused.

"Neither do I," agreed Marybeth, still shaken.

12

I-90, WEST OF MISSOULA, MONTANA
June 27

THE OLD MAN AWOKE to the sound of the early morning

news playing on the pickup radio. He had been having a dream that he was evil. It was a dream like any other dream, but it was from a different perspective. It was on the outside looking in, and his thoughts in the dream were dark, breezy, and grotesque. He saw other people, strangers, in the dream as vacant stooges to be bent to his will or disposed of if they got in the way. There were men, women, and little children and they were crying out. He had pure contempt for them and their suffering, which he saw as weakness. He had never had a dream like that before, and it unsettled him.

He grunted and pulled himself into a sitting position before readjusting the truck seat. It was a beautiful day in Western Montana and it wasn't raining. The Old Man was more comfortable here than in Washington State. The Clark Fork River was on their right. It was fast, white, and tumbling with early summer runoff. Mist hung low and stayed in the valley like a relative. The forested mountainsides were still and dark because the morning sun had not yet lit them, and they were shot through with a mosaic pattern of burn from the fires that had ripped through the land two summers before.

Through bleary eyes he looked at Charlie Tibbs, who was driving. Tibbs nodded good morning, then gestured to the radio. The Old Man yawned and listened. The huge black Ford pickup with smoked dark windows shot through the Lolo National Forest.

It was toward the end of the national news: U.S. Congressman Peter Sollito of Massachusetts had been found murdered in his Watergate apartment in Washington, D.C. The District of Columbia police and the FBI were investigating. Sollito's body had been discovered by his longtime housekeeper. The woman had come in to give the apartment a final cleaning as the congressman had called her the previous week to tell her that he would be going home to Massachusetts in a few days for summer recess. The police were investigating, but so far they had no suspects. The cause of death was not revealed.

But it *would* be, the Old Man said to himself. The news that Sollito was strangled to death by a pair of panty hose in his own bed, and that he was intoxicated at the time of his death would soon be splashed all over the headlines. Trace evidence of lipstick, long, tinted hair, and fibers from a cheap, loud miniskirt would be found in the sheets; a woman's shoe with a long spike heel would be discovered under the bed. The police would have certainly noted the singles' tabloid on Sollito's kitchen counter with the pages opened to listings of prostitutes and escort services. The conclusion to be drawn from all of this was very simple: Sollito had been playing sex games with a woman and the game got out of hand. It would be embarrassing, of course, and humiliating. He was not known for this kind of thing.

The important thing about all of this, as Charlie Tibbs had pointed out to the Old Man as they entered the elevator at the Watergate dressed in maintenance uniforms, was that Sollito would only be remembered for how he died, not for what he did in Congress.

Rep. Peter Sollito, with his position on the Natural Resources Committee and his relationship with the media, was by far the foremost advocate of environmental legislation in the House. Sollito introduced bills halting timbering, mining, natural gas, and petroleum exploration on many federal lands. He killed a proposal to declare a moratorium on grazing fees. He was the most visible "green" Congressman, and the most vocal. Environmental groups loved him and showered him with awards. His constituents were proud of his tough stands on the environment and his high profile.

In Charlie Tibbs's toolbox, in the elevator, had been an envelope with the fibers and hair, the shoe, the singles tabloid, and the pair of black panty hose. The Old Man carried a small daypack containing three bottles of cheap champagne, and he had the pistol. Sollito had opened the door after looking at them through a peephole and deciding they were legitimate. They were just two old guys, after all.

"That took a while, didn't it?" Charlie said after the news was over. "Four days to find him. You'd think a congressman would be missed."

"It seems like months ago," the Old Man said. They had crossed the country from Washington, D.C., to Washington State in the meanwhile. And now they were back in Montana.

"Charlie, don't you ever sleep?" the Old Man asked.

Charlie Tibbs clearly disliked personal questions and so he ignored this one as he had all of the other personal questions the Old Man had asked.

The Old Man shifted his weight and looked through the back window into the bed of the pickup.

"Where did the computer and all that other stuff of Powell's go?"

"Dumped them in a canyon by Lookout Pass," Charlie said. Lookout Pass was on the Idaho-Montana border.

"I didn't even know we stopped."

"I know."

Charlie seemed to resent the fact that the Old Man slept at night. Charlie seemed to resent anything that suggested human frailty of any kind. The Old Man recalled the look Charlie gave him back at Hayden Powell's house when the Old Man didn't want to see Powell's injuries.

"There's some coffee in the Thermos," Charlie said.

"Charlie, do you dream much?" the Old Man asked, finding the Thermos of hot coffee and pouring the remainder into their cups. He knew the question would annoy Tibbs, which was why he asked it. Waking up to the news of Sollito had unsettled him and brought it all rushing back. The situation in Washington, D.C., had been especially troubling to the Old Man. It was much worse than what had happened in the Bighorns or at Hayden Powell's house. Sollito had begged, and had continued begging, for his life even after he was forced to drink the second bottle of champagne and his voice had become a slurred whine. He had tried, unsuccessfully, to escape. He had looked deeply into the Old Man's eyes and asked for mercy, mercy that wasn't granted.

Charlie didn't respond to the question. He seemed uncomfortable with it, and shrugged.

"I had a hell of a dream," the Old Man said, sipping the coffee. "I dreamed I became an evil man. Then I woke up and I still feel evil."

The Old Man watched for a reaction. He knew he was pushing it with Charlie.

"That's a bad dream," Charlie said, finally. "You should just wash that right out of your mind. You are not an evil man."

"Didn't say I was," the Old Man said. "Just said I woke up feeling that way."

"You are a noble man. What we're doing is noble work." It was said with finality.

The Old Man rubbed the sleep from his eyes. "I think I need a real bed and a real rest. I hope I can get both when we get to where we're going."

"I hope you can, too," Charlie said. It was another shot at the Old Man's weakness. The set in his face made it clear that as far as he was concerned the topic was finished.

After a lapse of some time, Charlie cleared his throat to speak. "Our employers have heard rumors that some environmental whackos believe that Stewie Woods is still alive because they never found a body."

The Old Man snorted. "He was blown to bits."

"That's how goddamned nuts some of those people are, though. I guess they've got stuff on the Internet about it."

The Old Man just shook his head and chuckled. The early morning sun heated the tops of his thighs through the windshield.

"They don't believe it, do they?" the Old Man asked. "Our employers, I mean."

"No."

The Old Man sipped his coffee and watched Charlie Tibbs drive. He enjoyed watching Tibbs drive. There was such a display of competence, and competence was something the Old Man admired because it was so extremely hard to find. With Charlie Tibbs you always knew where you were going and why. The fears he had the night before about Tibbs he dismissed as manifestations of stress and fatigue.

But the feeling the Old Man had from the dream lingered.

13

ON THE SAME MORNING, 580 miles to the southeast of Missoula, Montana, Joe got a call about a mountain lion from a homeowner who lived in Elkhorn Ranches. The homeowner claimed he had been stalked. Joe took down the address and said he would there soon.

"You better be quick or I'm going to shoot that son-of-a-bitch," the homeowner told Joe.

On his way out, Joe stopped at the breakfast table to kiss the girls and jokingly complained about "sloppy milk kisses," which set them to howling. Even Sheridan, at the ripe old age of ten, still participated in the mock outrage over their dad's early morning taunts. It was either about "breakfast kisses" or when he complimented them all on their lovely early morning hairdos before they got dressed and groomed themselves for school.

Marybeth followed him out the front door. Joe was already at his green Game and Fish pickup before he realized she was still with him. Maxine bounded out of the house and launched herself into the cab of the truck.

"I'm still disturbed about what happened yesterday in the library," Marybeth said. Joe hoped for more.

He nodded, and turned to her.

Marybeth shook her head. "I feel horribly sorry for that woman, but she scared me."

"What she looked like or what she said?" Joe asked, putting his arms around her, tucking her head under his chin and looking out toward Wolf Mountain, but not really seeing it.

"Both."

Her hair smelled fresh, and he kissed the top of her head.

"She scared the hell out of me the first time, too," Joe said. "She was sort of hidden in the curtains at their house."

"I feel bad about being so repulsed," Marybeth said quietly. "A disease like that could afflict any of us."

Joe wasn't sure what to say. He rarely thought in those terms. Right now, he only wanted to keep her close. He was grateful for the moment.

"That Tom Horn business puzzles me," she said. "I'm still not sure if Ginger Finotta is just crazy, or if she's trying to tell me something."

"Maybe we ought to read up on the guy," Joe offered.

"I'm waiting for her to return the book," Marybeth said. "It's the only copy the library has. I did a search on the computer trying to find it in another collection, but the book is really obscure. I found a copy in Bend, Oregon, and sent them an e-mail but haven't heard back."

He hugged her tightly. After a moment, she pulled away, but gently.

"Any chance you'll get home early this afternoon?" she asked slyly. "The girls all have swimming lessons after school and won't be home until five."

Finally, Joe thought.

He smiled at her. He was wearing a department baseball cap until he could get his hat reshaped.

"Sounds like a proposition."

Marybeth smiled mysteriously and turned toward the house.

"Get home early enough and you'll find out," she said over her shoulder.

• • •

THE THREE-STORY RED BRICK HOME was easy to find because it was the only house on Grand Teton Street in Elkhorn Ranches. All three acres had been recently landscaped with grass, mature Caragana bushes, and ten-foot aspens. The sod was so new that Joe could still see all of the seams in the yard. Joe couldn't see a mountain lion anywhere.

As he pulled into the driveway from the road, one of the four garage doors began to open. As the door raised Joe saw a pair of fleece slippers, pajama legs of dark blue silk, a thick beige terrycloth robe cinched tight around a large belly, and the rest of a large gray-bearded man holding the garage door opener in one hand and a semiautomatic pistol in the other. The gun startled Joe and he froze behind the wheel. One arm was raised toward Joe. Luckily, it was the remote that was raised, not the pistol. Beside Joe, Maxine growled through the windshield.

Both Joe and the homeowner, at the same instant, realized that if Joe drew and fired, the shooting would be considered justified. The homeowner was armed and standing in the shadows of his garage. The man's raised arm could have easily been mistaken for a threatening gesture. Quickly, the homeowner sidestepped and placed the pistol on a workbench. The man then shook his empty hand as if he had dropped something too hot to hold and an embarrassed look passed over the man's face. Joe let his breath out, aware for the first time that he had been holding it in. If he had been out to get me, Joe thought sourly, it would all be over and he'd be the one left standing. Joe wasn't even sure where his pistol *was* at that moment. In the field, where nearly every human Joe encountered was armed, Joe was duly cautious and kept his gun with him at all times. But at this huge new showplace home, in a perfectly square three-acre oasis of textured and manicured greenery, in the middle of a huge sagebrush expanse, he had not expected to run into an armed man.

The homeowner approached Joe's pickup with a forced smile.

"Do you need to change your pants inside?" the home-owner grinned at Joe as if sharing an inside joke. Joe knew he must have looked terrified for a moment, and he felt an embarrassed flush crawl up his neck.

As Joe stepped out and shut the door to the pickup, he shot a glance inside the cab. His holster and gun belt were on the floor where he had left them the night before, the belt buckled around the four-wheel-drive gearshift.

"You okay?" the man asked, thrusting out his hand. "I'm Stan Wilder."

Joe shook it and said he was just fine. Joe guessed that Stan Wilder was in his late sixties and new to the area. His accent was Northeastern and his words came fast. He had perfect big teeth that he flashed as he talked. The faded blonde-gray mustache and beard that surrounded the man's mouth looked dull and washed out in comparison with his gleaming teeth.

"I was walking out to get the newspaper," Stan Wilder nodded toward the red plastic Saddlestring *Roundup* box mounted on a T-post at the end of his driveway, "when the hair on the back of my neck stood straight up. Then I looked over there"—Wilder pointed toward a new row of spindly aspen trees—"and saw the mountain lion stalking me. I'm not ashamed to say that I was about as scared as you were just a minute ago!" He clapped Joe on the back.

Joe stepped far enough away so that Stan Wilder couldn't do that again.

"How long ago did you see the mountain lion?" Joe asked. He chose not to reciprocate Stan Wilder's banter.

"Must have been about seven this morning."

"Did you see him run off?"

Wilder laughed, throwing his head back showing his teeth again. Joe guessed that he must have been in sales and marketing before he retired and moved west to Elkhorn Ranches.

"Nope, but he saw *me* run right back into the house! That's when I got my weapon out and called you."

"You didn't take any shots at him, did you?"

Somehow, Joe knew he had. Stan Wilder's face betrayed the answer.

"He was on my property, Warden," Wilder explained. "I popped a couple of caps. But I didn't hit him."

Joe nodded. "You ought to reconsider the next time you want to fire your pistol out here. The highway is just over the hill and there are construction workers framing a house in the next draw. You could hit one of them and you could also hit one of Jim Finotta's cows. They graze fairly close to here."

Stan Wilder snorted and rolled his eyes heavenward.

Joe walked over and checked the ground around the aspen trees. Because the trees had been planted just a few days before, the earth around them was still soft. A four-inch-long cat track was obvious and fresh near one of the trees.

"Big cat," Joe said.

"Damn right," Wilder agreed. "I need him removed."

Joe turned and sighed. "Removed?"

"Damn right. I don't mind the antelope and the deer. I see them all the time. I *paid* for antelope and deer and access to the trout streams. Finotta told me that elk sometimes come down this far and I'd like to see a few of them. That'd be added value.

"But I didn't pay for this," he swept his hand toward his new house, "to have mountain lions stalking me."

Joe said it was unlikely that the lion was stalking him. He told Stan Wilder that he had never heard of a mountain lion actually stalking and attacking a full-grown man.

"What about those babies in Los Angeles?" Wilder asked aggressively. "Didn't a mountain lion come down from the mountains and kill some babies?"

Joe said he thought he remembered something about that story, but the predator was a coyote and the circumstances were questionable.

"Well, I remember it being a mountain lion," Stan Wilder said gruffly.

"Look, Mr. Wilder, mountain lion sightings are rare. There's no doubt you saw one, but he didn't do any harm. Up until a year ago this was probably his range. These cats cover about two hundred miles. He was likely as surprised to see a big house and a lawn here as you were to see him. I know *I* was surprised to see this place out here."

Stan Wilder told Joe that he had just heard a perfect load of bureaucratic bullshit.

"If he comes back can I shoot him?" Stan Wilder asked. "I mean legally?"

Joe grudgingly said that yes, if the cat was actually close enough to do real harm, he could shoot him.

"But I would advise against it," Joe cautioned.

"Whose side are you on here, Mr. Game Warden? The cougar's or mine?"

Joe didn't answer that question.

"That mountain lion better watch his step," Stan Wilder cautioned, nodding his head toward the handgun in the garage. "If you catch my drift."

"Like I said, there are cars on the highway, workers at other lots, and cows all around."

Wilder snorted again.

"You should be aware, Mr. Wilder, that some of these cows have been known to explode," Joe said soberly.

That got Wilder's attention.

"What in the hell are you talking about?" Wilder asked, trying to gauge Joe's demeanor to see if he was being made fun of.

"Don't you read the paper?" Joe asked, then walked back to his pickup.

A BIG GREEN SUBURBAN with license plates reading "VBarU-1" turned from the highway onto the ranch road as Joe approached the turnoff. Joe stopped his pickup, and the Suburban slowed until the two driver's-side windows lined up. A dark power window lowered and Jim Finotta, looking patiently put upon, asked Joe if he could be of help.

"Yes, you can," Joe said. "You can help me out with a couple of things."

Finotta raised his eyebrows, but said nothing.

"First, you might want to advise the owners of the starter

castles out here that in addition to this being a place where the deer and antelope play, that there might be the occasional bear, badger, skunk, or mountain lion."

Finotta nodded and smiled with condescension.

"Second, you can let me get that sample of bone or antler from that bull elk mount in your office. I'll send the sample to our lab in Laramie and we should be able to clear this all up in two or three weeks."

Finotta's eyes became hard.

"Did you forget what we talked about?" Finotta asked Joe.

"Nope."

"Then why are you bothering me about this elk again?" Finotta asked in a barely controlled tone. "You can't be that stupid."

"I don't know," Joe said, "I can be pretty stupid."

Finotta's window began to rise.

"I talked to Matt Sandvick," Joe said quickly.

The window stopped just below Finotta's chin. Finotta's lips were now pressed together so tightly that they looked like a thin white scar. He was obviously furious, but fighting it. When he spoke his voice was oddly calm.

"Just leave it be, Warden."

Joe shrugged. "I'm doing my job. It's important for me to check these things out."

Finotta sneered. "Important for who? The Governor won't care and therefore your director won't care. Judge Pennock won't give a shit."

"It's important for me," Joe said, and he meant it.

"And just who in the hell are *you?*" Finotta asked with such contempt that Joe felt as if he had been kicked in the face.

"I'm the game warden of Twelve Sleep District," Joe said. He was fully aware of how lame that sounded, how weak it had come across.

Finotta glared at him. He began to say something, then thought better of it. The window closed and Jim Finotta drove away, leaving Joe sitting in his pickup with a sick feeling in his stomach and the premonition that he was going to be real alone in this.

THAT AFTERNOON, as he drove home, Joe called County Attorney Robey Hersig on his cell phone, only to get Hersig's voicemail. Joe outlined what he suspected regarding Jim Finotta's elk and what he had learned from taxidermist Matt Sandvick.

"I'm ready to move on Finotta but need Sandvick's affidavit and your okay," was how he ended his message.

14

TO JOE'S SURPRISE, Marybeth had both horses in the corral and saddled when he got home. She was bridling her paint, Toby, as he walked up. She looked at him provocatively and said: "Let's go for a ride."

"Sounds real good to me," Joe grinned.

Joe rode his buckskin, Lizzie, who was happy to follow the gelding, and they wound up the old game trail behind their house through the Sandrock Draw.

While they rode, Joe watched his wife and her horse and admired them both. Marybeth had taken an interest in horses in the last year, and he had learned things about them through her. Previously, he had always thought of horses the same way he thought about an all-terrain vehicle. A horse was a tool; a way of getting to places without roads, of accessing rough country. In Joe's opinion, a horse would lose in many, if not all, of the straight-up comparisons with an ATV, in fact. Although the initial investment was about the same, horses required daily maintenance and care. ATV's could be parked in the garage and forgotten. Hay, grain, and vet bills were expensive, and horses were always breaking things in the corral or injuring themselves in ridiculous ways. ATV's just sat there. If a single stray nail flipped into the corral, there was a 100 percent chance that a horse would step on it, eat it, or puncture himself on it while rolling. Horses could be counted on for eating things that would make them sick or not eating enough to keep them healthy. They were magnificently proportioned and heavily muscled and all of that bulk was held up by four thin bony legs that could, and did, snap at any time. And despite their size and heft, a horse was a prey animal. In the face of a real threat like a grizzly bear or a perceived threat like a motorcyclist on a side road or even a plastic bag blowing in the wind, a horse could bolt and take off like a rocket. Most of the injured hunters Joe encountered in the mountains had been injured by horses. He couldn't even guess the number of times that horses simply ran off from camps or makeshift corrals. Lizzie had once trotted miles away after Joe dismounted to look through his binoculars, and he spent the rest of the day chasing her on foot. In comparison, ATV's sometimes ran out of gas or broke down, although not very often.

But through Marybeth, Joe was starting to think about horses differently. She was firm with them, but nurturing.

She brought out their personalities. Toby had been an impetuous youth. He was never mean or dangerous, but he preferred his own company and was loath to do anything he didn't want to do—and what he wanted to do, primarily, was eat and rest. But she worked with him for months. Unlike old-time horsemen who were quick to reach for a whip or a two-by-four, Marybeth "asked" the horse to do things and he eventually did them. It was amazing that a woman Marybeth's size could gain the trust and respect of a big lazy gelding like Toby who weighed 1,100 pounds. It was as if she had convinced him—connected with something somewhere in his cloudy, preconditioned, herd-instinctive brain—that she was bigger and more dominant than he was.

All these years, Joe had simply been *using* Lizzie, not *riding* her. She was a good horse, trouble at times, but generally docile. He had been lucky she was so easy to manage because he was no horseman. Through watching and admiring Marybeth he was coming to appreciate true horsemen and horsewomen. And horses.

And there was something to be said for the feeling he got when he was riding a horse. That feeling—Marybeth called it "equine communication" or "being one with the horse"—could not be replicated in an ATV.

They cleared the Sandrock Draw and emerged on a grassy bench strewn with glacial boulders. The Bighorn Mountains, as well as the distant encroaching foothills furred with early summer grass were in the distance in front of them and the view was awe-inspiring. A fading jet trail cut across the sky, calling attention to the lack of clouds. Joe urged Lizzie forward so he could ride side-by-side with Marybeth.

That's when she told him about Stewie Woods and Hayden Powell and the reporter who kept calling.

Joe listened, asking only a few questions, steering away from the one he really wanted to ask.

"I slept with him once. Only once," Marybeth said, wincing, anticipating Joe. On cue, Joe moaned and slumped in his saddle as if hit by a rifle bullet.

"Aaugh," he groaned. "Yuck. Yipes."

She stifled a smile.

She told him that she had read in the library that Hayden had died recently as well; killed just a week ago in a fire in his home. Joe said he had learned of the fact from two anti-globalist drifters.

"So were you an ecoterrorist?" Joe asked, still wounded. This was a disquieting circumstance to be in, asking his wife about things he had never known about her.

"No, I never was," Marybeth answered. "But I was with them a few times when they did things like pull up survey stakes and pour sugar in gas tanks. I never did any of those things, but I was there. And I never told on them."

Joe nodded.

"This reporter," he asked. "Has he called back?"

"Twice," Marybeth said.

"Do you want me to talk to him? Would that help?"

She waved her hand. "He'll go away. I'm not worried about that."

Joe fell behind because they had to thread through two boulders, then caught up again.

"So why didn't you ever tell me any of this? Stewie Woods was a pretty famous guy in his way."

Marybeth thought for a moment. "It just didn't seem necessary. How could it have mattered?"

"It might just have been good to know," Joe said, unsure of whether or not that was true.

"Why?"

Joe shrugged. Like most men, he had a tough time believing that his wife had had any kind of interesting life before she met *him*. Which was ridiculous on its face.

"The good part of my life started when I met Joe Pickett," Marybeth said, looking deeply into his eyes. Joe felt his face go red. He knew what that look meant. He had just never seen it on horseback before.

"I brought a blanket," she said, in a tone so low he hoped he had heard her correctly.

THEY APPROACHED THE CORRAL as the school bus stopped and the door opened and the girls ran out. Lucy and April ran into the house to dry their hair from swimming. Sheridan, with her towel and sack of clothes in her arms, walked up to meet them, her thongs snapping on her bare feet.

"Hi, darlin'," Joe greeted her, leading Lizzie into the corral.

Sheridan just looked at him. Her gaze moved from Joe's face to her mother's. Joe noted that Marybeth's face glowed and she looked very pleased with herself, although she now sternly returned Sheridan's gaze.

"What?" Joe asked.

Sheridan slowly shook her head. It was the same gesture Marybeth used when she couldn't believe what her children had just done.

"You still have grass in your hair," Sheridan told her mother, her voice deadpan.

Marybeth gently scolded Sheridan. "You should be happy that your mom and dad like each other so much that they go on a ride together." While she talked she self-consciously brushed through her hair with her fingers to remove the grass.

Then Joe got it. For the second time in an hour, he flushed red.

From the house, Lucy yelled out that there was a telephone call for Marybeth.

"Go ahead," Joe said. "I'll untack. Sheridan, why don't you go with her?"

He didn't want Sheridan staring at him anymore. She was getting too old, and too wise. She huffed and went into the house, making sure to stay several feet away from her mother.

AS JOE WAS HANGING THE BRIDLES on a hook inside the shed, Marybeth entered the barn. Joe assumed she was there to talk about how Sheridan had reacted. He was wrong.

"It happened again," Marybeth said.

"That reporter?"

"I think so . . ." Marybeth looked troubled. "But this time he was posing as Stewie. He said he wanted to see me again."

"Are you sure it was the reporter?"

Marybeth held up her palms. "It had to be."

Joe carried the saddles to the saddletrees and folded the warm, moist horse blankets over a crossbar to dry.

"Did he *sound* like Stewie?" Joe asked.

Marybeth let a chuckle creep into her voice. "I haven't talked to Stewie Woods in years. It kind of sounded like him, but it didn't sound right. It was sort of as if someone were trying to imitate his voice."

Joe stopped and thought. He gripped his chin in his hand in a pose that made the girls whisper, *"Dad's thinking!"*

"It was weird," she said. "I just hung up on him."

"Next time," Joe said, "Don't hang up. Keep him talking until you can figure out who it is. And if I'm here, let me know so I can get on the other line."

Marybeth agreed, and they walked back to the house together. Before they opened the door, Joe reached out for her hand and squeezed it.

THAT NIGHT, in bed, Joe lay awake with his hands clasped behind his head on the pillow and one knee propped up outside the sheets. It had been the first warm evening of the early summer and it hadn't cooled off yet. The bedroom window was open and a breeze ruffled the curtains.

"Are you awake?" he whispered to Marybeth.

Marybeth purred, and turned to look at him.

"Sometimes I wish I were smarter," he said.

"Why do you say that?" Her voice was hoarse—she had been sleeping. Marybeth was a light sleeper, a carryover from when the children were younger.

"You're one of the smartest guys I know," she said, putting her warm hand on his chest. "That's why I married you."

"I'm not smart enough, though."

"Why?"

Joe exhaled loudly. "There's something big going on all around us, but I can't connect the dots. I know it's out there, and I keep trying to look at things from a different angle or perspective, thinking maybe then I'll see it. But it's just not coming clear."

"What are you talking about, Joe?"

He raised his hand and counted off: "Stewie Woods, Jim Finotta, Ginger Finotta, that Raga character and his friends, the reporter, Hayden Powell, Jim Finotta—"

"You already said Jim Finotta," she murmured.

"Well, he really pisses me off."

"*Anyway*—" she prompted.

"Anyway, I think that if I were smarter I could see how they all connect. And there *is* some kind of connection. That I'm sure of."

"How can you be sure of that?"

He thought, rubbed his eyes. The breeze was filling the room, taking the temperature down to comfortable sleeping conditions.

"I just am," he said.

She laughed softly. "You're smarter than you think."

"You're shining me on, darling."

"Good night." She hugged him and rolled over.

"That was fun this afternoon," he said. "Thank you."

"No, thank *you*. Now, good night."

Joe remained awake for a while longer. He recalled Raga saying the "people who did this will come back." He wondered if he would recognize them if they did.

15

Charlie Tibbs and the old man were parked behind a chain-link fence bordering an airstrip near Choteau, Montana. To the west were the broad shoulders of the Flathead range under a bleached denim sky. A morning rain—one of those odd ones where the bank of clouds had already passed out of view before the rain finally made it to earth—had dampened the concrete of the two old runways and beaded the black hood of the pickup.

Three-quarters of a mile away, a door opened on the second of four small private airplane hangars. Charlie Tibbs raised binoculars to his eyes. He would provide the commentary.

"They opened the door."

"I see that," the Old Man said.

The Old Man was, if possible, even more miserable than he had been the week before. Even though they had eaten a real dinner at a truckstop (steak, mashed potatoes, corn, apple pie, coffee) and had taken a break en route to Choteau to sleep the night at a motel in Lewistown, he didn't feel like he had gotten any real rest. His mind was doing things to him that were unsettling and unfair. He had nightmares about Peter Sollito, Hayden Powell, and Stewie Woods, as well as dreams peopled by friends and neighbors he hadn't seen in forty years. Everyone seemed to disapprove of him now. They clucked and pointed, and shunned him when he walked over to them. His own grandmother, dead for twenty-two years, pursed her lips defiantly and refused to speak to him. He'd had the same kind of disturbing, unconnected, fantastic dreams before, but only when he was feverish. His back was sore from sitting in the pickup and even the real bed two nights before hadn't helped unbend him. His back muscles were in tight knots and it hurt to raise his arms. His eyes were rimmed with red and they burned when he opened them. He wouldn't have been all that surprised if his reflection in the visor mirror showed two eyes like glowing coals. He had taken to wearing dark glasses. It flabbergasted him that Charlie Tibbs did not seem to require sleep. This must have been what the Crusades were like, the Old Man thought.

Now they were here in Choteau, 150 miles south of the Canadian border, waiting for a woman to get her airplane out of a hangar and fly away so she would die. The world did not seem particularly real to him this morning.

Their target was an effective and obsessive wolf-reintroduction advocate named Emily Betts. Betts had almost single-handedly brought about gray wolf reintroduction into Yellowstone and Central Idaho through her writings, protests, website, and testimony at hearings. The reintroduction was violently opposed by ranchers, hunters, and other locals. She had been photographed several years before walking side-by-side with the Secretary of Interior when he helped carry the first reintroduced wolves through the snow to their release pens in Yellowstone Park. The Old Man had once read the transcript of a speech Emily Betts gave before the Bring Back the Wolf Foundation in Bozeman. She had said that if the Western ranchers and Congress would not allow nature to exist in the sacred circle of predator and prey, then the same disgusting breed of animals that eliminated the predators in the first place must take the responsibility for their animal genocide and legally or illegally reintroduce the species they had destroyed. By "disgusting breed of animals" she meant humans, and by "animal genocide" she meant the poisoning, trapping, and shooting of wolves in the late nineteenth and early twentieth centuries.

But the reintroduction by the federal government wasn't happening fast enough for Emily Betts, and so she was now running a secret operation of her own, funded by donations. Wolves were being trapped in Canada where they were plentiful, transported to Choteau, and reintroduced throughout the mountain West by Betts in a private plane.

REMARKABLY, WHEN THEY ARRIVED at the hangar at three A.M., the Old Man and Charlie Tibbs had found an unlocked side door and they quietly entered, shutting the door behind them. It was completely dark inside.

Before the Old Man could thumb the switch on his flashlight, there was a desperate scramble of sounds. They were not alone in the hangar.

The Old Man had instinctively dropped to one knee, and Charlie Tibbs did the same. The Old Man heard the distinctive sound of Charlie working the slide of his pistol to jack a cartridge into the chamber and fully expected a blaze of light to suddenly reveal them—*caught at last!*—followed by a volley of explosions as Charlie blazed away. But instead of light, there was a low rumbling growl that had chilled the Old Man to his bones.

They were frozen in place, completely in the dark, all senses tingling. The Old Man imagined the yawning muzzle of Charlie's pistol sweeping across the inside of the hangar.

Finally, Charlie whispered for the light. The Old Man lowered the toolbox until it settled silently on the concrete floor and then unsnapped his gun holster. The Old Man aimed the unlit flashlight toward the sounds with his left hand and with his right, parallel to the flashlight, pointed his 9mm. He snapped on the flashlight and beyond the beam, in the gloom, eight dull red eyes looked back. The growl tapered into a whine.

Four full-sized gray wolves, ranging in color from jet black to light gray, their heads hung low, stared at Tibbs and the Old man with pagan laser eyes reflecting from behind the bars of a stout metal cage. The wolves had no doubt been live-trapped in Glacier Park or Canada, and transported to Choteau. From there they would be loaded on Emily Betts's aging Cessna airplane and flown south to the unknown mountains to further reestablish the breed.

Tibbs and the Old Man stood up, their old bones crackling. Tibbs holstered his revolver and followed the Old Man toward the airplane.

It was simple work, but it required skill. The Old Man held the flashlight while Tibbs took a razor blade utility knife to a half-dozen black hydraulic hoses snaking out from the motor. He shaved long slices from them, but was careful not to cut through the hoses completely. The idea was to weaken the hydraulic hoses so that under pressure, in the air, they would burst. It wouldn't do to cut all the way through the hoses and leave telltale puddles of hydraulic fluid beneath the aircraft that might be seen in the morning. The hoses need to burst in flight, while Emily Betts was flying down the spine of the Rocky Mountain front.

Whether Emily Betts would realize she was out of fluid from the gauge and turn back or continue on would make no difference. Either way, she wouldn't likely be able to land safely, unless she was just one hell of a pilot. Tibbs had said he doubted that was the case.

LOOK. THERE SHE IS," Tibbs said, and leaned back. The Old Man rubbed his eyes beneath his dark glasses, trying to see.

The propeller of the small airplane was nosing out from the dark inside, as Emily Betts and a man pushed it out. Betts was wearing an olive-drab flight suit. She was a heavy woman, and looked strong as she bent forward, pushing the strut. The Old Man could not see her face clearly from such a distance.

"They must have already loaded the wolves in the air-plane," Tibbs said. "I wonder what kind of ruckus they make inside."

"She's opened the door and about to climb in," Tibbs continued. "She started the engine. Oh-oh, there is fluid coming out of the engine. One of the hoses already broke."

The Old Man felt himself tense up. The plan could go awry. If it did, they would have to stay until the job was done. The thought of that possibility nauseated him.

"It's pouring out of the airplane," Tibbs said. "I can't tell whether her assistant can see it or not."

"She's going to check the gauges," the Old Man specu-lated. "She's going to know there's something wrong."

"The plane's moving," Tibbs countered.

The Old Man watched. The airplane was moving too quickly now for Tibbs to keep the binoculars on it. The Cessna built up speed on the runway. Both of them knew it still wasn't too late for Emily Betts to notice the leakage and abort the takeoff. The sound of the engine wound up to a high pitch.

The Old Man held his breath and watched the airplane, and saw its shadow form below it as it moved down the runway. The shadow began to shrink, and then it shot away into the sagebrush. Emily Betts was airborne. Back at the hangar, the man who had helped Betts push the Cessna stood by the open door, watched the plane with a hand at his brow, and then went inside. The hangar door closed. He had obviously not noticed anything wrong.

They watched the Cessna turn south until it was a shiny white speck above the mountains.

THE BIG BLACK FORD was approaching the town of Augusta, Montana, from the north when the Old Man rolled his head over in the seat to address Charlie. The headrest pinched the bow of his dark glasses so that the lenses shifted on his face to the right, making his face look lopsided. He didn't care.

"How many more, Charlie?" He asked.

Tibbs didn't respond with his usual glare. He was always in an especially good mood when his plans worked out as intended.

"One," Tibbs said. "Just one more."

The Old Man let his breath whistle out through his teeth. "Thank God for that," he said.

"You won't mind this one," Charlie said. "This one is a *lawyer.*"

The Old Man smiled, more at Charlie's rare attempt at levity than the fact that the next target was a lawyer.

Tibbs turned and smiled an awkward smile back at the Old Man. "We've done good work. We've been losing for thirty years. We've just been sitting back and taking it and taking it and *taking it* because we think that somewhere, somehow the politicians or judges will wake up and set things right. But we've waited too long and we've been too quiet. We've let them have just about everything they want from us. It's about damn frigging time our side went on the offensive. And you and me are the front line. *We are the warriors,*" Charlie's voice hissed.

"We've opened a gaping hole in the front line of the environmentalists. All of those bastards with their sandals and little glasses and lawsuits and trust funds don't even know what's hit them yet. Now it's up to our employers to take advantage of that gap in their front line and ram straight the hell through it. This is the first step in reclaiming our land, and our West."

The Old Man was speechless. Since he had met Charlie Tibbs three months before, throughout the training and the traveling, Tibbs had not spoken this much in a single week. Charlie Tibbs was eloquent, determined, and filled with righteous vengeance and passion. He was also, the Old Man reflected, the most terrifying man he had ever met.

16

THE NEXT MORNING, Twelve Sleep County Attorney Robey Hersig looked up from his desk, saw Joe Pickett standing at his door with his hat in hand, and sighed theatrically.

"Joe, come on in and please close the door," Hersig said,

pushing his chair back. "You're not going to like what I'm going to tell you."

Joe entered and sat down in a worn hardback chair facing Hersig's desk. The office was tiny and claustrophobic. Even with his knees tight up against the desk, Joe could still be hit by the door if someone opened it. Three of the four walls in the office were covered with bookcases of legal volumes. An old beige computer monitor, stained with fingerprints, sat lifeless on the desk. Behind Robey was his framed University of Wyoming Law School diploma and a photo of his young son holding a thirteen-inch brown trout. Hersig was in his first term of office but was well known throughout the county because his father and uncles were third-generation ranchers. Hersig had rodeoed in college until he broke both his pelvis and sternum at the Deadwood rodeo, which was when he decided to get serious about law school. Joe did not know Hersig well on a personal level, but they had gotten along professionally. Joe had come to Hersig with two previous cases. Hersig had aggressively prosecuted a local pilot who used a helicopter to herd elk into a clearing so his thirteen-year-old son could shoot them. In the second case, Hersig hadn't had any qualms recommending high fines for a fisherman Joe caught with fifty-seven trout—fifty-one over the limit.

Hersig was tall and balding, with short salt-and-pepper hair and a close-cropped beard. He liked to wear his large rodeo buckles with his suit in court. He was methodical and persuasive, and the only criticism Joe had heard about him was that he was extra cautious, that he insisted the sheriff bring him only cases that were airtight.

"I was going to call you," Hersig said.

"I was in the neighborhood and thought I'd see if you were in," Joe explained. "I need to ask Sheriff Barnum a couple of things about that Stewie Woods incident." Barnum's paper-strewn office was down the hall in the county building.

"I hope to hell that's the last exploding cow in my county," Hersig lamented.

"So what is it that I'm not going to like?" Joe asked.

Hersig leaned back in his chair and put his boots up on the desk. He looked squarely at Joe.

"Jim Finotta is an asshole. Everybody knows that."

Joe nodded.

"But we're not going to take these poaching charges against him any further."

Joe waited for a punch line. There wasn't one. He felt anger start to well up, but he stayed measured.

"Yes?"

Hersig swung his feet down and leaned forward. "I went and talked to Matt Sandvick so we could prepare his affidavit. He denies that he ever did any work for Finotta and denies he even talked with you about the man. He no longer has that photo you told me about, and his records from June suddenly can't be found."

"I can't believe it," Joe said, stunned.

"You should have kept that picture, Joe," Hersig said.

Joe looked away. Of course he should have. But he had taken Sandvick at his word.

"Did you tell Finotta that Sandvick was going to blow the whistle on him?" Hersig asked, cocking an eyebrow.

Joe thought for a moment, then: "Yup. I did tell him that when I saw him the other day."

Hersig raised his hands in a "what can I do?" gesture.

"I trusted Matt," Joe said.

"What's not to trust about Matt?" Hersig said cynically.

"Finotta got to him, didn't he?" Joe asked.

Hersig looked thoughtful. "Probably. But there's not a whole hell of a lot we can do to prove it unless Sandvick changes his mind again. And believe me, if he changes his mind, Finotta will slaughter him in court and point out that Sandvick changed his story three different times. That's not real credible."

Joe shook his head. "What kind of a guy are we dealing with here? Finotta, I mean. Would he intimidate a witness over a poaching charge?" Joe knew that if Finotta were convicted, he would, at best, lose his hunting privileges and have to pay $10,000 in fines. Finotta could certainly afford *that.* Game violations were shamefully lenient compared to other crimes, Joe thought.

Hersig smiled ruefully. "You know about those big hunters he hosts every year. He's got the governor, both senators. Lawyers and judges from all over. It would be a real loss of stature if word got out that he was convicted for poaching. That's a crime for low-lifes, not big-time lawyers and developers. It would get press attention and embarrass the hell out of Finotta in front of his big-shot pals. So you bet he'll fight it. He's the kind of guy who will work behind the scenes and call in all his chits to get what he wants. Finotta isn't the kind of guy to just accept a bad hand."

"Look, Joe," Hersig said, "Finotta's made most of his money by settling cases out of court. He's merciless in working the system and putting pressure on people. He's even been officially warned about intimidating those who plan to testify, but never brought up on charges, and no sanctions have ever been filed against him."

Joe sighed. Then he thought of something.

"I still have the DNA sample of the dead elk," Joe said eagerly. "We don't need Sandvick if we can get that mount and prove that it's a match."

Hersig shook his head. "I thought of that. I brought it up with Judge Pennock and he won't sign a warrant to go get that elk. He told me he thinks you've harassed Mr. Finotta quite enough."

"He said *that?*"

"It's a direct quote."

Joe banged the desk with his knuckles. "Finotta is Pennock's pal. Pennock has an interest in Elkhorn Ranches." Finotta, Joe thought, played in a different league than he or Robey Hersig.

Hersig held up his hand to caution Joe. "It's best not to cast aspersions on the judge in this office."

"Shouldn't Judge Pennock give this one to another judge? Isn't this a conflict of interest?"

"Recuse himself, you mean?" Hersig said, raising his eyebrows. "Do you actually want me to suggest that to him?"

Joe read in Hersig's expression that challenging Judge Pennock was absolutely the last thing Hersig wanted to do.

"Yup," Joe said. "That's exactly what I want to do. What about Judge what's-his-name in Johnson County?"

"Judge Cohn?" Hersig placed both of his hands on his face and rubbed his eyes as if Joe were torturing him.

"There isn't a person in Twelve Sleep County that wouldn't think it was wrong for Judge Pennock to preside over a crime involving his business partner," Joe said. "Even Pennock can understand *that*."

"Joe—"

"So you need to ask Pennock to assign the case to another judge," Joe said, and stood up.

/ Hersig looked up and spoke sharply. "Joe, what you're talking about will get you in all kinds of trouble. You think Finotta is going to give up? He's got a personal line to the governor, and to your director. I've got to tell you this case is really weak. You've got a witness who recanted and the only way you can prove anything is to get an order from a judge in another county to search the home of a Twelve Sleep County rancher and lawyer. Do you really think that mount will still be on the wall when you go to get it? My guess is that instead of that elk, there will be a charming English hunting print or some damn thing."

Now Hersig stood up, his face softening. "Joe, I like you. You are one of the few good guys I know. But this has turned into one of those cases where a truck backs up to the courthouse and dumps a huge pile of steaming shit on the floor. My job would be to try to convince the judge and jury that somewhere in all of that shit a gem of a case is buried, if they'll just be patient and get used to the smell. And to tell you the truth, if you were to keep pressing, it *would* start to sound a little like harassment."

Joe listened. He was surprised how vehement Hersig was.

"Keep this up and I might be prosecuting *you*, Joe."

"This just really makes me mad," Joe said. "The guy killed the biggest elk in the Bighorns and left the meat."

Hersig waved Joe away. "I know. I know. You already

129

told me that. There's just not much I can do here."

Joe turned and fumbled to open the door without banging the chair he had been sitting in.

"Joe!" Hersig called after him.

Joe leaned back into the office.

"I hate to say this, but usually the assholes win."

Joe stood silently for a moment, then put his hat on his head.

"Seems like, in this county, they do," Joe said, and closed the door hard.

SHERIFF O. R. "BUD" BARNUM was in his office and Joe walked in as Barnum checked his watch.

"I've got a lunch meeting planned," Barnum said, raising his heavy-lidded eyes. "You should have called ahead."

"This will take five minutes," Joe stated. The meeting with Hersig had battered him. He was humiliated, angry, and frustrated with how it had gone. He was mad at himself for trusting Sandvick and not anticipating how slick and effective Finotta could be. He wondered how much time Finotta had spent in the last week anticipating Joe's moves and countering them, and wondered what Finotta was telling the judge, the governor, and the director of the agency about him.

Joe decided to start the conversation with the less incendiary topic and told Barnum about the branch in the tree and asked if it had been examined for blood, hair, or fiber. Barnum looked at Joe with barely disguised impatience.

"You're here to ask me about one particular branch in a particular tree?"

"It's in the shape of a fishhook," Joe said.

Joe accepted how silly it sounded. But after the meeting with Hersig, his well of embarrassment was dry. Joe described the location of the tree, how the branch could almost certainly support the weight of a man, and how the branch was stained dark red. He left out his feeling of being watched that night.

Barnum shook his head slowly, as if Joe Pickett had disappointed him.

"So you're cowboying again, huh?" Barnum asked. "Following up on my investigation like you did when those outfitters got killed?"

Joe fought the urge to bring up the fact that Barnum had botched that investigation and had reached the wrong conclusion well before Joe ever got involved.

Barnum stood up and looked at his watch again. "The state crime lab boys photographed, tested, and measured everything up there. I would guess they looked at your branch as well. However, I will ask my deputy to send them an e-mail to confirm that. Are we through?"

"We're through except for one thing."

"And that is?" Barnum asked, reaching for his jacket.

"I'm going to petition Judge Cohn in Johnson County for a search warrant for Jim Finotta's residence," Joe said flatly. "Then I'm going to arrest that son-of-a-bitch for poaching."

This froze Barnum. Slowly, the sheriff swiveled his head toward Joe. Barnum's eyes, which had seen just about everything, showed surprise.

"I just thought you ought to know, so that when you hear about the arrest, you can say you were officially forewarned," Joe said calmly.

A crooked smile formed on Barnum's face. "I'd sure miss that half a beef at Christmas," he said. "But something tells me I don't have much to worry about in that regard."

Joe ignored the insult. "And when I bring him in I'm going to ask him how he knew about that exploding cow before I told him about it."

THERE WAS A "CLOSED" SIGN in the front window of Wolf Mountain Taxidermy and a hand-lettered sign taped to the inside of the front-door window.

Joe stopped to read it.

GONE FISHING UNTIL SEPT. 1.
CAN'T WAIT UNTIL HUNTING SEASON!
FOR RATES AND ORDERS, SEE
WWW.SANDVICKTAXIDERMY.COM

Joe slumped against the doorframe and looked down the empty Main Street of Saddlestring. At the end of the street, on the bridge, a knot of teenage boys were cheering on a buddy who was underneath them in the river. The boy had tied a rope to the railing on the bridge and was waterskiing in place on the fast summer runoff of the Twelve Sleep River. Joe suddenly felt very old.

MARYBETH WAS AT THE MASTER BATHROOM SINK, cleaning her face for bed and thinking about the day, when Joe came and flopped down on their bed. He was in a foul mood.

"Finotta outmaneuvered me," he said bluntly. "He was ten steps ahead of me all the time, and he got to Sandvick. I really screwed that one up by not getting that photo from

Sandvick on the spot."

Marybeth sighed inwardly. Sometimes her husband was a little too quick to take people at their word and it frustrated her. She hated it when he got taken advantage of. "You're too trusting, Joe." She looked at him in the mirror. "You're not cynical enough sometimes."

"I'm working on that."

She turned, the washcloth still poised near her cheek. "Finotta is a reptile, but you need to give up on him right now, Joe. He could buy and sell us if he wanted to. And if he's as bad as we think he is, you'll get another crack at him some day."

Joe grunted.

Marybeth thought of Ginger Finotta and about their aborted conversation in the library. She thought about the Tom Horn book, which hadn't yet been returned.

17

THERMOPOLIS, WYOMING
July 1

THROUGH BILLOWS OF SULFUR-SMELLING STEAM, the Old Man watched and waited for Charlie Tibbs. The Old Man reclined on the mineral-slick steps of a very hot pool and closed his eyes. He willed the muscles in his neck and back to begin to loosen up and untie what he imagined as a series of complicated, technical knots. He sighed heavily, and slid forward another step so the hot water lapped at his chin.

They were in the Central Wyoming town of Thermopolis, hard against the border of the Wind River Indian Reservation. Thermopolis claimed to have the "largest hot springs in the world," a claim based not on the number of spas or facilities but on the volume of hot water that poured from the earth.

The Old Man slid forward on the step and leaned further back. His mouth was now under water, then his ears. Total submersion created a static whooshing sound. He breathed slowly through his nose. He was big and white and the hair on his legs and chest riffled beneath the water like a bed of kelp. In addition to helping his sore back, the Old Man hoped the water would somehow purge his wracked, tormented soul. But that was a lot to ask of Thermopolis.

It had been the Old Man's idea to drive to Thermopolis and he had been mildly surprised that Charlie had agreed. The Old Man had limped from the pickup, rented a suit at the counter, and located the hottest and calmest water. In another part of the complex, children and families splashed and shrieked and funneled down a water slide. The pool he sat in was for old people. The Old Man's only company was an ancient Shoshone woman with jet black eyes and droopy, chocolate-colored skin. Occasionally, she coughed wetly. After half an hour, she left the pool and the Old Man was alone.

From the corner of his eye, the Old Man saw the black Ford pickup come into view through the chain-link fence that surrounded the pools. The truck parked against the curb. Afternoon sunlight penetrated the smoked windows enough that the Old Man could see Charlie inside the cab talking on the cell phone. The Old Man had not expected that Charlie would join him and was relieved that he hadn't. They had been spending too much time together and the Old Man couldn't even imagine what Charlie would look like in a swimsuit. Charlie had said he would try to contact their employers, and apparently he had. The cell phone was a technologically advanced model that scrambled voices so that eavesdroppers, or innocents with FM-band radios, could not overhear the conversation.

The pickup truck was a wonder and a virtual weapon in itself. Although from the outside it simply looked like an intimidating late-model four-by-four, the truck had been customized to serve as a rolling armory capable of "taking on an entire police department if necessary," as Charlie had put it. Even though the job was nearly finished and they had so far accomplished what they had set out to, they hadn't used even one-tenth of their available firepower and equipment. Apparently, Charlie said, their employers had listened to him when he told them he believed strongly in the old Western maxim about never being caught outgunned. And they hadn't been.

In addition to the pickup truck, they were also armed with shotguns and hundreds of rounds of double-ought buckshot shells, a MAC-70 machine pistol, plastic explosives with both altitude-sensitive and remote-control detonation devices, a 400-pound crossbow with telescopic sites, night-vision goggles and scopes, remote audio transceivers, nerve gas, and concussion grenades. Charlie Tibbs was especially proud of the custom-made, machine-tooled Remington Model 700 .308 sniper's rifle with the Leupold 4 x 14 scope. The rifle had been built to his specific demands and specifications. It used custom match .190 grain boattail bullets that were accurate beyond 1,000 yards, even after the slug began to flip end over end. The rifle could be steadied by bolting it to a special pole-mounted stand in the bed of the black Ford pickup. The stand itself was connected to a small atmospheric theodolite computer that gauged wind, altitude, trajectory, and distance to enable incredibly long-range shots.

Under hidden panels beneath the bed of the pickup was a shoulder-fired rocket launcher as well as an armored pod of pressure-sensitive and frequency-activated land mines.

The cab of the pickup had the scrambled cell phone, handheld wireless e-mail, and a pager, as well as an experimental computerized GPS directional mapping system loaded with American backroads and routes. They had only used the road-map computer once, and that was on the streets of Washington, D.C. Both the Old Man and Charlie Tibbs knew the Rocky Mountain region well enough that the computer was not necessary.

Their employers had supplied them with a lockbox of cash—thousands of dollars in used bills. Charlie kept track of their expenditures, but there was nothing they were prevented from buying at any time. They paid for everything with cash and cashiers often acted as if they didn't know what to do when, for example, Charlie counted out $400 in bills to pay for hotel rooms. They left no paper trail, no credit card receipts anywhere in the United States.

Originally recommended for this job by Charlie Tibbs himself, who had already been hired to oversee the field operations, the Old Man had been contacted late at night by a man who wouldn't leave his name. When the Old Man stated that he was interested in hearing more, a meeting with Charlie Tibbs was arranged at a local Denny's Restaurant to fill him in on the details. Tibbs told him that their employers had recommended at least six operatives, and possibly two different teams, but Charlie had convinced them that everything could be accomplished by two experienced men. Since then, only Charlie Tibbs had been in contact with their employers. The Old Man was not included in these conversations by design, to minimize the number of people involved in the planning of the operations. It was understood that Charlie would speak to the intermediary, who would then speak directly with their employers. The Old Man was kept in the dark except for the details of the operation most immediately at hand. The Old Man had agreed to this, but now wished he had a better idea, overall, of what was going on. Obviously, they were targeting high-profile environmentalists. But how many? And for how long? He had expected their work to take about two weeks going in, and they were now into their second month.

He had no idea what Charlie Tibbs had told their employers about him. He wondered if his recent doubts and complaints were being reported. Charlie could honestly say that the Old Man had recently shown more reluctance on the job. Would they relieve him if the complaints got too loud? Would they pay him off? Would they have Charlie Tibbs walk up behind him and put a bullet in the back of his head?

The Old Man had begun to question Charlie Tibbs's sanity. One of the reasons for this was that Tibbs had recently insisted on replaying a CD of *Oklahoma!* over and over again while they drove. Tibbs sang along with full force. And even before Emily Betts crashed, Charlie seemed to like this job way too much. He *enjoyed* what they were doing. It was as if Charlie had been given the opportunity to vent a lifetime of rage, and he just got a big old kick out of it. Charlie was driven by something, and absolutely relentless. He believed in this cause even more, he said, than their employers believed in it. And he still did not sleep.

Charlie emerged from the pickup and signaled through the fence for the Old Man.

Grunting, and moving very slowly, the Old Man pulled himself out of the hot pool and trudged over to the fence where Charlie was waiting. He left wet splayed footprints on the pavement behind him. His skin had turned bright pink in the hot water. As he approached the fence, he bowed his wet head to listen.

Charlie spoke softly. "They've located the lawyer so we have to get going."

"Please tell me he's close," the Old Man said, dreading another cross-country trip.

"Yellowstone," Charlie said. "Very close."

"In the park?"

Charlie nodded yes.

"Then we're through?" the Old Man asked with hope.

"Not quite."

The Old Man felt as if Charlie had reached through the fence and punched him in the side of the head. Charlie *knew* how the Old Man felt about this. He had told Charlie countless times in the last few days: he wanted this job to be *over.*

The Old Man shook his head. "I can't see our luck holding out forever, Charlie. They can't keep adding targets to the list. They just can't." His voice was anguished.

"Just one more after the lawyer," Charlie said. "And

please keep your voice down."

The Old Man looked up. Charlie was staring at him coolly, evaluating him. Under this withering glare, the Old Man capitulated.

"But this will have to be the last one, Charlie. Any more, and so help me, I'll quit. And you can tell our employers that. This is *it*." The Old Man spat out the last word.

Charlie Tibbs was silent.

"So after the lawyer where do we have to go? Who is the target?"

Charlie hesitated. The Old Man understood why. This was violating their agreement not to discuss the details of more than one job at a time. It had probably been a good idea, the Old Man conceded, since he wouldn't have stuck with it this long if he had known in advance how elaborate and twisted their mission would become. The Old Man wished he were stronger, more sure of himself and their cause—more like Charlie.

Charlie quickly looked left and right before speaking, and then leaned closer until his hat brim touched the fence.

"Our duty isn't to question." Charlie bit out the words. "We don't know the reasons these targets were chosen and that's good. All we know is that a lot of thought has gone into this and they've got the whole thing figured out. We just follow orders."

"No one's questioning anything," the Old Man answered, his tone deliberate. He wondered why Charlie seemed so defensive.

Charlie sized up the Old Man again, his light blue eyes raking across the Old Man's face like talons.

"Saddlestring, Wyoming," Charlie spoke in a voice that

was barely audible over the amplified swimming pool sounds from elsewhere in the complex. "That rumor about Stewie Woods isn't going away. Now it's that he—or somebody pretending to be Stewie Woods—is contacting his old colleagues."

The Old Man felt a rush of anger. "That's not possible. You *know* that's not possible."

Charlie nodded. "It's probably one of his hangers-on trying to get something going. But we have to check it out."

"It's not possible," the Old Man said again, shaking his head, trying unsuccessfully to come up with a scenario where Woods could have walked away from that explosion.

"And there's something else," Charlie said. "Because this guy, whoever he is, is pretending to be Stewie Woods, the local game warden in Saddlestring is snooping around. Other law enforcement might follow. That's heat we don't need. So we need to squash this pretender as quickly as possible."

"Do they have any idea who the pretender is?" the Old Man asked.

"Not yet," Charlie answered, narrowing his eyes. "But they expect they will shortly."

Part Two

Early in April of 1887, some of the boys came down from the Pleasant Valley, where there was a big rustler war going on and the rustlers were getting the best of the game. . . . Things were in a pretty bad condition. It was war to the knife between cowboys and the rustlers, and there was a battle every time the two outfits ran together. A great many men were killed in the war.

FROM TOM HORN,
THE LIFE OF TOM HORN:
GOVERNMENT SCOUT AND INTERPRETER, 1904

18

IT WAS A MONTH after elk-calving season in the Bighorns and Joe Pickett was doing a preliminary trend count. The purpose of the trend count was to assess how the elk had wintered, and how many babies had been born to replenish the herd. The season for calves was generally May 20 through June 30, so all of the new ones should have dropped. He rode near the tree line on his buckskin, Lizzie, looking down the slope into the meadows and brush for the elk. It was one of those rare, perfect, vibrant July mornings that pulsed with color and scent. Wildflowers were bursting open in the meadows like strings of mute fireworks, and saplings were stretching sunward after recently breaking out of the solitary confinement of the snowpack. Swollen narrow streambeds were flexing their muscles with runoff. Summer was here, and it was in a hurry.

The cow elk used the tall sagebrush just below the tree line for calving, and Joe had found seven elk cows and six month-old newborns so far. It was a good year for elk given the fairly mild winter and the moist spring. He could smell their particular musty presence even before he saw the first mother and calf. The mothers eyed him warily as he quietly rode by in the shadows of the trees. One tried to lure him away from her calf by fully exposing herself in the meadow and trotting through the open field toward the opposite rise. She stopped in clear view to look over her shoulder, and snorted when Joe rode on and didn't pursue. Her calf looked at him through a fork in the tall brush. The calf was all eyes and ears, and Joe was close enough to see a bead of condensation on the calf's black snout.

Joe rode deeper into the trees and further up the mountainside until the mother elk turned back to her calf. He goosed Lizzie through the timber, toward a patch of sunlight that became a small grassy park and dismounted. He tied up his horse and sat on a downed log, where he stretched out and let the sun warm his legs. Pouring a cup of coffee from his battered Thermos, he tipped up the brim of his hat and sighed. The coffee was still hot.

Joe had put off doing any serious thinking until he was in the mountains, hoping the quiet solace of the outdoors would help him find the answers he was looking for. Now, he reviewed the particularly odd chain of events that had that started with Jim Finotta getting to Sandvick and Judge Pennock's refusal to advance Joe's charges against Finotta.

Judge Cohn in Johnson County had reluctantly agreed to review the charges against Finotta but had yet to take any action. It was very likely that the charges, and the case, would go nowhere. The previous day, Joe had received a call from Robey Hersig saying that Judge Pennock was furious with him—and Joe, for taking the case out of the county. Hersig reported that Finotta was burning up the telephone lines between his law office in Saddlestring and the governor's office in Cheyenne. Joe was being accused of engaging in a vendetta against Finotta. Words like "harassment," "land owner abuse," and "bureaucratic arrogance" had been used. It wouldn't be long, Joe knew, before he heard something from Game and Fish headquarters in Cheyenne. He could imagine the furtive meetings and hand-wringing that was almost definitely going on at headquarters over what he had done. If the governor got involved, which was likely, the issue would be elevated immediately, probably to the office of director. It wouldn't be the first time he'd gotten in trouble, and probably wouldn't be the last time. He hoped if the boys at headquarters in Cheyenne decided to admonish him that they'd do it in a straightforward manner, but sometimes that was too much to expect from them.

If it weren't for mornings like this in a place like this, Joe thought, they could have this job.

He was not very good about letting things drop, Joe decided. It wasn't as if elk were an endangered species. There were tens of thousands of elk in the state, and probably more than there should be. Elk were killed every day by cars, disease, and predators. Hunters harvested thousands every fall. Other elk would replace dead elk.

But a huge bull elk had been killed out of season by a man who simply wanted the head of the animal on his wall. The elk's headless, massive body was left where it fell, and seven hundred pounds of meat left to rot. And nobody, it seemed, was as outraged about the crime as Joe Pickett was. For reasons he had trouble defining, he had taken this particular offense personally.

It wasn't that Jim Finotta was a millionaire lawyer, or a rancher, or a developer. Joe didn't harbor any ill will toward successful men. What outraged Joe was the casualness of the crime and Finotta's reaction when accused.

Most poachers Joe caught lied about their crime when

confronted. But Finotta lied with contempt and a haughty arrogance that suggested that it was somehow beneath him to have to waste his good, valuable lies on the likes of Joe. Jim Finotta didn't need a trophy head on his wall for any other reason than to impress his guests and boost his own sense of worth. He certainly didn't need the meat, like a lot of poachers and hunters, but instead of giving it away or donating it to a shelter in town, he left it. If it was just a trophy Finotta had wanted, he could have hired a guide and hunted the elk in season like a sportsman. Instead, Finotta chose to shoot the bull elk off season, when no one else could hunt it, order his lackeys to behead it, cover up the crime when accused, and use his influence and connections to discredit his accuser. As Robey Hersig had put it, the ass-holes usually won.

But Joe had more than just Jim Finotta on his mind.

TWO DAYS BEFORE, "Stewie" had called again. This time Sheridan had answered the telephone. When she asked who was calling, the caller had, at first, refused to tell her. But when Sheridan said she would have to hang up, the man identified himself as Stewie Woods and said he would be calling back when her mother was home. Sheridan wouldn't tell him when that would be.

Marybeth confided that evening when they were in bed that she had a strange feeling about this. If it were some kind of joke, there was nothing remotely funny about it. She said it didn't make sense that even the most dogged reporter would call twice using the same ruse. It had to be someone else, she said, calling for some other reason. She hoped it wasn't some morbid follower of One Globe.

But it *couldn't* actually be Stewie Woods. That was one thing both Joe and Marybeth left unsaid. There wasn't any reason to speculate further.

Whoever it was, Joe was irritated by the calls. They had requested Caller ID in the hope of tracing the number, but it not yet been installed. He hoped he would be there the next time a call came so that he could snatch the telephone away and try to determine what was going on. It offended him that a stranger would call his wife, and it offended him even further that the reason they were calling was because of her past relationship with another man. As innocent as Marybeth made it out to be, it made him grit his teeth when he thought about it. It was hard to imagine her in her high school and early college days laughing and trading jokes with two guys like Stewie Woods and Hayden Powell. Both of those men would later become well known, at least in the environmental community. They were semifamous and charismatic. *And both of them had loved his wife.* However, Marybeth had chosen Joe and opted out of her potential life of excitement and notoriety. He hoped like hell she didn't regret the path that she had chosen. Instead of hanging out with two big-shot environmentalist celebrities, Marybeth got to move around the state of Wyoming with Joe Pickett from one falling-down state-owned house to another. Choosing Joe had resulted in discontinuing her legal career and adopting severe month-by-month budgeting to make ends meet, not to mention getting shot in her own house and being left for dead.

Joe sighed, smiled grimly to himself, and tried to calm down. But he vowed that when he found out who was calling Marybeth he would punch him right in the nose.

. . .

LEADING LIZZIE DOWN to the stream so she could get a drink before he continued his ride up the summit, Joe marveled at the very bad run of luck the environmental community was having of late. First there was Stewie Woods, right here in his own district, blown up by a cow. Then their champion, Rep. Peter Sollito and his scandalous death. Then Hayden Powell is killed in a house fire in Washington State. Powell's publisher claimed that Hayden had been two weeks away from delivering his book but no trace of the manuscript could be found.

Joe climbed back into the saddle and clucked at Lizzie to go. The string of bad luck had been capped this last week by the discovery of the body of wolf advocate Emily Betts. Her small private airplane had crashed in the Beartooth Mountains southwest of Red Lodge, Montana. Hikers found her body. They reported that upon approaching the wreckage they had seen two wolves emerge from the cockpit and flee. Emily Betts, likely dead on impact, had been partially devoured by her cargo.

Joe Pickett was not the only one to wonder if this series of deaths had a common thread. Speculation ran rampant in both the environmental community and over coffee in Saddlestring's local diner. But each incident was vastly different from the others. If there was a pattern it was incomprehensible. There was nothing about any of the deaths that suggested murder, except perhaps for Rep. Sollito's, and Joe had read that a prostitute had recently been arrested who was accused of the murder—although she was denying it and had hired a celebrity lawyer.

Now Emily Betts had joined the list; a wolf advocate

who died while trying to illegally transplant wolves into Wyoming.

But even devoted conspiracy theorists could not connect the deaths in any way other than the fact that they were recent and all involved high-profile environmental activists. And that most of the deaths were, in some way, humiliating to talk about.

Joe had heard stories, though, of locals high-fiving each other in the bars. Apparently, there were allegations being made on a national level within the fringe environmental groups, accusations of conspiracies, calls for a congressional and FBI investigation into the string of deaths.

Reining Lizzie to a stop, Joe pulled his notebook from his shirt pocket, and flipped it open to a fresh page. He drew a crude outline of the United States. Then he drew stars and dates at four locations: Saddlestring, Wyoming, June 10; Bremerton, Washington, June 14; Washington, D.C., June 23; and Choteau, Montana, June 29. There were four days between the deaths in Saddlestring and Bremerton; nine days between Bremerton and Washington, D.C.; and six days between Washington, D.C. and Choteau.

If a killer or killers were responsible, Joe thought, then they had been criss-crossing the country by air or road for almost a month. And there could possibly be two, three, or even four of them, each with a separate assignment. That seemed unlikely, he thought, simply because it was too complicated, with too many factors and possibilities where something could go wrong. But if it were one killer or a team of killers, they were having a hell of a busy month. He thought about the time lapses between the incidents and concluded that it was possible, although unlikely, that one team could have done all of the killings. The longest span of time between incidents was between Bremerton and Washington, D.C., which was also the longest distance by car, which meant it was possible the killer or killers were traveling by car.

He stared at the drawing, thought about the dates.

He was getting nowhere.

JOE TURNED LIZZIE back into the trees. He planned to work his way up to the summit and back down toward his pickup and horse trailer through a drainage on the other side of the mountain. He expected to find, and count, additional elk calves. He might find some fishermen as well near the road, or campers setting up early for the weekend. He would take the long way.

He remembered to lean forward in the saddle and stroke Lizzie's neck and tell her what a good horse she was. He didn't used to do that.

19

SHERIDAN PICKETT ANSWERED the telephone Thursday during breakfast, listened for a moment, made an unpleasant face, and then handed the receiver to Marybeth.

"It's that man again," Sheridan said with distaste.

Joe and Marybeth exchanged worried glances and Joe mouthed, "Keep him on the line." He pushed back from the table to go upstairs to get on the other extension.

"Can I talk to him?" Lucy asked through a mouthful of breakfast cereal. Lucy wanted to talk with anyone who called.

Joe bounded up the stairs and closed the door in the bedroom. He sat on the unmade bed and gently lifted the receiver to his ear. The conversation had already begun. The connection was poor and filled with static. The baritone voice of the man sounded drugged-out, slurred. The words came slowly as if through a mouthful of pebbles, the tone distorted.

"This is Stewie again, Mary," the man said. "Please don't hang up again."

"Who is this really?" Marybeth demanded.

Through Marybeth's phone in the background, Joe could hear Lucy asking again as if she could talk on the telephone and Sheridan telling her to be quiet.

"Stewie. Stewie. Come on, Mary, you know who it is." He paused for a long beat. "I'm trying to think of how to prove it to you."

Her name is Mary*beth*, Joe thought.

"That would be a good idea," Marybeth said, "since Stewie Woods is dead."

The man chuckled. "The old Stewie might be dead, but not the new one. Hey . . . I know. I wish I would have practiced for this quiz, but it looks like I have to do it off the cuff." His words tumbled out and ran into each other. Joe guessed that the caller would be easier to understand if he could see him gesticulate. He imagined hands and arms flying through the air, the telephone pinned in place between jaw and shoulder, and determined pacing.

"Anyway, in high school you drove a yellow Toyota. Whenever it got cold, it wouldn't start, and I figured out how to get it going by taking off the air cleaner and opening up the intake valve with a screwdriver. Who else could possibly know that?"

Joe felt his face go slack.

"Just about everybody in high school," Marybeth answered, but her voice was tentative. "And it was a Datsun, not a Toyota."

"Whatever," the caller said, then bulled ahead with the confidence of a telephone solicitor trying to get as much across as possible before the phone went dead in his ear: "Okay, here's another one. Our football team, the Winchester Badgers, once played in Casper and you and Hayden Powell drove down on a Friday to see the game. After we won—I think the score was 27 to 17 and I intercepted a pass and ran it in for a touchdown—the three of us drove up on top of that hill on the east side of Casper and pulled up all of the survey stakes for their new mall. Remember?"

Marybeth was silent. Joe could hear Sheridan and Lucy squabbling at the kitchen table, and Marybeth's breathing.

"Who would possibly know that happened except you, me, and Hayden?"

"Maybe you told someone about it," Marybeth said, her voice weak. "Or you wrote about it in your newsletter or something."

Joe, Marybeth, and the caller all realized at once that Marybeth had said "you." Joe was stunned.

"Did you just hear yourself?" the caller asked.

"I . . . I did," Marybeth answered.

"Do I need to go on?"

"I'm just too shocked to answer right now," Marybeth said. Joe wished he were with her. He hoped she wouldn't hang up the telephone.

"Mary, I just want to see you again," his voice was kind.

"I'm married," Marybeth stammered. "I have three children eating breakfast at the table right in front of me."

"Everyone's married," Stewie said slyly, "but the big question, the one I've learned to ask is: are you *happily* married?"

You bastard, Joe thought. *I can't wait to punch you right in the nose.*

"Of course I'm happily married. To a wonderful man named Joe Pickett."

Stewie sighed. His voice changed. "I kind of figured that would be the case but I guess I hoped it wasn't."

Stewie was distancing himself. Now Joe hoped Stewie wouldn't hang up. Joe quickly buried the receiver in blankets from the bed so Stewie wouldn't hear the click of him hanging up, and scribbled a note in his spiral pad. He descended the stairs and handed it to Marybeth. Her face was pale and her eyes were vacant.

Joe had written: *Keep him talking—Ask him where he is.*

Marybeth read the note and frowned, and looked to Joe for confirmation. Joe nodded yes. Faintly, Joe could hear Stewie talking to Marybeth again.

"How can it possibly be that you're still alive?" Marybeth asked.

Now Joe could only hear one side of the conversation.

"What do you mean when you say that?"

The school bus honked outside the house and all three girls scrambled as if an electric current had been simultaneously shot through their chairs.

They were suddenly grabbing backpacks, sack lunches, jackets, shoes. Joe signaled to Marybeth that he would take care of things. He opened the front door, waved at the driver, and shooed his girls toward the front gate. Sheridan gave him a look to indicate that she was getting a little old for shooing. The driver, a retired lumberjack named Stiles, leaned out of the door and asked Joe about the mule deer count in his hunting area.

"I'll have to talk with you tomorrow," Joe said, trying not to dismiss Stiles out of hand. "I've got a little bit of a situation inside I need to handle."

Stiles waved him off and Joe literally ran back to the house. Marybeth, with wide, disbelieving eyes, was gently replacing the receiver on the cradle.

Joe and Marybeth simply stared at each other.

"Did that actually happen?" Joe asked.

Marybeth shook her head, stunned.

"He wants to meet me Saturday," she said. "I wrote down the directions."

"It just doesn't make any sense," Joe said, as much to himself as anyone. "I saw where he died."

Marybeth smiled cryptically. "Joe, Stewie said that he *did* blow up. But that he was *reborn*."

"He actually said that?"

She nodded, and started across the room toward Joe.

THAT EVENING, in the library, Marybeth saw the handicapped-accessible Vee Bar U van cruise through the parking lot. The sight of the van froze her to her spot behind the counter, her fingers poised and still over the keyboard of the computer. She slowly swung her head toward the front doors, anticipating the arrival of Ginger Finotta and Buster. But Ginger didn't enter and the van was no longer in sight.

Instead, in the side office behind the counter, Marybeth

heard the metallic clunk of returned books being dropped into the drive-up return. The sound, familiar as it was, startled her.

She waited for the van to pull away from the building and didn't move until the sound of the motor had vanished.

She quickly finished her entry, then went into the side office. On top of the pile of returns was the single, aged, dog-eared copy of *The Life and Times of Tom Horn, Stock Detective.*

20

YELLOWSTONE NATIONAL PARK, WYOMING
July 5

IT WAS DUSK when the Old Man realized he had truly become evil.

The setting had nothing to do with it. The heavy evening sun had painted a wide bronze swath through the tall buffalo grass of the clearing below them and had fused through the lodgepole pines that circled the clearing like a spindly corral. Breezes so gentle they could barely be felt rippled across the top of the grass and looked like gentle ringlets on water. The air was sweet with pine and sage but there was an occasional whiff of sulfur from seeping, newly punctured pockets in a swampy hot spring flat where they had ridden the horses a few minutes before. And there was another smell, too. It was the smell of slightly rancid pork.

Earlier that day they had located Tod Marchand, attorney at law, near his tent on the bank of Nez Perce Creek. Marchand had been remarkably easy to find. He had checked in at the ranger station the day before at the

South Entrance of the park and noted where he intended to camp. Tibbs had found the entry while the Old Man chatted with the female ranger and filled out the forms that permitted them to transport their newly acquired horse trailer and horses through the park.

They had ridden up on Tod Marchand just after noon, while Marchand was scrubbing his lunch plate clean with biodegradable soap. Marchand had looked back over his shoulder when he heard the horses approach, and stood up and turned around just in time for the butt of Charlie Tibbs's rifle to crack down hard on the top of his head.

"Counsel, approach the bench," Charlie Tibbs had said, without explanation, as Tod Marchand crumpled to the grass.

They had gagged and hog-tied Marchand and thrown him across the back of the Old Man's saddle. They took the horses up into the trees far away from the trail and the creek—away from the places other hikers or trekkers might be.

Yellowstone was remarkably big and wild beyond the tourist traffic that coursed along the figure-eight road system in the park. As they rode up into the timber and over a rise, the sounds of the distant traffic receded, replaced by a light warm breeze wafting through the treetops. The chance of anyone seeing them, or of the two men stumbling upon another person, were remote.

Still, to the Old Man, Yellowstone Park was a disquieting place to do business. Despite unreasonable demands by environmentalists and mismanagement by the federal government, Yellowstone was a special place, in his opinion. It was somehow sacrosanct. It had just felt wrong to be riding through the lodgepole pine with a bound and gagged lawyer on his horse.

They had ridden down the slope to where the trees cleared and the creek wound through a draw with very high eroded banks. They let their horses droop their heads to drink. It was then that they heard a splash upstream, somewhere over the high bank and out of view. The instant they heard the sound, Charlie Tibbs slid his big .308 Remington Model 700 rifle out of his saddle scabbard. The Old Man fumbled for his pistol.

Within two minutes, the water on the stream was covered with floating feathers within a swirl of a dark oily substance. They watched the feathers float by in front of them. It was as if a duck had exploded on the water less than 100 yards away.

Both horses had begun to snort and act up. When the Old Man's horse reared and turned back the way they had come, he muscled the horse around to face the water. The Old Man knew well enough that even experienced horses might be uncontrollable this close to bears.

They had quickly retreated back into the trees, tied off the horses, and tried to calm them. Marchand had been thrown to the ground when the Old Man's horse spooked, but as Charlie said, he probably couldn't feel it anyhow. Armed, they walked back down to the stream and cautiously climbed the bank. They heard muffled grunting and woofing even before they actually saw the bears—grizzlies, a sow and her two cubs. The sow was a shimmering light brown color with a pronounced hump on her back. Her snout was buried in the rotting bark of a downed tree, feeding on larvae. The cubs, already over a hundred pounds each, were further down on the tree trunk taking off shards of bark with lazy swipes of their paws. Apparently, the duck hadn't been much of a meal.

TOD MARCHAND WAS PROPPED against a tree trunk when he regained consciousness. The Old Man and Charlie had carried Marchand across the stream through a swampy meadow and into the timber on the other side of the slope. The bears had remained across the river. The first thing Marchand did when he awoke was pitch over sideways into the grass and throw up. When he was through, the Old Man helped him sit up again with his back against the tree. It took a while for Marchand to seem lucid.

The Old Man studied Marchand, while he waited for him to fully regain his senses. Marchand was, by all accounts, a good-looking man, the Old Man decided: tall, with thick blond hair cut into an expensive, sculpted, swept-back haircut. He was tanned and fit and he looked much younger than his fifty-three years.

The Old Man had, of course, seen his photograph in the newspapers and had watched him several times on television news shows. Tod Marchand was the most successful environmental lawyer in America when it came to winning court decisions. Marchand had been the lead attorney in the five-year case that forced the National Park Service to dismantle several recreational vehicle campgrounds because the area the campgrounds were located in was thought to be prime grizzly bear habitat. The RV campgrounds had, in fact, been within ten miles of where Marchand was camped.

The Old Man distinctly remembered a shot of Marchand standing outside the federal courthouse in Denver talking to reporters after successfully arguing for a halt to a multi-million-dollar gold mine about to be started up in southern Wyoming.

"Gold is a matter of perception," Marchand had told reporters. "Gold for many of us is wildlife running free in untrammeled wilderness."

Marchand had paused for effect and looked straight into a major network's camera (he was so experienced at this sort of thing that he knew by sight which were the network's cameras and which belonged to local stations), *Our gold won,* Marchand had said, which had since become a rallying cry.

Tod Marchand looked much different now, the Old Man thought. The lump on his head from Tibbs's rifle butt was hidden under tinted layers of hair, but a single dark red track of blood from his scalp had dried along the side of Marchand's sharp nose.

Tod Marchand also looked different because he was now tied up with a thin horsehair cord. The horsehair cord bit into Marchand's shoulders in several places, and continued down his waist and then was crisscrossed around his legs from his thighs to his ankles.

Horsehair was good, Charlie had said, because the bears would eat every inch of it and leave nothing. To make sure the bears would be attracted, Charlie had bound thick slabs of raw, uncured back-bacon under each of Marchand's arms and between his legs. The pork was pungent.

Now fully awake, Marchand looked slowly at the cord and the bacon. His thoughts were transparent. He was very scared, and not in a noble way, the Old Man thought. Marchand was scared out of his wits.

Charlie Tibbs walked past the Old Man and squatted down in front of Tod Marchand. Tibbs tipped his Stetson back on his head, then pulled an envelope with a sheet of paper from his pocket and unfolded it.

"I found this in your pack," Tibbs said, in his low deep drawl. "It says: 'Dear Tod: We need your help fast. Run like the fucking wind.' It is signed 'Stewie.'"

Marchand's eyes were white and wide. It reminded the Old Man of the look the horses had when they first smelled the bears.

"Then there are some directions to a cabin. This Stewie wouldn't happen to be Stewie Woods, would it?" Tibbs asked. "How come you're up here camping, if your celebrity client needs you so badly?" Tibbs said, not unkindly.

Marchand's eyes darted from Tibbs to the Old Man and back.

"I've been planning this long weekend all year," he said.

"Some pal you are." Tibbs snorted. "Unless you're not really sure that Stewie Woods is even alive. Unless you think someone mailed you this as a joke."

Marchand quickly broke down and nodded his head yes. "It's Stewie," he said. "I know exactly where he's at. I'll tell you if you'll let me go. I'll never say a word about this to anyone."

The Old Man dropped his eyes and stared at the ground for what became an interminable amount of time. Marchand shook visibly. Marchand looked to the Old Man for some kind of reassurance or humanity, but the Old Man refused eye contact. The Old Man knew Tibbs well enough to know that Tod Marchand had said exactly the wrong thing, and much too fast.

Finally, Tibbs swiveled slightly and looked back at the Old Man. "This is going to be a good one," Tibbs said. "Maybe the best one yet."

The Old Man nodded blankly. Charlie Tibbs, he suddenly knew, was a man beyond his own understanding. This would be ugly to watch. He was sure Tod Marchand felt the same way. The Old Man decided at that moment that things had gone too far. Maybe so far into evil he could never go back.

"I smell bacon," Tibbs said, turning back around to Tod Marchand. "It makes me kinda hungry. D'you suppose those grizzlies over the hill smell it, too?"

CHARLIE TIBBS WAS EATING piece after piece of beef jerky and drinking from a Thermos of iced tea. Periodically he would lift his binoculars to his eyes. Below them, in the swampy meadow, the grizzlies were eating Tod Marchand.

The sow had found him quickly after Tibbs had dumped the lawyer in the grass between her and her cubs and ridden away on horseback. She had killed Marchand by taking his entire head into her mouth and shaking it violently from side to side, like a puppy with a knotted sock. Marchand's scream stopped so suddenly that it seemed to hang in the air like a lost ghost. A powerful swat from her paw had sent the body flying end over end. The strength of the bear was awesome.

"The cubs are feeding now," Charlie Tibbs said, lowering the binoculars. "It would be a shame if those cubs ate every bit of the lawyer and nobody ever found him out there."

Since they had ridden up on him that day, Tibbs always

referred to Tod Marchand as "the lawyer." He had never once spoken his actual name.

The Old Man felt sick. He had waved away the offers of jerky and iced tea by saying he thought he thought he was coming down with the flu.

"If folks just knew that the lawyer vanished and not that he was attacked by the grizzlies he saved, it would be a shame," Tibbs said.

"I understood the first time," the Old Man said with irritation.

Tibbs's face had a way of going dead that had unnerved a lot of people. It unnerved the Old Man now.

"I just don't like this, Charlie," the Old Man said.

"It's nature at work, is all," Tibbs said, his face assuming life again.

Nature and four pounds of bacon, the Old Man thought.

"Far as I can tell those cubs gobbled that horse hair straight away," Tibbs said, still peering through the binoculars. "No one'll ever know he was tied up."

I WONDER WHO IS IMPERSONATING Stewie Woods?" Tibbs asked suddenly, lowering the binoculars. It had become so dark that the Old Man could no longer make out the individual forms of the bears in the clearing, but he knew that Tibbs's glasses gathered what little light there was, so he could still see. Tibbs also had a night-vision scope in his saddlebag. "Whoever he is, he was trying to draw the lawyer into some kind of situation."

It was so still that the Old Man could hear the bears feeding, hear bones crunching.

"Who would do a thing like that?" the Old Man asked.

His mouth was dry and he had trouble speaking. If Tibbs knew what he had been thinking, the Old Man figured he'd be in danger.

"Don't know," Tibbs shrugged.

"We couldn't have screwed up with Stewie Woods, could we?"

Tibbs snorted. The question was beneath him.

From the clearing they could hear the sound of the two cubs fighting over something.

"I like this," Tibbs said. "Great Grizzly Bear Savior Eaten by Bears in Yellowstone Park."

"Yup," the Old Man said, not agreeing, not disagreeing. He slowly stood up.

"Charlie, how much longer you going to wait here?"

"Couple a hours. Just to make sure."

"Make sure of what?"

Tibbs didn't answer. Long enough to make sure you see everything there is to see, the Old Man thought.

"I think I might ride back and get some sleep in the truck. My stomach's doin' flip-flops and I think I'm coming down with something."

Tibbs leveled his gaze on the Old Man. The Old Man was glad it was almost dark, but knew he looked miserable anyway.

"It's not a good idea to split up," Tibbs said.

"Yeah, I know," the Old Man said. "But it's not a good idea to move in on that pretender tomorrow with me feeling like I do now. I need some rest."

The Old Man sensed Tibbs giving consideration to the argument. Then without a word, Tibbs turned back to the bears.

"See you in a little while," the Old Man said. "I'll just stretch out in the horse trailer in some blankets. Don't forget to wake me up."

Tibbs said nothing. They both knew that the Old Man wasn't going to get away, that he was in this until Charlie let him go. Charlie Tibbs had the keys to the truck, and the Old Man had never had a set. Tibbs didn't offer them now, and the Old Man didn't ask. They also knew how unlikely it would be for the Old Man to try to ride the horse away. Charlie was twice the tracker and horseman the Old Man was, and would be upon him within a few hours.

The Old Man mounted after being sure his horse had calmed down and likely wouldn't bolt because of the bears. The horse was still spooked and white-eyed, but was under control.

Before he left, he looked over his shoulder. He could see Charlie Tibbs's wide back in the moonlight, his shirt stretched tight between his shoulder blades. For a brief moment, the Old Man thought of how easy it would be right then to put a bullet in Tibbs's back. Right into his spine, between the shoulder blades. Then he considered the possibility of the horse bolting as he fired, or of simply missing. He knew if either happened, it would be his last act on earth.

The Old Man had literally felt himself cross over a line and truly become evil. He knew it for a fact. There was nothing he could do to redeem himself in full. But he could, at least temporarily, stop the killing. He wasn't doing it for Stewie Woods or Hayden Powell or Peter Sollito or Emily Betts or Tod Marchand. He still didn't like what any of them stood for. He was doing it for himself.

Someday, in some place, he would need to answer for what he had done these past two months. He at least wanted to be able to tell the inquisitor about one good thing.

He shifted in his saddle and rubbed the right thigh of his trousers. The keys for Tod Marchand's green Mercedes SUV, that the Old Man had found back at the Nez Perce Creek campsite, made a hard little ball in his pocket.

21

EARLY ON SATURDAY MORNING, Joe Pickett finished his monthly report for his area supervisor, Trey Crump. In it, he dutifully explained the status of the situation regarding Jim Finotta. At the conclusion of the report, after a summary of elk herd trend counts and citations issued, he wrote that he had reason to believe that someone impersonating the environmental terrorist Stewie Woods was holed up in a remote cabin somewhere in the Bighorn Mountains. He said he planned to investigate the possibility later that day.

When the report was complete, he attached it to an e-mail and sent it to Crump's office in Cody.

Joe rolled his chair back and exited his tiny home office. Both Lucy and April had been picked up earlier for a weekend church camp, leaving ten-year-old Sheridan (whose age group would go to the camp in the next week) alone and in front of the television watching morning cartoons and enjoying her solitude.

Marybeth was descending the stairs. Joe stopped and watched her, then whistled. She waved him away. She had already been out to the stables to feed the horses. She had returned, showered, and changed clothes. Her hair was up and she wore a white blouse and pleated khakis. She would be working at the library today until three. She looked concerned.

"Is it still your plan to see if you can find that cabin today?" She didn't say "Stewie" or "Stewie's cabin," Joe noted. She spoke low enough not to be overhead by Sheridan in the other room.

"I'm going to leave as soon as I finish getting ready," he said.

She met him at the base of the stairs and stopped on the last step. "I don't like the idea of you going up there alone."

He reached for her and put his hands on her hips. "Are you afraid I'm going to punch him in the nose? I just might, you know."

"Joe, I'm not kidding. He's expecting me and if you show up . . . well, who knows?"

Joe sized up Marybeth. "You look good today," he said. "What time do you need to leave for the library?"

"We don't have time for that." A look of exasperation came over Marybeth's face. "I'm not kidding you, Joe. It's not a good idea for you to go up there without any backup. You *know* that."

Joe thought about it for a moment.

"You're letting your feelings cloud your judgment," Marybeth said. "That's not like you."

Joe had to agree. "I'll call Sheriff Barnum."

She nodded. "Good."

"And I'll run it by Trey in Cody."

"Better still."

He stepped aside so Marybeth could get her purse and sack lunch for her day at the library.

Before she left, she wrapped her arms around his neck and kissed him deeply. It was much more than a morning good-bye kiss.

"I've never seen you jealous before, Joe, and don't get me wrong . . . it's flattering," she said, holding his face inches from hers. "But you have nothing to worry about. You're my man." Then she smiled.

Slightly flustered, Joe smiled back.

"I should be back by dark," he said. "I'll call as soon as I'm back in cell phone range."

She fluttered her eyes coquettishly. "I'll be waiting."

Sheridan overheard her mother and moaned from the living room.

MARYBETH'S CAR WAS PULLING OUT onto the Bighorn Road when Trey Crump called Joe on his office telephone. Crump was a game warden with twenty-one years of experience and was known as one of the real good ones. He was tough, fair, independent, and knowledgeable and as area supervisor he had the reputation of standing by the wardens he oversaw. It was rare for him to call, and even rarer for Crump to read Joe's monthly report the day Joe sent it.

"Before we get to this part about trying to find Stewie Woods," Crump said gruffly, "what in the hell did you do to piss off this Jim Finotta guy so bad?"

Joe said there was nothing more than what was in the report; he suspected Finotta of poaching and was trying to pursue the case.

"I hear he's an asshole," Crump said.

"What you hear is correct."

"There's all kinds of heat and light going on at headquarters over this," Crump sighed. "The director has called me twice in the last week to ask you to cool it. He kind of wanted me to agree that you're being overzealous and need to be reined in."

Joe smiled to himself. "But you didn't call."

"Hell no, I didn't call. I don't raise hell with game wardens for doing their jobs. If a guy shoots an elk out of season, I don't give a shit how much a guy has contributed to the governor's campaign or who he knows in Washington."

"So why are you calling now?"

He could hear Crump shuffling papers. "How much credibility do you give this Stewie Woods thing?"

"I'm not sure," Joe answered. "Marybeth isn't sure, either, and she actually knew the guy. I mentioned those phone calls she's been getting in my report. So I'm going to check it out."

"It would be a hell of a note if this guy was still alive," Crump grumbled. "Most everybody I know would look at that as bad news."

Joe laughed. "That's how most of the folks think around here, too. But it sure is curious, isn't it?"

Crump had to agree with that. He asked Joe to call and let him know what he found out.

SHERIFF BARNUM wasn't in and neither was Deputy McLanahan. Joe left a message with the dispatcher for either man to call him and left his cell phone number. He was secretly pleased they were both unavailable. The last thing he wanted to do was turn this over to them or to get their assistance.

JOE HOOKED UP the two-horse slant-load trailer, saddled Lizzie, and loaded her in. After starting the engine of his pickup, Joe paused to take inventory. The radio, GPS unit, cell phone, and light-control switchbox mounted to the dashboard were all operational. His Redfield spotting scope was on the console next to his file of maps, as well as his Steiner binoculars. Under his seat was the department-issued M14 carbine, and the short .12 gauge shotgun was mounted upright in back of the passenger seat. A .22 revolver loaded with blanks, for the purpose of scaring game animals out of private pastures or other places they didn't belong, was in a holster on the floor. The evidence kit, camera and lenses, first-aid kit, rain gear, and flares were packed into the center console. He checked the batteries on the small tape recorder he used for interviews. On his belt were handcuffs, a thin canister of pepper spray, a Leatherman, and his holster with the .357 Magnum Smith and Wesson revolver. Joe's personal weapon of choice, his Remington Wingmaster .12 gauge shotgun, was behind the seat, secured by Velcro straps. His water bottle and Thermos of coffee were full, and he had packed a lunch of salami, cheddar cheese, and an apple.

From inside the house, Maxine howled a pathetic, mournful wail. She did not like to be left behind. Joe looked up to see Maxine being pulled away from the front window by Sheridan, who waved at him.

"Bye, babe," Joe waved back at Sheridan.

He unfolded the paper with the directions to the cabin that Marybeth had been given over the telephone.

Then he pulled his hat brim down low, backed the pickup

down the driveway to the Bighorn Road, and pointed it toward the mountains.

22

NORTHWEST OF SADDLESTRING, WYOMING
July 6

DRIVING FOUR MILES OVER the speed limit with the Mercedes SUV set on cruise control, the Old Man noticed a small tape recorder pressed upright between the seats and pulled it out. Lawyers liked to talk in these things, he thought, and later give their valuable musings to their secretaries to decipher. Then he remembered the microcassette tape they had taken from Hayden Powell's telephone answering machine. With his left hand on the wheel he dug through his daypack on the passenger seat until he found the cassette, then inserted it into the player. It fit.

He rewound the tape and glanced again at the rearview mirror. He had been driving all night. The Old Man continuously watched for the black Ford pickup to come roaring up behind him. Every time a dark-colored vehicle approached, he reached for his handgun on the console. He had absolutely no doubt that Charlie Tibbs was somewhere behind him, and the two-lane highway he was on was the only southbound route. It could be later today, or tomorrow, but Charlie would come. The Old Man hoped like hell he would be in and out of town by then. If he wasn't, the Old Man would be dead. It was as simple as that.

He listened to the tape from the beginning, getting insight into Hayden Powell's life for the week prior to the night when Charlie Tibbs and the Old Man showed up to end it.

There were several messages from Powell's New York editor asking for selections from *Screwing Up the West* so he could send them out in the hope of getting good quotes from other authors and environmentalists for the book jacket and publicity kit. The editor told Powell not to worry about having the entire manuscript complete and to send chapters that could stand alone and garner praise.

There was a message from Powell's attorney warning Powell that the SEC had called and requested an interview because of the failing dot-com company. The attorney said he recommended delaying the interview as long as possible, but that the two of them would need to get together soon to decide on a strategy for dealing with the allegations.

There were several curt "Call me" messages left by a woman the Old Man guessed was Powell's ex-wife.

It was near the end of the tape that Charlie Tibbs called. There was silence except for traffic sounds. The Old Man had been seated next to Tibbs when he made the call as they entered Bremerton.

Assuming that this was the last of the messages, the Old Man reached to stop the tape. But now he heard one more.

The last message was a bad connection, with static in the line. The voice was thick and slurred.

"You know who this is. You need to get out of here as fast as you can. First they tried to get me, now Peter Sollito is dead. These things work in threes, and who knows who might be next. Hayden, it might be *you.* We need to get together and think this thing out, come up with a strategy before it's too late."

The Old Man was stunned. That message could have been left only by Stewie Woods.

The Mercedes topped a hill on the highway. The Bighorn Mountains loomed ahead; they were light blue, peaked, and crisp in the morning sun. The small town of Saddlestring, from this distance, looked like a case's worth of glinting, broken bottles strewn across the hardpan at the base of the foothills.

23

SHERIDAN PICKETT, STILL IN HER PAJAMAS, was nestled in a pile of couch cushions in front of the television when Maxine began barking at the front door. This ruined Sheridan's perfect Saturday morning. She tossed candy wrappers and a half-eaten bag of chips aside and scrambled out of the cushions, wrapping herself in her terrycloth bathrobe as someone knocked heavily and then rang the doorbell.

Sheridan had been instructed never to open the door for strangers and she was rarely tempted. Ever since the man had broken into their house and hurt her mother she had been especially cautious.

People often came to the door looking for her dad, because his office was in the house. Sometimes they were ranchers who wanted to file damage claims or complain about hunters or fishermen, and sometimes they were hunters or fishermen who wanted to complain about ranchers. Her dad always asked people to call first and set an appointment, but sometimes they just showed up. Since it was her dad's job to serve the public, her parents had told her that if she was home alone and someone stopped by, she should be polite and get a telephone number where her dad could call them.

She cinched her robe tightly and approached the window. Pulling aside the front window curtains, Sheridan peeked outside.

An older, portly, pear-shaped man stood on the front porch. He had a round, full, red face and was not shaved. He wore a low-crown gray cowboy hat, and a weathered canvas ranch jacket and blue jeans. Scuffed lace-up outfitter boots with riding heels poked out from the bottom of his Wranglers. Sheridan always noted the boots men wore because she thought that boots, more than anything, defined who a man was.

The man stood looking at the door, his shoulders slumped, his head tipped forward, as if he were very tired. She looked out through the yard and could see the roof of a car over the fence but couldn't tell what kind of car it was. Sensing her eyes on him, the man turned his head and saw Sheridan looking out at him. He smiled self-consciously at her. Sheridan thought he had a friendly face and that he looked like somebody's grandfather.

Nevertheless, she made sure the door chain was secured before opening the door the several inches the chain would allow.

"Is your father the game warden in this area?"

There was a wooden sign out front on the fence that said exactly that, but oftentimes strangers either didn't see it or chose not to acknowledge it.

"Yes, he is," Sheridan said. "He's not here right now but he'll be back soon." This is what she was supposed to say, that he would be back soon. Sheridan's mother had drilled this into her, this deliberate vagueness.

The man seemed to be thinking. His brow furrowed and

he stroked his chin.

"It's important," he said, looking up. "How soon will he be back?"

Sheridan shrugged.

"Do you think it will be in a few minutes or a few hours?"

Sheridan said she didn't know for sure.

The man rocked back on his boot heels and dug his hands into the front of his jeans pockets. He looked annoyed and troubled, but not necessarily with Sheridan as much as with the circumstances in general. She had not been much help to him, but she would only say what her parents had told her to, nothing more.

"I can give you his cell phone number," Sheridan offered. "Or if it's an emergency you can call the 911 number and ask the dispatcher to radio him." She wanted to be helpful.

The man didn't respond.

"I suppose you can't let me come in and wait for him?"

"Nope," Sheridan said flatly.

The man smiled slightly. It was clearly the answer he expected.

"If I leave him a note, would you make sure he gets it?"

"Sure."

"Back in a minute."

The man turned and walked through the picket fence gate toward his car. Sheridan went into her dad's office and got a business card from the holder on his desk. She waited at the front door. Then she saw the man emerge from his car. As he came through the gate he was licking the back of an envelope.

"Here's his card," Sheridan offered, exchanging it for the

envelope through the crack in the door.

The man's handwriting on the envelope was wavery and poor but it said "Game Warden," followed by the word "Important," which was underlined three times. She read the return address on the envelope.

"Are you a lawyer?" she asked. The printing was for the law offices of Whelchel, Bushko, and Marchand, Attorneys at Law, in Denver, Colorado.

When the man looked at her there was something very sad in his eyes.

"No, I'm not. I just borrowed the paper."

"Okay."

"Make sure you give that to him the minute you see him, little lady," he said as he backed off of the porch.

"My name's Sheridan Pickett."

He stopped before opening the gate and looked over his shoulder.

"My name is John Coble."

Sheridan shut the door and threw the bolt home as he slowly walked to his car and got in. Through the windshield, she watched him as he collapsed into the driver's seat. He seemed exhausted. Then he rubbed his eyes with both of his hands, ran his fingers through his gray hair, and reached forward and started the engine. He backed up and drove away on the Bighorn Road.

Sheridan took the envelope into her dad's office and put it on his computer keyboard where he would see it right away.

JOHN COBLE, THE OLD MAN, felt remarkably good about what he had just done. It was the first thing he had felt really good about in two months. It was possible, he hoped, that he had set some wheels in motion. The girl had been suspicious of him, which was a sign of both intelligence and smart parents. She was a good girl, it seemed to him.

But there was more to be done. His next trick would be harder, and much more unpleasant.

Luckily, he knew these mountains well, and after seeing the crude map that Charlie had pulled from Tod Marchand's pack, he had a very good idea of where Stewie Woods's cabin would be.

24

JOE WAS APPROACHING the grade that would lead to switch-backs up the mountain, when he looked in his rearview mirror and saw the horse trailer listing to the side. There was Lizzie, who liked to thrust her entire head out of the false window opening in the trailer as if she was desperate to force air in through her nostrils, leaning to the left.

He pulled over onto the shoulder and got out. Curls of acrid dark smoke rose from the flattened right tire. He'd been riding a flat for a few miles. The bearings were white hot and smoking in their sleeves of steel and the asbestos brake pads had sizzled and melted.

He unloaded Lizzie and picketed her in tall grass, which she munched as if she had never eaten before. With her weight out of the trailer, Joe assembled the jack and raised the trailer into the air to change the tire. He barely even noticed the green Mercedes SUV that roared by him on the highway.

JOHN COBLE SAW THE HORSE TRAILER and the familiar

pronghorn antelope decal on the door of the pickup as he passed and he took his foot off of the accelerator.

It had to be the game warden, he thought.

Coble studied the reflection in his rearview mirror as the Mercedes began to slow. The driver of the truck was in the ditch next to the trailer, working the handle on the jack. Behind the man, a buckskin horse was staked down, contently grazing.

Coble looked at his watch. It was approaching eleven. He had no idea how far behind him Charlie Tibbs was but he still expected to see the black Ford at any moment.

He had already wasted time in Saddlestring finding the game warden's house. He had left his message for the game warden, done his good deed. Coble had been a little reluctant to meet the game warden face to face in the first place, having no idea how that would go.

Coble made the decision to continue on to the cabin. He pressed on the accelerator and his head snapped back into the headrest as the Mercedes rocketed up the base of the mountain.

THREE MILES PAST CRAZY WOMAN CREEK, Joe slowed and pulled off the highway onto a gravel two-track. The thick lodgepole pine trees formed a high canopy above, casting deep shadows over the road. The crude map he had drawn from Marybeth's directions was on the console between the seats. He had never been on this particular road before, but knew it led through the National Forest to several sections of state and private land where there were old hunting lodges and mining claim cabins. As he drove further up the mountain, the road worsened, pocked now with spurs of granite that slowed him down considerably.

Because of the thick trees, Joe was surprised when he crested the mountain and a massive valley opened up before him. He stopped before he had completely emerged from the forest, put the truck in park, and grabbed his binoculars from his pack on the seat beside him.

It was a beautiful valley, pulsing with summer mountain colors. The two-track wound down the mountain and along the length of the valley floor before disappearing into a grove of shimmering aspen. The groves fingered their way down the slope to access a narrow serpentine creek. On Joe's left, to the south, the mountainside was rugged, marked by cream-colored granite buttes that jutted from the summer grass like knuckles of a fist straining against silk. Between the knuckles were dark stands of spruce in isolated pockets.

A shadow from a single high cumulus cloud scudded slowly across the valley from east to west, its front end climbing up tree trunks while its mass engulfed entire stands of timber, darkening them, before sliding back over the top of the grove to hug the ground again.

On his right, to the north, the mountain was heavily forested. A few grassy parks could be seen through breaks in the timber where tree branches opened up. Matching the terrain to a worn topo map he pulled from his map file, Joe guessed that the lodges and cabins were tucked into the trees to the north.

Through the binoculars he could find only one structure, an ancient log cabin that was leaning so far to one side that it looked like it could collapse any minute. The door gaped open and the windows were gone. This was obviously not the place.

Joe eased down the road into the valley with his hand-drawn map on his lap. Whatever would happen this afternoon would happen here in these mountains and forests, he thought. Either Stewie would be waiting for Marybeth in the cabin he had described to her or this was a hoax of some kind. And if Stewie was in fact alive, what would his reaction be when instead of his old girlfriend, he met the girlfriend's husband?

Joe scanned the trees and undergrowth that lined the edge of the road, looking for an old, lightly used road that supposedly broke off from the two-track and headed north to the top of the mountain. The road would be blocked by trees that had been dropped across it, the directions said, so it was necessary to approach the cabin on foot.

As he descended further into the valley, Joe watched the signal strength on his cell phone dwindle to nothing. He tried his radio to contact the dispatcher and heard only static in return. He was effectively isolated and out of contact, and would remain so until he eventually emerged from the mountain valley.

IT WAS WARMER on the valley floor and Joe unrolled his window. His slow drive toward the aspen was accompanied by the low hum of insects hovering over the carpet of newly opened wildflowers, with spasmodic percussion from small rocks being squeezed and popped free under the weight of his tires. He noticed, as a matter of habit from patrolling, that there was already a fresh tire track on the road—which was unusual in such a remote area.

He followed a road through the trees where the noon

sun dappled the aspen leaves, looking for a turnoff to the right.

When he saw the glint of steel and glass—a vehicle—deep in the Caragana brush through the passenger window, he immediately tensed up, but kept driving slowly as if he had seen nothing at all.

A half-mile from the vehicle, the aspen began to thin, and Joe eased to a stop off the road and turned off his motor. If the person in the car was trying to hide from him, Joe expected to hear a car start up and retreat up the mountain. But it was silent.

Quietly, Joe got out of his pickup. He slipped his .12 gauge shotgun from behind the seat, loaded it with three double-ought buckshot shells, and filled his shirt pocket with additional shells. Then he eased the pickup door shut.

Lizzie anxiously backed out of the trailer, and he was grateful she didn't slam a shoe against the metal floorboard or whinny when she was free. He mounted, secured his hat tightly on his head, slid the shotgun into the saddle scabbard so only the butt of it showed, and nudged Lizzie back toward the road. He kept her in the trees with the road on his right, and she picked her way back to where he had seen the vehicle.

Joe narrowed his eyes as they entered the alcove where the old road was and leaned forward in the saddle to avoid a chest-high branch. It was quiet here, away from the stream, and Lizzie's footfalls were the only sound. He was tense, his senses tingling, and he could feel his heart beat in his chest.

As he approached, Joe could see that the car was a dark green, late model SUV with Colorado plates. Someone had broken leafy aspen branches and laced the hood and windshield with them in an attempt to hide the car. Joe recognized the familiar Mercedes logo on the grille. Because he couldn't call a 10-28 in to the dispatcher, he noted the license plate number in his notebook for later, when he would have a radio signal again.

He dismounted, reins in hand, and peered through the branches at the leather interior. There was an open backpack on the front seat, but there was no one in the car. He felt the hood with the palm of his hand—it was still warm. That puzzled Joe because he had assumed that the vehicle belonged to Stewie, or whoever was posing as Stewie, and therefore that it would have been parked for some time. But the cuts on the branches were fresh as well. Joe squatted and confirmed that the vehicle's tire tread matched the tread pattern he had noticed out on the road.

Joe stepped back and, with his eyes, followed the old road through the trees until it ended beneath two massive spruce trees that had fallen—or were dropped—over it. A single footprint in the loose dirt of the old road pointed up the mountain. This had to be the place, he said to himself. But someone had gotten here before him.

Joe mounted Lizzie and nudged her out of the shaded alcove into the grassy park where the old road led. Riding parallel to the two downed trees, he finally reached their crowns, then turned Lizzie to go back down, along the other side of the trees, to get back on the road.

He wasn't sure what he should do now, how he should proceed. His original plan was that he would ride up to the cabin, find out who was in it, and make a report. But circumstances had changed. The SUV meant that a third party had entered the picture. He was out of radio contact and the threat that he could be entering a situation, alone, that he wasn't prepared to handle was very real. Everything he had ever learned told him he needed backup and that the smart thing to do right now was to retreat back to the road, drive to the top, and call the dispatcher for assistance.

That's when he heard a truck rumbling down the two-track.

CROUCHED BEHIND THE WALL-LIKE BRANCHES of the downed trees that blocked the road, Joe waited for the vehicle to drive by. He saw flashes through the trees as it came down the road from the east, the same direction Joe had come. When it passed by the alcove he saw it in full: a sleek, massive black pickup with dark windows, pulling a horse trailer. Then, almost immediately after it passed him, Joe heard the low hiss of brakes and saw brake lights flash through the brush. The truck was backing up.

Joe turned to check on Lizzie and saw that she was feeding on grass just behind him. He hoped against hope she would keep her head down. If she heard or sensed another horse in the trailer, it would be just like her to raise her head up and call to it. Horses were like that, mares especially, he had noted. They wanted to connect with other horses.

"I'm sorry, girlie," Joe whispered in her ear as he unlashed a coil of rope from the saddle horn and slipped it down over her head as she ate. Then he circled the coil around her front legs with his right hand, caught the loop with his left, and pulled it hard and fast. With a double hitch, he tied her head down against her ankles so she couldn't raise it.

Lizzie's nostrils flared and her eyes flashed with white. Joe tried to keep her calm, patting her shoulder and whispering to her, so she wouldn't panic and try to buck the rope off. He could feel her muscles tense beneath his hand, but kept talking to her in what he hoped was a soothing voice, telling her he was sorry but it was for her own good, telling her that there would be some good grass to eat at the end of the day.

She calmed, exhaling with resignation, and Joe briefly closed his eyes with relief.

When he turned back to the tree and the alcove beyond it, he saw that a tall man wearing a gray Stetson had emerged from the black Ford and was now studying the SUV.

Joe considered calling out to him, but something about the man precluded it. Joe watched as the man approached the vehicle, much as Joe had, but the man did it looking down the sights of a semi-automatic pistol he held stiffly in front of him. Joe watched as the man circled the SUV, nudging branches away so he could see inside. The man was now on the driver's side of the car. If the man were to look up, Joe thought, he would see Joe in the trees. But the man didn't look up because he was busy smashing in the driver's side window.

The Stetson twisted and lowered as the man reached inside the car toward the dashboard. Then Joe heard a small pop and saw the hood of the SUV open.

The old man strode to the front of the vehicle, raised the hood, reached inside, and stepped away with a fistful of loose wires. To ensure the car was disabled, the man bent

181

over and twisted the air valves out of both front tires with a Leatherman tool he had pulled out of a case attached to his belt.

The way the man moved was fluid and calculating, Joe thought. He wasn't quick, but he was deliberate and purposeful. This man did not hesitate; he didn't stop and think about what he was going to do next. He had dismantled the SUV in a couple of minutes without even looking over his shoulder to see if someone was watching. He knew what he was doing, Joe thought, as if he had done this kind of thing before. Joe realized, with a shiver, that he was watching a professional.

Suddenly the man turned from the car, pliers still in his hand, and a pair of icy blue eyes seemed to bore a hole through the branches into Joe. Joe froze, his breath caught in his throat. It was as if the man had heard Joe thinking, sensed Joe's fear the way a predator sensed prey. Joe lowered his hand to the butt of his revolver and felt his thumb unsnap the strap that secured it in his holster.

Only when the blue eyes raised over the top of the trees did Joe realize that the man was following the road, past the downed timber and into the spruce. Joe found he could breathe again and his breath shuddered out.

The man stood staring into the trees above Joe for a moment, then turned and peered through the opening in the alcove at the other mountain, the one on the east side with the granite knuckles. It was as if he were taking a measurement, comparing this mountainside with the other.

The man turned on his heels, without a glance back, and Joe heard the engine of the truck come to life. But instead of proceeding down the road, the pickup turned sharply and started climbing up the other side of the mountain, straight away from Joe. A plume of dirt shot out from the Ford's tires as the black pickup shifted into four-wheel-drive low.

Joe untied Lizzie, ignoring her glare, and swung himself into the saddle. He could breathe again, but the terror he had felt when he thought the man saw him had not yet released its grip.

He could hear the Ford as it climbed, but could no longer see it through the trees. He was surprised there was a road over there because he hadn't seen it.

Then he had a thought, and it chilled him. The man had estimated where the cabin was located in terms of elevation on the mountain. Joe guessed the man was working his way up the facing mountainside to take a position directly across from where he thought the cabin would be.

Joe had a decision to make, but none of his choices were worth a damn. "Joe," he could almost hear Marybeth telling him, "You have *really* done it this time."

"Let's go, Lizzie," Joe barked, turning her and spurring her on so she loped up the mountain road in the direction of where the cabin was supposed to be.

25

TWENTY MINUTES BEFORE Joe had discovered the Mercedes SUV, John Coble had drawn his gun, stepped up on the slatboard porch of the low-slung log cabin, and kicked the door open. He had entered and had pointed his pistol at the man inside, who was seated at a table eating his lunch. Coble was winded from the climb so he leaned back against the doorframe to rest. The cabin was simple: a single large room with a kitchen, dining area, fireplace, and desk. A darkened doorway led to the only bedroom.

"I know you were expecting your lawyer, Stewie, but let me introduce myself," Coble wheezed. "I'm Mr. John Coble, and I've spent the last two months trying to kill you and others of your ilk."

Stewie Woods was frozen where he sat, a spoon filled with soup raised halfway to his mouth. Stewie's face was hard to see because Coble's eyes had not yet adjusted to the darkness inside the cabin.

Coble paused to take a couple of deep breaths of air and then continued. "What I have to say is simple. Get out of this place as soon as you can and don't look back. Don't ask a bunch of questions because we don't have the time. A manhunter named Charlie Tibbs could show up here any minute. Don't stop until you're out of the country; get yourself to Mexico or Canada or wherever you can get to fast. Get on a plane and go overseas if you can. Contact no one and *just flat run*."

Stewie lowered the spoon into the bowl. His words were raspy and filled with air when he spoke, as if his voice box was a carburetor that had the mixture set too lean.

"I guess I've been expecting you. I just didn't realize you would be so old," Stewie rasped. "Somehow, that makes it worse."

A woman stepped from the bedroom rubbing sleep from her eyes. "Stewie, I . . ." she said before she noticed Coble and gasped.

"Britney, this is John Coble," Stewie said, looking stiffly over his shoulder at her and wincing in pain as he did so. "He is one of the men I told you about." Stewie Woods is in bad shape, Coble thought.

Britney's face drained of color as she stared at Coble.

Stewie turned back in his chair. "This is Britney Earth-share. She lived in a tree to protest the logging of an old growth forest. She's famous."

Coble squinted at her. "Yeah, I remember. I remember I thought that was stupid."

Stewie chuckled at Coble. "Britney's been helping me out while I recover. She's a saint."

Coble grunted.

"Why don't you sit down and talk to me for a few minutes?" Stewie asked politely. "You've probably got a pretty good story to tell."

Coble's eyes were still adjusting to the darkness in the cabin. As Stewie Woods's features began to appear, it seemed to Coble like a Hollywood special effect where the closer he looked, the worse it got. Stewie was horribly disfigured. His face was monstrous. His prominent features had once been a jutting jaw, well-defined cheekbones and languid blue-green eyes, but now those outstanding features were ragged mutations. One eye was completely closed, the lid concave over an empty, seeping socket. Stewie's nose was flattened to one side of his face, and the exposed nostril burred and flapped like the beating of a hummingbird wing when he exhaled. Coble cringed and looked away. Britney took a position in back of Stewie with her chubby hands on his shoulders. Her eyes were still wide.

"I don't blame you," Stewie said to Coble. "I still scare myself sometimes. Especially in the morning when I look in the mirror and expect to see the old Stewie. I used to be a pretty good-looking guy, you know."

Coble looked back but focused on a spot somewhere above and to the left of Stewie's head so he wouldn't have to look at him again.

"I don't have time to sit down and chat."

"You're doing a good thing, aren't you?" Stewie asked. "That's impressive."

"I'm not here to save you or protect you. I don't want to be your friend. I still think you and your ilk are shitheels." Coble shook his head. "I'm amazed that you are still alive."

"Me, too," Stewie said. "So why are you doing this?"

Coble had a strange thought. He had not yet holstered his gun and it was at his side in his hand. It would take no effort to raise it, shoot Stewie and the tree-loving woman, and return to Charlie Tibbs. He could tell Tibbs he just wanted to finish this job himself. Tibbs may or may not believe him. There was comfort in evil, Coble thought. It was simpler.

"I'm doing this for me, not you," Coble snapped. "Our job seemed right at first. It seemed like the only way left to strike back. You people threatened our way of thinking and our way of life. All you environmentalists just showed up one day and told us that everything we've done for years was now wrong, and that everyone living in the West was a stupid ignorant criminal.

"You people expect everyone out here to suddenly give up the only jobs they've ever known in mines and the fields," he shot a dirty look at Britney, "and the forests. Somehow, all of us are expected to get jobs working out of our homes with computers, telephones, and modems. That's all you've offered up as an alternative, you know. Like lumberjacks and cowboys can just change over to being software programmers."

Coble's voice began to rise, and his face began to flush. "None of you know or appreciate how tough and raggedy-assed it used to be in this country. Hell, a hundred and forty years ago this was still a wilderness out here. Indians ran the show. Even thirty-odd years ago when I started working for the state of Montana as a brand inspector, it was rough and it was real out here. There was bad weather and bad land and no water. If you looked over your shoulder the country was gaining on you and ready to wipe you out at any minute. The last thing anybody ever thought of was that they were *ruining the earth.* Hell, we all thought the earth was ruining *us.*"

Coble gestured to Stewie: "You people want to stop us from doing everything we know. You do it just so that if you ever want to travel out here from the East in your new car, you might be able to see a wolf out of the window. You're trying to make our home a real-life theme park for environmental whackos. You don't give a shit how many people lose their jobs or are displaced—just so you can see a goddamn wolf that hasn't lived here in over a hundred years."

Coble caught himself. He realized he was giving a speech, one that had been put together in bits and pieces in the pickup and rehearsed in silence as he and Tibbs drove across the country. Although he believed in what he said, he didn't have time for it. He stood and looked at Stewie Woods. Stewie stared back. The man was grotesque.

"But as Charlie and I began to do what we were hired to do, it didn't seem so damned noble to me anymore. In fact, I started feeling like the worst kind of criminal."

Coble paused and shook his head.

"Not Charlie, though," Coble said, grimacing. "Charlie enjoyed it more as we went along, and got more and more excited. He got righteous about it. We started getting sloppy, starting with your friend, Hayden Powell, that writer. There was no planning, no strategy, no nothing except Charlie and me turning into animals trying to kill somebody as fast and as nasty as we could. And we had no idea that our first project failed," he said, looking at Stewie, the first project.

"Charlie Tibbs really does think he's doing righteous work, you know," Coble said with caution. "Charlie's lost something in his head along the way. Something's malfunctioned. His moral compass is gone, and that fact is very frightening, given Charlie's skills and abilities. Charlie's the best tracker and hunter I've ever seen, and I've seen one hell of a lot of 'em. Charlie thinks he's doing this not just for the Stockman's Trust, but for America."

Britney Earthshare was horrified by what she had heard. She covered her mouth with her hand.

"You got paid for this," Stewie said. "You didn't do this entirely for your beliefs."

Coble nodded uncomfortably. He didn't like talking about the money. "I was going to get three-quarters of a million dollars," Coble said flatly. "Two-hundred and fifty thousand was up front, the rest will be sitting in an escrow account for me once the list is cleared. Charlie is probably getting at least double that. We never discussed how much each of us was getting."

Stewie whistled.

"You've got to understand something," Coble said.

"When I worked for the state of Montana I maxed out in salary at $30,500 per year. That was the highest annual salary I ever got. My state retirement is half of that a year. Charlie always made a lot more in his work as a stock detective, but I have no idea what that amounted to."

Stewie said he understood.

"It wasn't hard to recruit us," Coble said, challenging Stewie with an arched-brow glare. "But the difference between Charlie and me is that Charlie Tibbs would have done this for free. It's not a money thing with Charlie. It's never been a money thing, and they knew it when they hired him. I don't see him stopping even when he's sure he's got everybody on the list."

Stewie's unblinking eye had been boring into Coble as he spoke. "So the purpose," Stewie said, "was to eliminate each person on your list in the most humiliating way possible so they would avoid martyrdom, and only be remembered for the ridiculous way they died."

Coble stared back.

"You were pretty successful at that, John Coble," Stewie said.

"Yup," Coble agreed.

"But what is the Stockman's Trust?"

Coble was about to answer but stopped himself and rubbed his eyes. He was absolutely exhausted, completely spent.

"Who is in charge? Who are your employers?"

One of Coble's old hands weakly waved Stewie away. The other hand continued to rub his eyes.

"I've stayed too long and talked too much," Coble said, grunting and pulling himself to his feet. "You two best get out of here. I need some air."

John Coble opened the door and leaned against the inside of the door frame.

26

JOE TRIED TO STAY in the trees, avoiding the grassy open meadows, as he rode hard up the mountain. Lizzie was tiring, her easy lope giving way to lunges, and she was throwing her head in annoyance. Her hooves launched chunks of wet black earth into the air behind them.

He tried to anticipate and play out the scenarios that might occur when he reached the cabin. Should he ask them to come out with their hands up or yell for them to get down on the floor? Should he tell them about his suspicions in regard to the man in the alcove? A stream of sweat trickled down the back of his neck from his hatband.

Sensing that Lizzie was just about to give out, Joe reined her to a stop in the shade of a tree. While she rested, her nostrils billowing, Joe raised his binoculars and looked across the valley to the opposite mountain. He swept the binoculars over the mountain parks and granite spires, looking for the black Ford truck. A glimpse of movement in a meadow startled him, but when he looked back he saw it was only a cow moose grazing at the edge of a treeline.

Then he saw a flash of glass. Fumbling, he dialed the focus in tighter and tried to concentrate his view while Lizzie heaved, breathing hard, and his own heart whumped against the inside of his sternum. He found it. The glint was from something in the rear of the black Ford truck.

Joe reached out to grab a branch to steady himself and raised himself up in his stirrups so that he could see better.

He took a sharp intake of breath. The man in the Stetson was in the back of the Ford, leaning over a long rifle mounted in the bed of the pickup. The glint was from the telescopic site. Joe imagined a line of fire from the black Ford to the cabin, which must be just above him through the trees.

Joe heard the bullet before he heard the shot; a sound like fabric ripping that suddenly ended in a hollow and sickening *pock* sound.

IN THE DOORWAY OF THE CABIN, John Coble flipped backward through the air and landed heavily on the table where Stewie Woods sat. Britney screamed and backpedaled until the wall stopped her. Her T-shirt and face were spattered with blood and bits of bone and tissue.

Stewie kicked back his chair and scrambled to his feet, looking down at Coble. The top half of Coble's head was gone.

Outside, a heavy rifle shot rolled across the valley, sounding like thunder.

CROUCHING FORWARD IN THE SADDLE like a jockey, Joe spurred Lizzie out of the trees and into the open meadow that rose up the mountain to culminate at the shadowed front of a dark cabin. The boom of the shot swept through the timber.

"Get down!" he shouted at the cabin, not knowing how many people were inside. *"Get down on the floor!"*

And suddenly Joe felt an impact like an ax burying itself into soft wood. Lizzie stumbled, her front legs collapsing as her rear haunches arced into the air, her head ducking as she pitched forward, throwing Joe. He hit the ground hard, crumpling against the foot of the steps to the porch of the cabin, his chest and chin taking the brunt of the fall. Lizzie completed her thousand-pound somersault and landed so hard, just a foot short of Joe, that he felt the ground shudder.

BRITNEY WAS STILL SHRIEKING inside but she had screamed herself hoarse and was practically soundless when the doorframe filled with Joe Pickett. The fall had knocked the wind out of him and he leaned into the cabin with his hands on his knees, fighting for breath. The rope he had looped around the saddle horn was tangled around one foot.

Stewie lurched around the table where Coble lay twitching and helped Joe inside, leading him from the open door, as a fist-sized hole blew through the front window and shattered all of the glass.

"Get down!" Joe barked, as he dropped to his hands and knees, pulling Stewie with him.

Methodically, bullets hit the front of the cabin blowing holes through the walls that looked alternately like stars, hearts, and sunbursts—followed by the rolling thunder sound of the heavy rifle fire.

"You must be Stewie Woods," Joe said, looking over to the man who had helped him inside the cabin.

"And you *aren't* Mary Harris," Stewie said.

"I'm her husband," Joe said, glaring at Stewie's disfigured face. Now was not the time to punch him in the nose, Joe thought. "Her name's Marybeth Pickett."

Stewie wheezed. "You're a game warden."

"Right."

"Do you know how many there are out there shooting at us?" Stewie asked with remarkable calmness.

"One older man in a black Ford pickup. He's got a hell of a rifle and he knows what he's doing."

"Look what he did to John Coble," Stewie gestured to the table above them. For the first time, Joe noticed the two boots that hung suspended from the edge of the table and a single still arm that dropped over the side. A stream of dark blood as thick as chocolate syrup strung from the table to a growing pool on the floor.

"Is he—"

"He's dead," Stewie said. Britney Earthshare had now crawled over to join them on the floor. Her face was a mask of revulsion and frozen shock. Joe sympathized. He couldn't yet grasp the magnitude and danger of the situation he was in.

"Do you have any weapons in the cabin?" Joe asked them both.

"No, but Coble has a pistol with him," said Stewie.

"Get it," Joe commanded. "Can you shoot a gun?"

"Of course," Stewie said. "I'm from Wyoming."

Stewie rolled toward the table and began to rise up. As he did, the kitchen window imploded with the force of another bullet and threw shards of glass skittering across the floor. Stewie dropped to a sprawl, his attitude accusatory toward Joe.

"Forget *that!*" Stewie yelled.

"What about you, Britney?" Joe asked. She was closer to Coble.

"I will not touch a gun."

Joe cursed. They were useless.

Joe's mind raced as he lay there, his cheek pressed to the rough wood. Stewie was a few feet away, and despite the immediacy and danger of the situation, he couldn't help staring. Stewie, Joe thought, was hideous. Seen in the dusty rods of light from the bullet holes in the walls, Stewie's face looked as if it were made of wet papier-mâché that had been raked from top to bottom with a gardening claw and allowed to dry. His mouth was misshapen and exaggerated, capable of making a perfect inverted U when Stewie was angry, like he was now. His mouth looked like a child's drawing of a sad face.

Under Stewie's rough, loose clothes, it was obvious that he had been bigger but had recently lost most of his muscle tone. Skin sagged on big bones. His left arm was limp and thin. Stewie's fingernails and toenails needed trimming, and a beard, once full and red, was now pink and wispy. The hair on his head grew in patches, like putting greens on a desert golf course.

Joe, however, pulled his attention away from Stewie as he realized that the gunshots had suddenly stopped. Joe guessed that the shooter was reloading. He reached down to make sure his .357 was still in his holster and was relieved to find it was. Unfortunately, Joe was a notoriously bad shot, and he knew that it would be close to impossible for him to hit the shooter at this distance.

The shots resumed, but inside the cabin nothing happened. The shooter had shifted targets. Joe heard a faraway shattering of glass, and a metallic clang from the impact of a bullet.

"He found my truck," Joe spat.

He remembered that his shotgun was in the saddle scabbard. On his knees and elbows he scrambled toward the open door.

"Where are you going?" Britney asked hysterically. "Are you leaving us?"

"Try to calm down, Britney," Stewie implored.

Joe crawled to the side of the doorframe and cautiously leaned forward. His face and head felt stunningly exposed when he peered outside. He wondered if he would hear the bullet before it hit him.

Joe was practically useless as well. The shooter was over 1,500 yards away on the other mountain. Joe's .357 Magnum was not capable of even half of that range. The fat, heavy bullets he fired would fall short at about the distance of the road.

LIZZIE WASN'T WHERE she had fallen, but Joe spotted her further down the meadow. She stood in a pool of shadow just inside the treeline. His saddle had come loose and hung upside down beneath her belly. She took a step, faltered, and stopped. She stood stiffly. He could see that the bullet had shattered her right rear leg. Her leg, from her hock down, hung like a broken branch.

Suddenly, there was a puff of dust and hair from her shoulder and the horse jerked and buckled into the summer grass as the reverberating sound of shot rolled across the valley.

That son of a bitch, Joe thought. *That son of a bitch killed Lizzie!*

Joe suddenly scuttled back as another .308 bullet blew a football-sized chunk out of the doorframe directly above where his head had been.

"Jesus Christ!" Stewie bellowed.

Joe knew his face was white and contorted with fear—he could feel his own skin pulling across his skull—when he joined Stewie and Britney Earthshare under the table. His voice choked as he asked them if there was another way out of the cabin.

Stewie said there was a side door but that Charlie Tibbs could probably see them if they went out that way.

"There's a window in the bedroom," Britney said, her teeth chattering as if the temperature were subzero.

They crawled across the floor of the cabin toward the bedroom over shards of glass, splinters of wood, and congealing globules of blood and tissue. A bullet tore through the wall a foot above floor level and smashed into the base of the stove where Britney had huddled just a few minutes ago. Joe felt the cabin shudder with the impact.

In the bedroom, Joe ripped the curtains and rod off of the only window and shoved it open. It faced the back of the cabin, away from where Charlie Tibbs was positioned on the mountain.

Britney was trembling beneath her T-shirt as Joe helped her out the window. There was a five-foot drop, and she landed awkwardly but recovered. Stewie sat on the sill and grunted, trying to fit his broad shoulders through the frame.

"I'm stuck, dammit," he complained.

With the heel of his hand, Joe thumped Stewie's left shoulder, forcing him through. Stewie dropped to the ground and landed gracefully.

A sound like a cymbal crashed in the main room as a bullet tore through the wall and hit a cast-iron skillet hanging above the stove.

Joe dropped through the window and his boots stuck fast to the soft earth covered with pine needles.

"Which way?" Britney asked.

"North." Joe pointed into the timber. "Keep the cabin between us and the shooter. Stay in the trees and don't look back until we're over the top of the mountain."

"I was really looking forward to seeing Mary," Stewie said. "What a shitty day this has turned out to be."

Joe wheeled and hit Stewie square in the nose. Stewie lost his footing and sat down.

Stewie reached up and covered his nose with his hand, then looked at the smear of blood in his palm. He glared at Joe with his one good eye.

"Enough about my wife," Joe commanded, shaking his hand that stung from the blow.

Britney ran to Stewie and helped him to his feet. Stewie rose with a twisted, manic grin that looked almost cartoonish.

"The man who is shooting at us," Joe asked, "do you know who he is?"

Stewie nodded, still rubbing his nose. "His name is Charlie Tibbs."

"Charlie Tibbs?" Joe repeated. "Oh, shit." Joe had heard of Tibbs. He hadn't realized the legendary stock detective was still working.

"Okay," Stewie said, shaking his head with bemused disbelief. "Let's resume fleeing now."

As THEY CLIMBED through the thick trees in back of the cabin, Joe grimly went over what had just happened, wishing he could call it all back, wishing he could start over from the time he saw the man he now knew as Charlie Tibbs.

Wishing he knew then what he knew now, Joe thought how easy it would have been to pump his shotgun and level Charlie Tibbs with a cloud of buckshot as the man stood in the alcove by the hidden Mercedes. If he had done that, Joe thought, John Coble would still be alive, Joe would still have his horse and his dignity, and he would not be deep in the timber, running north, with Stewie Woods and Britney Earthshare, into mountain country so rough and wild that no one had ever bothered to cut a road into it.

Behind him he heard another heavy bullet slam into the cabin, followed by another booming roll of a rifle shot.

27

AFTER ENTERING THE HOUSE and kissing Sheridan, Mary-beth asked if Joe had called. Sheridan, still lounging on her pillows in front of the TV, answered that he hadn't.

Marybeth dropped the Tom Horn book on the kitchen table and launched herself into scrubbing the counters and washing the dishes. It was a way of fighting off the sense of dread she had been feeling since the telephone calls and the incident with Ginger Finotta in the library. It was barely four in the afternoon and Joe had said he would be back by dark or call first. It was still early, and she had no good reason to feel such anxiousness.

Reading the book hadn't helped. Although it meandered through Tom Horn's Indian fighting days—he was one of those hired to pursue Geronimo—and his service with the U.S. Army in Cuba, what interested her were the chapters at the end of the book. Those chapters covered the period when Tom Horn was hired by Wyoming ranchers to clear out rustlers and homesteaders in southern Wyoming. The ranchers were a gentlemanly, genteel group. Many had nothing to do with day-to-day ranch work, which they hired out to their foremen, and they spent their days in the men's clubs wearing fashionable clothing and their nights in a cluster of beautiful Victorian homes in Cheyenne. Some had visited their vast holdings up north only for occasional hunting trips. They knew, however, that the presence of rustlers, outlaws, and settlers threatened not only their income but also their political power base and the concept of open range. The ranchers were all members of the nascent Wyoming Cattle Growers' Association. So it was decided among a cabal of association members that the rustlers had to go, and it would be best if it were accomplished ruthlessly, to send a powerful message. Based on the landowners' experience in the territory thus far, local law enforcement couldn't handle the job. The rustlers were local and their connections within the community were pervasive. For example, the rustlers knew well in advance when a sheriff's posse was forming or where deputies were going to be sent to try to break them up.

So Tom Horn was hired, supposedly to break horses for the Swan Land and Cattle Company. He lived alone in a rough cabin in the rocky Iron Mountain range, which was country better suited for mountain lions than for people. But there was no mistaking the real reason he was in the area, and it had little to do with horses.

One by one, men suspected of rustling turned up dead. They were found in the high sagebrush flats and amid the granite crags of the Medicine Bow Mountains. There was a pattern to their deaths. All were found shot in the head, probably from a great distance, with a large caliber rifle bullet. And under their lifeless heads, someone had placed a rock.

"You be good," parents of the time would say to their children, "or Tom Horn'll get you!"

AT FIVE, MARYBETH CALLED the dispatcher to find out if there had been any word from Joe. The dispatcher said that according to the log, Joe had not called in the entire day. At Marybeth's request, the dispatcher tried to reach him, but after several attempts, she reported that either Joe's radio was turned off or he was simply out of range. Both Marybeth and the dispatcher knew how difficult it could be at times to make contact with officers in the mountains.

At five-thirty, Marybeth called the Sheriff's Office. Joe had promised to call the sheriff and advise him of his whereabouts, as well as his agenda. Sheriff Barnum was out of town at the Wyoming Law Enforcement Academy in Douglas for firearms recertification, and Marybeth didn't trust Deputy McLanahan enough to tell him her suspicions. Barnum was not expected back until late Sunday afternoon. The Sheriff's Office told Marybeth that Joe had called early in the morning and had left his cell phone number for the sheriff to use when and if he called in.

Marybeth felt a flash of anger at Joe. Knowing Joe, he had probably been grateful that Barnum wasn't in. This way, he could investigate the cabin on his own. This was the kind of stubborn behavior that worried and enraged her. She tried to relax, telling herself that he was probably just fine, simply out of radio or cell phone range. He was probably rumbling up out of the trees with the horse trailer after having met Stewie Woods—or not. He would certainly call her when he could. But dammit, he had no right to put her through this.

She stepped out of Sheridan's line of sight while she composed her thoughts. She breathed deeply and calmed herself. The one thing she didn't want to do was to worry Sheridan, because the two of them would feed off of each other and their dual concern would escalate—which wouldn't accomplish anything of value. Marybeth was grateful that Lucy and April were both at church camp so there were two less children to hide her feelings from. But then, at times like these, she wanted all of her children around her. She wanted to be able to shelter and protect them.

She thought of Trey Crump, Joe's district supervisor in Cody. He was a good guy, and wouldn't begrudge her calling him for advice. It was still much too early to panic, but if Trey was aware of the situation he might have some ideas on how to proceed, and he was the closest to the mountains—although from the other side—if it were nec- essary to start a search.

Joe had taken a copy of the directions she had written down when Stewie called, but Marybeth assumed the orig- inal was still in the small desktop copier in his office. She noted that Sheridan's eyes were on her as she crossed the family room and entered Joe's office.

"Anything wrong, Mom?" Sheridan asked.

"No, nothing," Marybeth answered a little too quickly.

"Oh, I forgot to tell you," Sheridan said from her cush- ions. "A man came here today and left a letter for Dad."

Marybeth stepped from the office doorway holding the envelope that was printed with the return address of Whelchel, Bushko, and Marchand, Attorneys at Law.

"You need to tell me these things," Marybeth snapped.

Sheridan did her best "Hey, I'm innocent" shrug. "I just did," she explained. "Besides, people drop stuff off for Dad all the time."

Marybeth sighed, knowing Sheridan was right. Still holding the envelope, she found the directions in the copier, exactly where she thought they would be. Then she stared at the writing on the envelope.

Game Warden. Important.

Important enough to open now, she wondered? Important enough for the game warden's *wife* to open it?

"Tell me what the man looked like," she asked Sheridan.

"Jeez, chill, mom," Sheridan said, turning the television volume down with the remote control. "He was an older guy, probably sixty or so. He had on a cowboy hat and jeans. He had a potbelly and he seemed like a nice guy. He said his name was Jim Coble or something like that."

Marybeth thought about it. The description wasn't much help, except that the man wasn't someone they knew.

TREY CRUMP WASN'T AT HOME so Marybeth talked to his wife. They agreed that this kind of situation was maddeningly familiar and would probably reduce both their normal life expectancies. Mrs. Crump said she would have Trey call Marybeth as soon as she heard from him.

"Tell him I'm not panicking," Marybeth asked. "That's important."

Mrs. Crump said she understood.

· · ·

THE GENTLEMEN RANCHERS, the pampered sons of industrialists and shipping magnates and bankers from Europe and New York and Boston, had gotten together and conspired over brandy and cigars and had determined that the local authorities were too stupid, too ineffectual, and too familiar with the rustlers and the settlers to eliminate the problem. What they needed, to preserve the status quo and the dominant concept of open range, was a calculating hired assassin from the outside who would answer only to them.

So Tom Horn was brought in, hired by an associate who could not directly implicate them, to do the job.

The rustlers were criminals, but they were not treated with the condemnation by the public that they deserved, the ranchers thought. Rustlers were often portrayed as dashing cowboy rogues, the last of the frontiersmen. The settlers, who were building shanties (some actually burrowing into the earth like human rodents) and putting up fences on their open range, were thought of as rugged individualists. Public sentiment was growing against the gentlemen ranchers. Locals spoke of a distinction between the ranchers who lived on their land and took on the elements and the markets as opposed to the gentlemen ranchers who lived in Cheyenne and managed their affairs over fine dinners and liquor sent out daily on the Union Pacific.

So the ranchers started a small war. And they were very successful, at least for a while.

Marybeth lowered the book and her eyes burned a hole into the clock above the stove. It was six-thirty, and shadows were beginning to grow across the road on Wolf Mountain. Joe hadn't called in. Neither had Trey Crump.

Maybe this is what Ginger Finotta was trying to tell her. Maybe, she thought, the ranchers were going to war again.

She drew the envelope from her pocket. It could be anything. It could be a letter asking about where the man could get permission to hunt. In the Rockies, men generally thought that anything to do with hunting should be labeled "Important." And ranchers thought anything that had to do with their land was important.

She ripped open the envelope and pulled out a single folded sheet and read the wavering script.

"Oh My God," she said aloud.

"Mom, what is it?" Sheridan called from the other room.

Part Three

I'm not much of a prophet. I suppose the conflict between conservation and development will grow more intense each year with the pressure of a growing population and economic demands. That's all I can see in the future—more conflict.

EDWARD ABBEY, AUTHOR OF *THE MONKEYWRENCH GANG*,
NPR INTERVIEW, 1983

28

WITH THE CABIN BEHIND THEM, Joe Pickett, Stewie Woods, and Britney Earthshare ascended the first mountain. Joe led, keeping to the trees, and eventually found a game trail that switchbacked its way to the top. Descending, they plunged steeply into twisted, gnarled, almost impenetrable black timber. They crawled more than walked through it, sometimes covering much more ground moving sideways to find an opening in the trees than actually distancing themselves from the cabin.

The frequency of the rifle fire had slowed. Joe checked his watch. It was now three to five minutes between shots. Then the shots stopped altogether.

Finally, they reached the bottom of the slope. By then Joe was thinking about the probability of being tracked. While the black timber would be as difficult for a horse as it was for them, it would be obvious that the only place they had to run was downhill. There was no reason to flank the cabin or try to work their way back to the road where they could possibly be seen. The best strategy, Joe figured, was to get as far away as possible, as quickly as possible.

Stewie was doing remarkably well, considering the circumstances and the tough climbing. As they crawled through the timber his chatter was nonstop. He filled Joe in on what John Coble had told them about how it had been he and Tibbs who had rigged the cow with explosives, and how boring it was to be a fugitive.

"If this was a movie, we would have stayed at the cabin and plotted and then set a bunch of booby traps," Stewie riffed. "You know, we would have dug a pit and filled it with sharpened sticks or fixed up a trip-wire on a bent-over tree or something so when Charlie came tonight— *whoops!*—he would get jerked into the air by his feet. Then we'd surround him and beat him like a piñata.

"But this ain't no movie, man. This is real life. And in real life when some dickhead is shooting at you there is only one thing you can do, and that is to *run like a rabbit. Like a scared fucking bunny.*"

Joe ignored him.

Occasionally, when a branch snapped dryly or two trees rubbed together with a moan in the wind, Joe would spin and reach back for his pistol. At any time, he expected Charlie Tibbs to appear above them or for long-range rifle shots to start cutting them down.

At the bottom of the slope was a small runoff stream that coursed through boulders. Joe stepped up on the rocks and led them downstream for half a mile before cutting back up the next slope.

Britney objected and Joe explained that the foray was meant to make them more difficult to track since they would leave no marks on the stones.

THEY STAYED IN THE SHADOWS of a steep granite wall and followed it up the second mountain until the wall finally broke and let them through. After five hundred yards of spindly lodgepole pines, the trees cleared and and they started toward the top of the mountain, laboring across loose gray shale. The temperature had dropped ten degrees as they climbed due to the increase in altitude, although it was still hot and the late afternoon sun was piercing.

Stewie's labored breathing and the cascading shale as it loosened under their feet were the only sounds as they hiked upward.

"Try to get over the top without stopping," Joe called over his shoulder to Stewie. "If Charlie Tibbs is going to see us with that spotting scope of his, it's going to be here, while we're in the open."

"Stewie can't get his breath!" Britney pleaded to Joe. She had dropped back and was climbing with Stewie, his good arm over her shoulder.

"He's fine," Joe grumbled. "Let's keep going. We can rest on the other side."

"What an *asshole*," Britney said to Stewie in a remarkably out-of-place Valley Girl intonation. "First he *hits* you and then he tries to *kill* you."

Stewie tried, between attempts to catch his breath, to reassure Britney that he was all right.

Joe sighed and waited for them to catch up, then pulled Stewie's other arm over his own shoulder. The three of them summitted the mountain and stumbled down the other side, again through loose shale.

Joe kept urging them on until they approached larger trees that provided some cover and shade. He stepped out from Stewie's arm, letting it flop down, and found a downed log to sit on.

Stewie crumpled into a pile of arms and legs and sat still while he slowly caught his breath. Britney positioned herself behind him in the crux of a weathered branch. Joe noticed that she had gouged her shin sometime while they were climbing and that blood from the wound had dried in two dirty streams running down her leg and into her sandaled foot.

Sitting back, Joe felt cool as the sweat beneath his shirt began to dry. He removed his hat and ran his fingers through hair that was getting stiff with salt from sweating beneath his hatband. Patting his shirt and trouser pockets, he did a quick inventory of what he had brought with him. While he had started the day in the cocoon of his pickup surrounded by radios, firearms, equipment, as well as Lizzie, he now counted among his possessions his clothing, boots, and hat, his holster and belt, the long coil of rope, small binoculars hung by a thong over his neck, and his spiral notebook and pen.

Looking at Stewie and Britney, he saw that they had brought even less with them from the cabin.

Stewie painfully untangled himself and sat up, his arms around his knees. He looked up at Joe.

"Thanks for helping me up the mountain."

"Sure."

Britney rolled her eyes.

"What do you think our plan should be?" Stewie asked. "How long should we hide out before we head back?"

Joe had been thinking about this on their long march up the mountainside.

"I don't know."

Britney huffed, blowing her bangs up off her forehead. The Valley Girl speech pattern was back. "What do you *mean* you don't know? Why did you *lead* us up that freaking *mountain,* then?"

Joe grimaced. This was not where he wanted to be, he thought, and these were not people he wanted to be there with.

"We don't know if Charlie Tibbs is tracking us," Joe explained patiently. "If he is coming after us, he has a horse and he seems to know what he's doing. Even I could follow our sloppy tracks up this mountain."

"I didn't know we were supposed to tiptoe," Britney whined.

"John Coble said that Tibbs was the best tracker he had ever seen," Stewie said.

Joe addressed Stewie. "If he turns away and goes back to where he came from, we'll know it tonight, I think. He might even follow our tracks down to the stream, where I hope he'll get confused about where we came out and turn back. I can't imagine him trying to run us down at night. If he leaves, we can sneak back to the cabin tomorrow. You've got a cell phone and a radio in there, right?"

Stewie nodded yes. *How do you think I called your wife?* was what Joe expected him to say. But Stewie wisely kept his mouth shut.

"The phone only works at certain times," Britney said. "Like when the weather is just perfect or the sunspots are lined up or something. Most of the time we can't reach anybody and nobody can call us."

Joe nodded. "I've got a phone and a radio in my truck, if we can get to it. Provided Charlie Tibbs doesn't get there first." He thought of Tibbs's methodical work on the SUV and imagined him doing the same to his pickup. "Plus they'll be looking for us by tomorrow, is my guess."

"At least when I was in the tree I had electricity and could use my cell phone to call my friends," Britney said, speaking as much to herself as to Stewie or Joe. "I had *food,* at least. But I guess that was California and this *isn't.*"

Stewie's misshapen mouth exaggerated his frown. "And if he comes after us?"

"Then we die," Britney offered.

IN A THICK POCKET OF ASPEN TREES below where Stewie and Britney were resting, Joe found a spring that burbled out of a granite shelf into a small shallow pool that had been eroded into the rock. From the shelf, trickles of water dribbled down the rock face and, with the help of other spring-fed trickles further down the mountain, worked their way in unison toward the valley floor to birth the next stream. Joe drank from the pool, pressing his cheek against the cool lip of it, sucking the water in through his teeth to catch the pine needles that floated on the surface. If there was bacteria in the water, he didn't care. Giardiasis was the last thing he was worried about right now.

He put his hat in the water, crown down, and filled it as much as he could. Holding it in his hands like a newborn puppy, he walked back up the mountain to give Stewie and Britney a drink.

Stewie accepted the hatful of water and Britney crinkled her nose at the very idea. She left to find the spring for herself.

After drinking, Stewie wiped his mouth with his sleeve.

"I'll bet you ten thousand dollars that he's already coming after us," Stewie said.

"No bet."

"A thousand?"

"No bet."

"Can you hit anything with that pistol?" Stewie asked, gesturing with his head toward Joe's holster.

"Nope."

"How well do you know this country?"

"Not as well as I wish I did," Joe confessed, sitting back down on the log.

Stewie cursed the fact that they didn't have a map.

He looked beyond Joe to the jagged peaks of the mountains, which were brilliant blue and snow-capped. "Unless I'm completely wrong, it seems to me if we keep going west we will hit a big canyon that will stop us cold."

Joe nodded. "Savage Run."

"I always wanted to see that canyon." Stewie's face screwed up in a clownish, pathetic grimace. "But not like this."

29

THE SUN BALLOONED AND SETTLED into a notch between massive and distant peaks, as if it were being put away for the night. There was a spectacular farewell on the westward sides of the mountains and bellies of the cumulus clouds as they lit up in brilliant fuchsia.

They were still in the tall trees below the rim, and Joe had searched in vain for a natural shelter of some kind. But he had not located a cave, or a protected wash, or even an exposed root pan large enough for the three of them. As the evening sky darkened, there were no signs of thunderheads, so he hoped there wouldn't be rain. The temperature had dropped quickly as the sun had gone down. At this elevation, there were wide swings of temperature every day. Joe had estimated that it had been about eighty degrees that afternoon, and he expected it to drop to forty by the predawn hours.

They were, by Joe's guess, only five miles from the cabin. That was all the progress they had made, despite an entire afternoon of climbing, hiking, and crawling over exceedingly rough terrain.

The place they had chosen to stop had its advantages. It was close enough to the top of the ridge that they could peer over it into the valley. Because they were on the other side of the second mountain, their camp could not be seen if Tibbs was glassing the country with his spotting scope. There was water nearby, and the grade of the slope behind them was not nearly as difficult as the two they had already come across. If Tibbs suddenly appeared, they could move into the trees and down the mountain fairly quickly. And if a helicopter arrived, on the remote chance that one had been called out, they could scramble out into the open areas and be seen from above.

JOE LAY ON THE STILL-WARM SHALE at the top of the ridge and looked through his binoculars at the first mountain and the valley below them. As it got darker, the forest appeared to soften. There was no way, looking at the country now, to know how rough and ragged it was beneath the darkening velvet green cover of treetops.

Joe looked for movement, and listened for sounds in a vast silence so awesome it was intimidating. Although he didn't expect to see Charlie Tibbs riding brazenly through an open meadow, there was the chance that Tibbs might spook deer or grouse and give away his location. That is, Joe thought, if he were out there at all.

Joe didn't turn when he heard the crunching of heavy steps as Stewie joined him on the top of the ridge.

"See anything?" Stewie asked, settling into the shale with a grunt.

"Trees."

"Britney's not in a very good mood, so I thought I would join you," Stewie said. "She tried to wash John Coble's blood out of her shirt but she couldn't get it all out."

"Mmm."

"Damn, it's beautiful, isn't it?"

"Yup."

"Do you ever actually talk?"

Joe lowered the binoculars for a moment. "I talk with my wife." Then he cautioned Stewie: "But I don't talk *about* my wife."

Stewie nodded, smiled, and looked away.

"Have you wondered how it is I came to be?" Stewie spoke in hushed tones, barely above a whisper. "I mean, now. After getting blown up by a cow?"

"I did wonder about that."

"But you haven't asked."

"I've been busy."

"It's an amazing story. A horrible story. You got a minute?"

Joe smiled in spite of himself. *Did he have a minute?*

"The force of the explosion pinned you to a tree trunk," Joe said. "I saw the branch you hung from. I even climbed up to look at it."

Stewie nodded. That's where it began, he said.

HE WAS ALIVE.

Either that, or he was in a state of being that was at least similar to being alive, in the worst kind of way. He could see things and comprehend movement. His imagination flowed around and through his brain, like warm fingers of sludge, and the sludge had taken over his consciousness. He imagined that a thin sinewy blue string or vein, a tight wet cord that looked somewhat like a tendon, tenuously secured his life. He thought that the tendon could snap and blink out the light, and that his death would come with a heavy thumping sound like a wet bundle of canvas dropped onto pavement. An impulse inside him, but outside his control, was working like mad to keep him living, to keep things functioning, to maintain the grip of the tendon. If the impulse ran out of whatever was fueling this effort, he would welcome the relief and invite whatever would happen next. And for a moment his senses focused.

Blood painted the trees. Bits of clothing and strips of both human and bovine flesh hung from branches. The smell of cordite from the explosion was overpowering and it hung in the air, refusing to leave.

He was not on the ground. He was in the air. He was an angel!

Which made Joe laugh out loud, the way Stewie said it.

He watched from above as the three men wearing cowboy hats approached the smoking crater. He could not hear anything beyond a high-static whooshing *noise that resembled the sound of angry ocean breakers. Red and yellow globules that his own damaged head had manufactured floated across his field of vision. It reminded him of the time he ate peyote buttons with four members of the Salish-Kootenai Nation in northwestern Montana. Then, however, he had been laughing.*

But he was not an angel—the thought of that alone was preposterous—and he was not having an out-of-body experience, although he couldn't be sure since this was his first. His soul had not left his body and had not floated above in the blood-flecked branches of the trees.

When the heifer went up, so did he. He had flown upward and back, launched out of his shoes until stopped fast, skewered through his shoulder by a thick pine bow. His feet, one sock off and one sock on, had floated below. They swung a bit in the wind.

He had not thought such things were possible.

What an awful tragedy it was that his wife was dead,
atomized, before he had really known much about her.
Conversely, he wondered if perhaps he had known her at
her absolute best and that he was blessed to have known
her at all. Nevertheless, she had done nothing to deserve
what had happened to her. Her only crime was to be with
him. Blinking hard, he had tried to stay awake and con-
scious.

The men below had stretched yellow tape around the
crater and had left in the dark. Two of them were talking,
their cowboy hats pointed at each other and their heads
bobbing. He waited for the man who was standing to the
side to look up. He wondered if the pattering of his blood
on the leaves far below the leaves made any sound.

"That was me," Joe said.

"I know that now."

I will be dead soon, he had thought, and sleep took him.

But he wasn't dead yet. The thoughts of his bride had,
strangely, given him strength. When he awoke, the men
were gone and the forest was dark and quiet.

A raven landed directly in front of him on the bloody
branch. Its wings were so large that they thumped both
sides of his head as it settled. He had never seen a live wild
bird this close. This was not a Disney bird. This was an
Alfred Hitchcock bird. The raven's feathers were black and
had a blue sheen, and the bird hopped so closely to Stewie's
face that he could see his reflection in the beads of water
on its wings. The raven cocked its head from side to side
with clipped, seemingly mechanized movements. The
raven's eyes looked intense and passionless, he thought,
like glistening ebony buttons. Then the raven dug its black

beak into Stewie's neck and emerged with a piece of red flesh.

He had closed his eyelids tightly so the raven could not pluck his eyes out. The raven began to strip flesh from his face. The raven's beak would pierce his skin near his jaw and clamp hard, then the bird's body would brace as it pulled and ripped a strip upward, where it would eventually weaken and break near his scalp. Then the raven would sit back calmly and with lightning nods of its head devour the stringy piece whole, as if it were a thick, bloody worm.

The thought he had, as the wind increased and his body swayed gently, was that he really hated this bird.

"I saw the same bird when I climbed your tree," Joe said. "The bird made me fall out of it."

He freed himself by forcing his body up and over the branch, sliding along the grain of the wood, in the single most painful experience of his life. Disengaging himself from the skewer left him weak and trembling, and he fell more than climbed from the tree. For ten days he crawled. He had become an animal and he had learned to behave like an animal. He tried to kill something to eat but he was hampered by his bulk and lack of skill. Once, he spent an entire agonizing day at the mouth of a prairie dog hole with a makeshift snare, missing the fat rodent though it raised its head more than forty times. So he became a scavenger.

As he crawled southwest, through the forest, he competed with coyotes for fresh deer and elk carcasses. Plunging his head into fresh mountain springs, he had crunched peppery wild watercress. He had stripped the hard shells from puffballs and had gorged on mountain mushrooms, grazing in the wet grass like a cow. A thick stand of rose hips near a stream had provided vitamin C. He had even, he was ashamed to say, raided a campsite near Crazy Woman Creek and had gorged on a two-pound bag of Doritos and six BallPark franks while the campers snored in their dome tent. He had seen the earth from inches away for weeks on end. It was a very humbling experience. His clothing was rags. He slept in the shelter of downed trees. He wept often.

He had purposely not crawled to a road or campsite where he could be found, because he thought to do so would be to invite his death—when the men who had already tried to kill him once found out about it.

At a ranch house near Story, Wyoming, a lovely woman, a widow, found him and took him in and agreed to keep it quiet. She fed him, let him use a guest room in the bunkhouse, and gave him her dead husband's clothes to wear. He gained enough strength to walk again. She had been a tough, independent rancher and a woman of strength. She was exactly the type of rancher he had convinced himself in previous years to despise.

Eventually, he was well enough to get a ride from her to the cabin. He had known about it from his youth and it belonged to a family friend who never used it. Slowly, he had initiated contact with colleagues. Britney had been the first to respond, and had come bearing groceries and communications gear. Hayden Powell said he was coming but he died mysteriously. Attorney Tod Marchand didn't make it, either. Both, he now knew, had been murdered by Coble and Tibbs.

"That's a hell of a story."

Stewie shrugged and looked away. His good eye was

moist. Joe couldn't tell whether the retelling of his story made Stewie cry or if it was something else.

"What's that glow over there?" Britney Earthshare suddenly asked from behind them. Joe had not heard her approach.

To the west, the peak of the first mountain was illuminated by a faint band of orange.

"That's your cabin burning down," Joe said, feeling the words catch in his throat. "That means Charlie Tibbs is still with us."

JOE'S EYES SHOT OPEN TO UTTER DARKNESS, his heart racing. Something had set off an alarm in his subconscious that had jolted him completely awake.

It took a moment to assess exactly where he was. He had fallen asleep in the camp beneath the ridge. The sky was brilliant with stars. There were so many of them their effect was gauzy. There was a blue sliver of moon like a horse's hoof print.

Stewie and Britney were huddled together near Joe's boots, their arms and legs entwined. They were both sleeping from sheer physical and mental exhaustion, like he had been.

Above him, somewhere near the tree line, Joe heard a muffled snap and the rustle of something heavy-bodied in the trees.

As quietly and deliberately as he could, Joe shifted his weight so he could unsnap his holster and slip out his .357 Magnum. His mouth was dry as cotton. With his eyes wide open, he tried to will himself to see better in the dark.

There was a footfall. Was it the step of a horse? Was

Charlie Tibbs on top of them already? Would Tibbs, on horseback in the shadows, suddenly appear before him?

He pulled the hammer back on the revolver, felt the cylinder turn, and heard it ratchet and lock. He raised it in front of him with two hands. Using the muzzle as a third eye, he moved the pistol as he swept his gaze through the darkness.

A large black form disengaged itself from the gloom and passed in front of the gray trunks of the trees. There was a snort and a cough, and Joe felt his face twitch involuntarily.

It was an *elk*. The form had a light brown rump that absorbed the starlight. Joe eased his finger off of the trigger. The elk continued to move through the trees until it was out of view. Joe noticed the familiar musky elk odor in the air.

Then something in the night seemed to snap, and it looked like the trees themselves were moving, the pale color of their trunks strobing light and dark, light and dark. Joe suddenly realized that it wasn't the trees that were moving but the elk—dozens of them—streaming across the mountain. They moved in a steady run, their ungulate hooves pounding a drumbeat. They were now all around him, passing through the camp like a ghost army. Four feet high at the shoulder, several huge bulls trailed the herd. Glints of their eyes were reflected in the moonlight and he heard the wooden click of massive antlers catching low branches.

Then they were gone. It wasn't as if he could see that last cow, calf, or bull elk pass as much as he could feel a kind of vacuum, an emptiness in the stand of trees that just a moment before was full.

He stood and let the gun drop to his side. Carefully, he

lowered the hammer back down. Stewie was now awake and sitting up. Britney rubbed her eyes.

But it wasn't over, as he again felt the presence of animals, this time swift and low to the ground. Shadows were moving through the grove in the same direction as the elk had, as quickly but with more stealth. Their movements had a liquid flow. He squinted and listened, his senses almost aching from the force of his effort. He saw a glimpse of long silver-black fur and a flash—no more than a half-second—of a pair of large canine eyes reflecting the slice of moon.

Wolves! It was a small pack of wolves, no more than five. They were following the elk, hunting for a calf or straggler to drop off from the herd.

Then as quickly as they had come, the wolves were no longer there.

Joe stood and waited, wondering almost absurdly what would happen next. Nothing did. He looked at his wristwatch. It was only ten-fifteen.

"There are not supposed to be wolves in the Bighorn Mountains," Joe said.

"Maybe they're Emily's wolves," Stewie answered, smiling so widely that Joe could see his teeth in the starlight.

Joe holstered his revolver and walked to the top of the ridge. In the darkness there was no definition to the land, no difference in degrees of blackness between one mountain and the other. There was only the horizon and the first splash of stars.

Charlie Tibbs, he knew, was out there and closing in on them.

Joe pictured his children as he last saw them that morning. April and Lucy had been silly, giddy, chattering as they waited to go to overnight church camp. Lucy was wearing a pink sweatshirt, denim shorts, pink socks to match her sweatshirt, and blue snub-nosed tennis shoes. April was wearing a turquoise sweatshirt and jeans. Their faces had been wide and fresh, their eyes sparkling, their hair summer blonde.

Sheridan stayed away from the fray, waiting until the littler girls left so she could take over the television and the house. Sheridan in her sleeveless shirt and Wranglers, starting to look like her mother, starting to molt from childhood. Sheridan, who had been through so much but had come through it so well.

And then there was Marybeth.

"Help me, Marybeth," he whispered.

30

THE STOCKMAN'S BAR IN SADDLESTRING was dim and smoky, and Marybeth wore her determination like an invisible suit of armor. As she closed the door behind her and absorbed the scene on this Saturday night, she confirmed to herself that the armor was necessary.

Ranch hands, mechanics, fishing guides, and flinty divorcées peopled the bar. Dark booths were behind them. The walls were covered with faded black-and-white rodeo photos and local cattle brands, and the support and ceiling beams were made of twisted and varnished knotty pine. In the back of the long and narrow building, low hanging lamps made fields of light green on three pool tables. Loose billiard balls in abstract geometrical configurations glowed beneath the lights. Eight-ball specialists in cowboy hats or backward caps either sipped from beer mugs or leaned across the pools of light to sight in on cue balls, like elk hunters aiming at a bull.

Marybeth sat on the first empty stool at the bar and waited for the bartender to work his way down to her. She ordered a glass of beer. Throughout the Stockman at least a half dozen sets of eyes were working her over. She felt the eyes on her in a way that made her think of her law career, the bar's patrons like judges waiting for her answer to a question.

She had been to the Stockman only once before, four years earlier, when Joe had brought her to meet with his supervisor, Vern Dunnegan, and Vern's then-wife, Georgia. Vern had a booth near the pool tables that he had claimed as his and where people met with him. Marybeth had smiled politely with Georgia as Vern and Joe discussed department policy and disputed directives, and she had nudged Joe with her foot to get his attention so they could leave. The Stockman was historic, dark, local, and corrupt, and she had seen enough at the time. Both Vern and Georgia made her uncomfortable, and the mounted elk, deer, sheep, and moose heads on the walls seemed to want to draw her back to an earlier, rougher era. She had not planned on ever coming back. When Sheridan, still outside in the car, had realized that her mom was leaving her to go inside the Stockman Bar, she had erupted.

"What if the sheriff comes by and sees me here?"

Marybeth had stopped with the door half open and the dome light on.

"Tell him I'll be back in a minute."

"What if he says it's child abuse? I mean, you *are* leaving your loving daughter outside in your car while you go into a saloon!"

"I'm investigating something, and I think there may be a man inside who can help us," Marybeth said patiently, but her eyes flashed. "Don't forget that your dad is missing."

Sheridan started to speak, but caught herself.

"There's somebody in there who might know where Dad is?"

Marybeth took a deep breath. There was a lot to explain.

"That's what I'm hoping," she said, almost pleading. "Please don't do your thing on me now."

Sheridan thought about it, nodded, then leaned forward in her seat to hug her mother's neck.

"You look like a fox," Sheridan said, leaning back and looking at her mother as a peer. "You're a hottie."

MARYBETH HAD DRESSED in new jeans, a dark French-cut T-shirt, and a denim ranch jacket. Her blonde hair was lit with the glow of the neon beer signs. She was here to meet with a rancher. Or ex-rancher, to be more precise. Only he didn't know it yet.

She recognized him, as her eyes grew used to the bar gloom. He sat at the farthest end of the bar, on a stool by the wall, which he leaned against. Although he was situated in the shadows and the only illumination of his features was from a small-watt neon tube in an aquarium on a shelf of stuffed prairie dogs playing pool, there was something foreboding about him. She felt it right away. He was avuncular, short, and solid. He had a large head with a bulbous, alcohol-veined nose. His head was mounted on a wide body, and he wore a silver-gray 24X short-brim Stetson Rancher that was sweat stained and battered, but had cost $400 new. He was in his sixties. When he ordered another bourbon he cocked his finger and raised an eyebrow almost imperceptibly and the bartender knew what it meant—and scrambled.

There was an empty barstool next to him, and Marybeth picked up her glass of beer and carried it there. She sat the glass on the bar, settled into the stool, and looked at herself and the ex-rancher in the mirror. He looked back, narrowed his eyes, and smiled with puzzled amusement.

"I'm Marybeth Pickett, Mr. McBride. Can I have a few minutes of your time for an important matter?"

"I know who you are." His grin grew, and he looked her over. "Babe, you can have as much of my time as you want. Call me Rowdy."

"Okay, Rowdy," she said. "Tell me about the Stockman's Trust."

Something passed over his face and his eyes inadvertently widened. He took a sip. "It seems kind of ironic that you're asking a man drinking in the Stockman's Bar about something called the Stockman's Trust, don't it?"

"I hadn't thought about that."

"What about it?" His voice was gruff.

"I received some information today that there are two killers who have been hired by the Stockman's Trust. My husband may be in danger."

"Killers?"

She withdrew the note written by John Coble from her jacket pocket and slid it over to him. He read it, then folded it and handed it back.

Dear Game Warden:

It is my understanding that you have been investigating the murder of Stewie Woods and that there is a possibility that someone is impersonating Woods and causing trouble. A man named Charlie Tibbs (stock detective) has been hired to rub out environmentalists and has done a good job of it. Stewie Woods was the first target on our list. I assisted him in this task, but I have quit.

Charlie Tibbs was last in the vicinity of Yellowstone Park, but I think he's coming here.

The men that hired us is the Stockman's Trust. I don't know the names of the men, but you should investigate.

I'm writing you this to help relieve my conscience.

Signed, John Coble

P.S. Don't try and look for me. I have left the country and changed my name and I done you a kindness here.

McBride seemed to be contemplating what he would say next.

"Before you sold your ranch to Jim Finotta, you were a member of the Stockman's Trust, right?"

"Before Finotta stole my ranch out from under me, you mean." His eyes flared.

"Whatever."

"Before I turned into a goddamned drunk at the end of the bar instead of a fourth-generation rancher?" he said bitterly. "If you'll excuse my French."

225

"That's not what I mean," she said softly.

He shook his head. "I know it isn't."

She drank from her glass of beer, giving him a moment to collect himself.

"Yup, I was a member. I was never on the board, but I was a member."

"Who else is a member?"

"What you need to understand is that there's an oath. I took that oath. Don't expect me to spill my guts out to you now, just because you look so fine, Marybeth Pickett."

She turned her head so he wouldn't see the look of distress on her face.

"Members of the Stockman's Trust are everywhere," McBride said after a beat. "Our bartender Jim might be a member. Your state legislator might be a member. Sheriff Barnum may be a member. In fact . . . never mind."

"But Sheriff Barnum wasn't ever a rancher."

"It's not just ranchers anymore. You just never know." He looked around them to see if anyone was paying undue attention to the conversation.

"Were you just kidding me about Sheriff Barnum?" Marybeth asked.

One of the ranch hands splayed in a nearby booth was ogling Marybeth, and McBride stared him down as he might a curious dog. "There's a lot of bitter men out here," he whispered. "Under the surface, there is real anger. They see their whole way of life getting undermined and laughed at. It's a real culture war."

Marybeth nodded.

"The Trust got started back in the Tom Horn days," he said. "That was the name of the group that hired Horn.

They were all members of the Cattleman's Association, but kind of a splinter group. They all chipped in, hired Horn, and then let the man work his magic on the rustlers down around Cheyenne."

Marybeth nodded, listening intently. He liked that.

"After Tom Horn got hanged, the Stockman's Trust kept on as a group. But instead of a bunch of guys who had come together for one particular thing, the Trust became sort of a secret men's club. They elected officers and met semiregularly to discuss the matters of the day." Rowdy paused and gestured at Marybeth's glass. "D'you want another beer?"

Marybeth agreed. Anything to keep him talking.

Up until the 1940s, McBride said, the Stockman's Trust membership was exclusively ranchers. It was a secret society, and new members swore an oath to keep it that way. Although all of the members knew why the organization had been formed in the first place, the Trust became a kind of salon. Because so many legislators, judges, oilmen, lawyers, and doctors were also ranchers, the organization prided itself in its old-fashioned exclusivity. It was an honor to be asked to become a member.

McBride's father had been a member, as had his grandfather. At one time his father had been vice-president.

The Stockman's Trust was financed by a voluntary levy by ranchers of a few pennies on every cow and by oilmen on barrels of oil they produced. Over time, quite a treasury was amassed. They used it to buy a discreet building in Cheyenne for a headquarters and to pay lobbyists to advance their agenda and protect their interests. The Stockman's Trust was as effective in its quiet way as Tom

Horn had been with his Winchester.

"Is it possible that the Stockman's Trust has turned a culture war into a real one? That they've gone back to their roots?" Marybeth asked.

McBride pushed the fresh beer the bartender delivered toward Marybeth and drank a long pull from his bourbon.

"I wouldn't put it past them," he declared. "You've got to understand that the Stockman's Trust had completely changed even before I got out of it. It wasn't that old gentleman rancher's club anymore. Most of the new board members were out-of-state absentee ranch owners. You know, the kind who likes to come out, put on his hat and boots, and play rancher a couple of times a year, so he can let it drop at cocktail parties in New York or L.A. that he owns a ranch in Wyoming. The old guys, like me, got pushed out. By the time I got out, I hardly knew any of them personally. They did all of their meetings by conference call instead of at the headquarters in Cheyenne. These jokers called in from their private planes or from cell phones in limos. They bitched about the bad PR ranchers were getting because of loudmouth environmentalists. It was getting to be a joke. These guys weren't *ranchers*. They just *owned* ranches."

"Did you quit?" she asked.

He stared into his drink. "I said some things I shouldn't have said when I was drinking. Called a couple of 'em out-of-state cocksuckers, pardon my French. They rescinded my membership after I lost the ranch."

"Why did those guys even want to be members?"

McBride was ready for that. "I kind of wondered that myself at first. Then I realized they liked the idea of the exclusive club just like they liked the idea of owning a third-generation Wyoming or Montana ranch. It's the same impulse to be a local big dick and to call the shots. You know, like Jim Finotta."

She nodded. She thought of what Ginger Finotta had been trying to tell her.

"He's a member, isn't he?" Marybeth asked.

"Shit," McBride snorted. "I wouldn't be surprised."

AT HOME, THERE WERE no messages from Joe. It was ten-thirty. Trey Crump had called and said he would be leaving in the morning for the cabin, and he had asked Marybeth to fax him a copy of the map. If Joe was still missing in the morning, he would notify the County Sheriff to organize a search and rescue team.

Marybeth sat alone at the kitchen table. Her palms left a moist smear on the surface. She stared straight ahead and fought an urge to cry out of sheer frustration.

Suddenly, she pushed away from the table and dug the slim Twelve Sleep County telephone book from a drawer. She looked up and dialed the number for the Finotta Ranch.

The phone rang eight times before it was picked up. The voice was cold and distant.

"Is this Jim Finotta?" She asked.

"Yes."

"May I please speak to your wife, Ginger?"

"Who is this?"

She told him. There was a long pause.

"Ginger is in bed."

"It's important."

He hung up on her.

31

ON SUNDAY MORNING BEFORE the sun rose, and cool air was flexing through the trees and over the mountainside, about the time Joe should have been home mixing pancake batter and frying bacon for his girls, Britney Earthshare came scrambling down from the ridge through the shale saying she had just seen Charlie Tibbs.

Stewie had been stretching and commenting how good bacon and eggs would be for breakfast.

"Show me where," Joe said, and followed her back to the ridge.

She pointed to a series of openings on the mountainside on the other side of the valley. Joe looked with his binoculars but could see nothing.

"He came out of the trees into the clearing and then he went back into the trees," she said , her teeth chattering from fright and the early morning cold.

"Where was it again?"

She pointed generally.

"Can you be more specific?"

She hissed angrily. "Damn you, I saw what I saw!"

"Was he on horseback or on foot?"

She glared at him. "Horseback, I think."

"You think," he repeated, still glassing the mountain. The binoculars gathered more light than his naked eye, but it was still too shadowy even in the meadows to see Charlie Tibbs. "Was he coming our way?"

"Straight at us," she declared.

Joe lowered the binoculars and looked at her, trying to decide if she had actually seen Tibbs or had only *thought* she had seen him. He had already been making plans about returning to the cabin and his pickup, plotting how they could travel up the ridge and work their way back through the heavy timber covering a massive saddle slope to the south. If the terrain was agreeable, they could be back by noon.

But if Tibbs was coming straight at them, had found their track, they would have to either make a stand or run.

"*There he is!*" Britney screamed, gesturing frantically across the valley. "Oh, my *God!*"

Joe wheeled and jerked his binoculars to his eyes. He saw a tiny movement on the edge of a far-off meadow. It was dark and passed into the trees before he could see it clearly. But it could have been the shoulders and head of a man on horseback.

STAY IN THE ELK TRAIL," Joe cautioned as they scrambled down the mountain, away from the camp and the ridge. "If nothing else, the trail may foul him up a little."

The path of the elk herd from the night before wasn't hard to follow. They had churned up a two- to three-foot swath of earth, mashing pine needles into the dark loam and littering the trail with upturned black divots. Joe was pleased by the way their own tracks blended into the elk tracks.

"I'm sure getting hungry," Stewie sang out. "If we catch those elk I might need to take a bite out of one of 'em."

"Yuck," Britney said. She had already mentioned that she didn't eat meat. She made a point about how the elk had become their metaphysical guides through the wilderness and how Emily's wolves played a part in providing the trail.

"Seeing those wolves running wild and free last night was, like, *awesome,*" Britney rhapsodized. "It was, like, *orgasmic.* These beautiful creatures were all around us and for a minute there, I felt like I was one of them. Once you've seen those magical creatures with your own eyes, it makes it really hard to understand why they were trapped and killed almost to extinction. It really makes you hate the people who did that. What were they possibly thinking, to want to kill a magnificent animal like a wolf?"

They walked.

"There's an irony to all of this whole situation that I bet neither one of you know about," Stewie said.

"What's that?" Britney asked.

"Whatever it is, I hope it's short," Joe grumbled.

Stewie giggled at that. "The irony is that just before I headed out here and got married to Annabel and got blown up by a cow, the executive board of One Globe had a meeting and *kicked me out!*"

"You're kidding!" Britney was outraged.

"It's true." He was starting to breathe hard with the exertion of the fast trek. "They met at the new headquarters on K Street in Washington, D.C., and voted me off of the board, eight to one. My old buddy Rupert was the only one who stuck with me. They said they didn't like my methods anymore, that I was an embarrassment to the organization. They said that direct action wasn't as effective as lawsuits and that my egomania was holding back membership funds."

"But you started One Globe!" Britney argued. "They can't kick you out of your own organization."

"Yes, they can," Stewie said. "And they did. The suits

took over. The fund-raisers beat the hellraisers."

"Shameful!"

"So," Stewie said, directing it at Joe, "the irony is that Charlie Tibbs is coming after a big, fat has-been."

"You're not a has-been," Britney cooed.

Joe, however, was too preoccupied with the scene in front of him to answer Stewie.

A COW ELK STOOD off of the trail, in a small clearing, in a yellow shaft of early morning sunlight. She was straddling what looked like a wet bundle of fur. She watched them approach with her large black eyes. As they neared, her big cupped ears rotated toward them. Her legs trembled, as did her moist black nose.

Joe stopped. Stewie and Britney froze behind him.

"Jesus," Stewie whispered.

The bundle of wet fur was the cow's dead calf. Joe could see now that the calf's throat had been ripped open and its lower jaw was gone. It lay dead in a slick pool of dark blood. Near the calf, tufts of long canine fur clung to shafts of the long grass.

The cow elk would soon die as well. She had been disemboweled as she fought off the wolves that killed her calf. Loops of intestine, like long blue ropes, hung from her abdomen. One of her front forelegs had been skinned to the bone. Dark blood clotted in the thick fur of her upper shoulder.

Joe had seen female elk fight; they sat back on their haunches and lurched forward, striking with their hooves. The power of their strikes could crush the skull of a badger or break the back of a coyote. The mother elk had connected with at least one wolf from the pack, hence the fur in the grass.

Britney broke down. She covered her face with her hands.

"You've got to *do* something," Britney sobbed. "It's horrible."

Joe scanned the trees that surrounded the clearing. The wolves were there, he was sure, but he couldn't see them. They were in the shadows, or hunkered down and still in the brush. He could feel their eyes on him.

"Do something," she begged, her voice wracked.

"Shoot that poor elk so she won't have to suffer," Stewie murmured.

"No," Joe sighed. "A gunshot will give our position away."

"Who cares about that?" Britney cried, her voice raising to an emotional pitch. "Who cares about that? *Do something!*"

Joe turned toward her, his face a tight mask. His glare was so intense that she involuntarily stepped behind Stewie for protection.

"Look away," he hissed, his voice coldly furious. He strode toward the cow elk and unsheathed his Leatherman tool, pulling out the blade. The mother elk turned her head away, but did not have the strength to run or strike out, and he reached out and grabbed her ear to steady her while he cut her throat.

Stewie stood with an ashen face, watching, while Britney buried her head in his back. As Joe walked back to them, he heard the cow elk gurgle and settle into the grass on top of her calf.

"This is what wolves do," Joe said, his voice calm, a betrayal of what he felt. "I'm not saying they shouldn't be here, but this is what they do. *They're wolves.* I know it sounds real nice to say they're magical and beautiful and they balance nature and restore an ecosystem—and it's true, they do that. But this is how they do it. They go after the weakest first. When the mother stays back, the wolves open a hole in her belly and pull out her entrails. Then they wait until she doesn't have the strength to protect herself, then they'll move in and tear her throat out."

Joe slid the sticky Leatherman back into its case and wiped hot blood on his pants from his hand and sleeve.

"You people just like the idea of things, like bringing the wolves back. It makes you feel better." He looked from Britney to Stewie, both of whom averted their eyes. "I agree that it is a beneficial thing overall. But you don't like to see what really happens out here when those grand ideas become real, do you?"

THEY FOLLOWED THE ELK TRAIL to the bottom of the mountain, through another small stream swelling with icy runoff. They drank, and continued up the next mountain through twisted black timber, crawling in and out of scalpel-cut ravines.

The terrain finally flattened as they rose, and the walking became easier. Joe was drenched in sweat, and light-headed from lack of food. The water sloshed in his empty stomach as he hiked. The incident with the elk had dampened the enthusiasm and frequency of Stewie's monologues, and Britney was still so angry with him that she didn't talk—which was fine with Joe.

Trees thinned in number but the ones they hiked through became thicker and taller. Joe felt as if they had entered a land of giants, their bodies becoming specks on the forest floor as they trudged on. He thought about Marybeth, and Sheridan, Lucy, and April. At times, the thought of them almost overwhelmed him.

The trees cleared enough that he could now see the mountain behind them. As Britney and Stewie rested, he glassed the forest with his binoculars, guessing where the elk trail switchbacked down the mountain, and followed it all the way to the top with his binoculars. He saw no movement.

Then, far to the right on the shoulder of the mountain, a flock of spruce grouse rose out of the trees. They glided over the treetops, veered, and settled back into the timber out of view. Something, or someone, had spooked them.

"The elk trail threw him off," Joe said, keeping his voice low. "He's way over there to the right coming down through the trees. Probably trying to pick up our track."

"Shit," Stewie hissed, angrily throwing a pinecone away from him. "How far?"

Joe tried to estimate the distance between the flock of pine grouse and where they now stood. Charlie Tibbs was closing in on them.

"An hour. Maybe an hour and a half."

"We can't keep running," Britney said, more to Stewie than Joe. "We're exhausted, and we keep getting deeper into the wilderness. Maybe we can just *talk* to him. That's something we haven't tried."

"You can stay and talk with him if you want," Stewie grunted, as he pulled himself back to his feet. "This is the same guy that blew up my bride and shot his friend's face off a foot away from me."

LIKE TRIBUTARIES FEEDING A GREAT RIVER, small individual tracks started to peel away from the elk trail. Joe noticed it first, how the once-prominent trail was diminishing as they walked.

He felt a sensation ahead of him that at first he couldn't comprehend. It was a sense of vastness, of openness, that belied the dark woods.

He pushed through a thick wall of Rocky Mountain juniper. The branches were so full and tough that it seemed they were trying to throw him back. Stewie and Britney complained behind him that they were having trouble figuring out which way he went. Britney cried out as a branch whipped back from Stewie and hit her flush in the face.

The juniper was sharp smelling and acrid, and the dusty clustered berries that fell to the ground looked like rabbit pellets. Joe ducked his head forward so the brush wouldn't knock his hat off.

With a hard push he cleared the brush wall and stumbled into the open and gasped.

One more clumsy step and he would have plunged seven hundred feet to the floor of the canyon known as Savage Run.

32

SAVAGE RUN WAS SHEER, sharp, beautiful, and, to Joe, virtually uncrossable, so they followed a game path that skirted the rim. Periodically, Joe would near the edge and look down. The Middle Fork of the Twelve Sleep River was a thin gray ribbon of water on the shadowed canyon bottom. Occasionally, he could see a twiggy falcon nest blooming out from the rock face below them.

The canyon was as unique a geographic phenomenon as Joe had heard it was. Instead of tapering down from an elevation, it was a sharp slice that cleanly halved the mountain range. The other rim was no more than two hundred yards away and it, like the side they were on, was brushy with juniper and old-growth spruce. Joe could clearly see the layers of geological strata that made up the mountain on the face of the opposite canyon wall. It looked as if the mountain had been pulled apart recently, instead of millions of years before. The undergrowth and exposed roots that snaked out from below the two canyon rims seemed to be reaching for their counterparts on the other side.

Beyond the other rim and two slump-shouldered mountains, the range descended into the Twelve Sleep Valley ranch land and, eventually, to the highway and on to the town of Saddlestring.

Joe knew what kind of trouble they were in. Now that they had found the canyon, they could only go either east or west, and it wouldn't be difficult for Charlie Tibbs to figure out which way they'd gone. Joe knew that an offshoot canyon intersected Savage Run a mile to the east and would have cut off progress in that direction. If they went that way, they would have, in effect, trapped themselves. So their only choice was a westerly route.

From where he had seen the birds rise from the forest and signal what he thought was Charlie Tibbs's location, Joe tried to determine where Tibbs was headed. Tibbs would either follow their track to the rim and ride up on the trail behind them or ride ahead and try to intercept them. Joe wished he knew more about Tibbs—how Tibbs acted and thought, his past tendencies—so he might have a better inclination of what Tibbs would do next. Professionals like Charlie Tibbs didn't just make things up as they went along. They stuck to procedures and maneuvers that had worked for them in the past. And whatever happened next, it seemed to Joe, a confrontation was inevitable. He wished he could be more prepared for it when it came.

It was essential to stay focused. He tried to trim all of his musings, memories, and daydreams into one central purpose: that of being ready to react. Joe tried to force his eyes to see better and his ears to hear more. He hoped that if Tibbs were near, he would be able to feel his presence and prepare. Staying in the heavy timber was no longer an option for them, Joe thought, which meant that Tibbs, with his deadly long-range rifle, could take out all three of them from a position with good sight lines.

Tibbs had the edge of being better prepared and equipped, and of being on horseback, so he was likely well rested, well fed, and well armed. Hunting down human beings was something Tibbs clearly had experience with. In any kind of encounter, Tibbs had the overwhelming advantage. Joe, with his .357 Magnum revolver and his history of missing whatever he aimed at, felt practically impotent.

If Charlie Tibbs suddenly bulled his way through the brush and cut them off on their trail, what would Joe do? He tried to think, tried to visualize his reaction so that it would be instinctual. He tried to envision himself drawing his pistol cleanly, raising it with both hands in a shooter's stance, and squeezing the trigger of the double-action until every bullet was fired. He would aim at the widest point of his target. The commotion, if nothing else, would divert Tibbs from aiming and give Stewie and Britney a fighting chance to bolt into the brush and back into the trees. Even if he were unable to hit Tibbs or his horse, there was the possibility that his booming shots might spook the animal, causing it to rear and tumble into the canyon with its rider. Targeting Tibbs's horse felt wrong to Joe, but in this situation soft sensibilities were not an option. Besides, Joe thought bitterly, that son of a bitch shot *Lizzie.*

"There is no way in hell that those Indians crossed this canyon," Britney declared. Joe had to agree, because he could see no possible way to the bottom of the canyon and up the other side. Even the falcon's nests in the rock walls seemed precarious.

"Don't give up, Miss Steinburton," Stewie cajoled.

"Is that your real name?" Joe asked. "Steinburton?"

"Margaret Steinburton," Stewie offered. "Heir to the Steinburton Chemical Company of Palo Alto, California."

"Shut up, Stewie," she said. "He asked me, not you."

Stewie giggled, and Joe continued on in silence.

Despite his almost constant monologues, his occasional whining, and his cocky attitude, Joe found himself warming to Stewie. He had gotten used to his freakish appearance and his face-splitting grimaces, and wasn't as alarmed at them as he had been at first. Stewie had a cheerful optimism about him that was reassuring, and helpful. Stewie seemed to be gaining in strength the more they traveled. While Britney (or Margaret, or whoever the hell she was) descended into a prickly dark funk, Stewie kept pointing out wildlife and points of interest (to him) as if he were on a nature walk and Joe was the stoic guide.

"If you had to run for your life," Stewie had declared happily that morning, "you just couldn't have picked a nicer day!"

No wonder Marybeth liked him, Joe thought.

Joe realized he had once again put too much distance between Stewie and Britney so he stopped, turned, and waited for them to catch up.

Stewie was marveling at the canyon as he walked. He was not watching in front of him, and didn't see the snout of a large rock that had pushed up through the trail. The toe of his boot thumped into the rock and tripped him, and he lost his balance.

Joe turned and lunged for Stewie but there was too much distance between them. Stewie's arms windmilled and one of his legs crashed into the other. Stewie tried to regain his balance by stepping into a thick tangle of juniper perilously close to the edge of the canyon only to have the branches give way under his weight.

Stewie dropped so quickly that the only thing Joe could reach for was the fleeting afterimage of Stewie's out-stretched hands.

Joe approached the juniper as Britney wailed, holding her face in her hands and retreating from the place where Stewie had fallen.

"Britney!" It was Stewie. "Stop screaming! I'm all right."

Joe kneeled and cautiously parted the stout, sticky branches. Stewie's large hand, like an inert pink crab, was in the bush, gripping onto its base so hard that his knuckles were blueish white. Joe braced himself, grabbed Stewie's wrist with both hands, and began pulling.

"Whoa, Joe!" Stewie said from over the rim. "Whoa, buddy! I'm okay. I'm standing on a ledge."

Joe sighed and sat back, and watched Stewie's hand unclench in the brush and slide down out of it.

"*Stewie!*" Britney cried in relief, leaning back against a tree trunk. "Don't ever do that to me again."

"Don't you want me to help you up?" Joe asked.

There was a beat of silence, and something small and brown was tossed up from below the juniper. Joe caught it, releasing a puff of dust.

It was an ancient child's doll. The head was a dried ball of rocklike leather and the arms and legs were stuffed with feathers and sewn from rough, aged fabric. The face, if there had ever been one, had washed clean over the years. The doll's matted black hair, sewn on the leather head, looked human. The doll, no doubt, had belonged to an Indian child.

Joe scrambled forward on his belly and pushed the juniper branches aside. Stewie looked up at him with a massive, radiator-grille grin.

Stewie stood on a narrow shelf of rock no wider than a stair step. The shelf ran parallel to the ledge, then switched back, still descending. Far below Stewie, trapped against the rock ledge by an outgrowth, were gray tipi poles that had come unbundled and fallen over the edge a hundred and fifty years before.

Joe studied the opposite rock wall as he hadn't before and now he saw it. A narrow shelf, a natural geological anomaly, barely discernible against the same yellow and gray color of the canyon wall and hidden in places by overgrowth, switchbacked up the other wall as well.

"This is the crossing," Joe whispered. "This is where the Cheyenne crossed the canyon."

33

DID I WAKE YOU UP?"

"Are you kidding? I haven't slept," Marybeth said, as she swung out of bed, the phone tight against her ear. The floor was cold beneath her bare feet. "Did you find Joe?"

Trey Crump hesitated.

"I located his pickup in the valley. It was parked just off the road."

The phone reception was crackling and waves of static roared through the receiver. Marybeth looked at the clock on her bed stand—it was five forty-five A.M.

"You haven't seen Joe?"

"Negative," Crump yelled over the static. "I had to drive back up to the top of the mountain to get any radio or telephone signal, Marybeth. I might cut out at any minute."

"I understand," she shouted, surprised at the loudness of her voice in the empty room. "Tell me what you found. "

"The pickup and the horse trailer are empty. The pickup's been shot up . . ." Marybeth gasped and covered her mouth with her other hand, "and somebody disabled the engine and deflated the tires. I found two other vehicles as well; one is a Mercedes SUV with Colorado plates and the other one I just located about a half-hour ago up on the other mountain. It appears to be a black pickup with a horse trailer. There's no one at the scene of . . ."

A whoosh of static drowned out the end of his sentence. Marybeth closed her eyes tightly, trying to hear through the roar and willing it to subside.

". . . The cabin was burned to the ground just last night. It's still smoking. There was a body inside that was not Joe. I repeat, it was *not* Joe!"

Marybeth realized that she was gripping the telephone receiver so tightly that she had lost feeling in her hand.

"Marybeth, can you hear me?"

"Yes, Trey!"

"I found your buckskin horse, and I'm sorry to say the horse has been killed. I searched the vicinity around the horse but couldn't find any sign of Joe."

She let out the breath she had been holding. It racketed out unevenly.

"Marybeth, I've contacted the sheriff and he is on his way now. He told me he will call for a helicopter out of Cody. It should be in the air above us by mid-morning."

"The sheriff?" Marybeth recalled her conversation with Rowdy McBride from the night before. She recalled that McBride never actually *confirmed* . . . "When will the helicopter get there?"

"A couple of hours. But the sheriff should be here any minute. I just talked to him."

"My God, Trey, what do you think happened?"

She missed the first part of his sentence. ". . . happened. I can't tell who is who with these vehicles up here or if they're even connected with Joe's disappearance. I ran the plates with dispatch and the SUV belongs to a Denver lawyer but they can't find anything on the plate on the black pickup."

"You mean it can't be traced to *anyone?*"

"That's what they tell me. But they're checking again."

"Trey," Marybeth said, increasing her volume again as a wall of static began to build, "It's the Stockman's Trust. That's who is behind all of this. The pickup belongs, I think, to the Stockman's Trust!"

". . . Say again?"

She cursed. Someone was knocking on her bedroom door. Sheridan.

"The *Stockman's Trust!*"

"I see Barnum's vehicle now, Marybeth," Trey Crump said, distracted. "I'll call you back when I know more."

"Trey!"

"Got to go now, Marybeth. Stay calm and don't panic. It's a good sign that I didn't find Joe here because it probably means he's in the area. Joe's a smart one. He knows what to do. This is big country, but we'll find him and I'll advise you of our progress."

The connection terminated and Marybeth couldn't tell if it was because the signal was lost or Trey Crump had hung up.

She lowered the receiver to her lap. Sheridan entered, and sat down beside her on the bed.

"No, they haven't found him yet," Marybeth said, finding the strength to smile with reassurance. "But they've located his pickup."

"Why were you yelling?" Sheridan asked.

"It was a bad connection."

34

ONCE THEY HAD CRAWLED down through the steep, narrow, and brushy chute to the trail, their commitment was made. The ledge Stewie had found was a seven-foot drop down a tongue of slick rock. It was clear to Joe that if the switchback ledge became impassable on the canyon wall, or had broken away somewhere below, it would be hard for them to turn back.

Because the ledge was so narrow, Joe did not try to shoulder around Stewie into the lead. Hugging the wall, Stewie sidestepped along the jutting fissure, calling out hazards such as a break in the trail or loose rocks. Joe followed, and Britney, with tears of fear streaming down her dirty cheeks, stayed close. They had tied the rope around their waists to each other.

"There's something, like, *cinematic* about this," Stewie called over his shoulder.

"Watch where the *fuck* you're going!" Britney hissed.

"Stay calm," Joe sighed. "We've got a long way to go."

Joe buttoned the doll into his shirt. If there was any luck or mystical charge emanating from the doll, Joe wanted as much of it as he could get. The doll rested against his sweating skin as a lucky talisman. He vowed that if he somehow made the descent and got back to his family, he would clean up the doll and give it to his girls.

After the first switchback, the trail widened and they were able to square their shoulders and hike down it slowly. Like Stewie, Joe kept one hand on the canyon wall at all times. If he slipped on loose earth, he wanted to fall into the wall and not plunge into the canyon.

"I swear if I get home I'll go to church," Britney promised. "I don't know which church yet. It needs to be spiritual, and healing, and forgiving. And without a lot of that religious baggage so many churches seem to have nowadays."

246

Joe's thighs began to burn as he descended. He perversely welcomed the sensation, because it took his mind off of other concerns. He was hungry, and his mouth was cottony with thirst. His clothing had been ripped by branches. His eyes burned due to lack of sleep, and despite his efforts to concentrate, there was a thick fog born of exertion, fear, and unusual self-doubt that was clouding his thinking.

They were far down the trail, which Stewie had taken to calling the Cheyenne Crossing, when Joe started to question if they had done the right thing. It would be amazingly easy to become rimrocked, that is, to get to a point where they realized they could not get back. Joe had been involved on a search-and-rescue effort of a bighorn sheep hunter who had meandered up a boulder-strewn mountain and found out he couldn't figure out how to get back down. He fell, and the hunter's broken body was found wedged beneath two upthrusts of granite, where he had been for seventy-two hours. The hunter died of exposure on the way to the hospital.

If suddenly the wedge of rock that served as a path ended, they would have to backtrack up the wall. Balance and gravity had helped carry them this far down, and going back up with aching muscles and minds dizzy with hunger and exhaustion would spell trouble. It would be extremely difficult to crawl up the slick rock chute they had used to slide down to the ledge.

Only when Joe looked across the canyon at the opposite wall did he realize that they had already dropped two-thirds of the way into the canyon. He looked at his watch and confirmed that it had only taken twenty minutes.

"When we get to the bottom," Britney asked, "will we go downstream or up the other side?"

"Up the other side!" Stewie shouted triumphantly. "Then on to Saddlestring and cheeseburgers! And beer! And chicken-fried steaks swimming in country gravy!"

"A shower would be nice," Britney said lamely.

Getting rid of you two nuts would be more than nice, Joe thought with such clarity that for a moment he feared he had actually said it.

Joe smiled, his spirits recovering. The exhaustion combined with their progress seemed to supercharge his emotions. His mood swung from the utter despair he had experienced a few moments before to near euphoria as they approached the canyon floor. It was a sensation he didn't welcome, or trust.

The path narrowed, now only slightly less wide than the length of his boots. He pressed his cheek against the cool rock wall and held its unforgiving firmness with outstretched arms as he shuffled along. Soon, he could hear the tinkling of the stream below, but he dared not readjust and look down.

Then he heard a splash and a whoop as Stewie dropped from the ledge into the Middle Fork and screamed, *"Hallelujah!"*

Joe followed, landing ankle-deep in snow-cold water that was a pleasing shock to his system. After helping Britney down from the ledge, Joe dropped to his knees in the stream, fell forward, and drank from it until the icy water numbed his mouth and throat.

He sat back, water dribbling down his shirt, while Stewie and Britney did the same. He looked at them on all fours in the water, sucking and slurping from the stream, and thought, *We look and act like animals.*

THEY WERE IN COMPLETE SHADE on the canyon floor. Joe looked up at the brilliant blue slice of sky. He guessed that because of the extreme narrowness of the walls, the floor got no more than an hour of full sunshine a day as the sun passed directly over. Then he heard the deep chopping sound of a helicopter.

Stewie rose, hearing it too. The sound reached its zenith as the helicopter, looking like the silhouette of a damselfly, shot across the opening above. The chopping slowly receded until it melded with the rushing sound of the stream.

"They're looking for us!" Stewie cheered, rising to his feet. "Just our luck we're down here in this hole, but they *are* looking for us!"

DOWNSTREAM, THE WALLS constricted and forced the mild Middle Fork river to boil and become whitewater. There were no banks, and therefore no place to walk, even if they had decided to head downstream instead of up the canyon wall.

Joe led the way, stepping up on the ledge that paralleled the wall they had just come down. He paused, sighed, summoned his strength, and began climbing. It was harder going up than down, and Stewie called out for frequent breaks. Joe's shirt was again soaked. Sweat streamed from his hatband into his collar and pooled on his temples.

Eventually, Joe passed from shade into sun and he could tell from looking at the other canyon wall that they were nearly to the top. While pausing to rest, Joe tried to survey the opposite rim. He could not yet see over the top, and couldn't tell if Charlie Tibbs had made it to the trail along the rim yet. If Tibbs were to find the trail, Joe thought, the three of them would be nakedly exposed to him. There was no place to hide along the ledge, and the rock wall would serve as a backstop to the bullets Tibbs would fire.

"Listen to me," Joe said to Stewie and Britney, who were resting on a ledge below him. "I know you're tired, but we need to get to the top of this canyon. No stopping, no resting. We can rest once we get over the rim. Okay?"

Britney shot a hateful look at Joe and cursed.

"Do you think he's close?" Stewie asked, concerned.

"I don't know," Joe answered flatly. "But let's go."

IT CAME QUICKLY, a feeling like a storm rolling through the mountains—the intuitive realization that Charlie Tibbs was upon them. Joe tried to look over his shoulder at the opposite rim. He could see nothing, but he could feel an impending force as if an invisible hand was pushing him down. He implored Stewie and Britney to pick up their pace.

Joe figured he was less than twenty yards from the top, and the ledge was narrowing. Ahead, Joe could see where the ledge receded into the wall and, for all intents and purposes, vanished from view. The last ten feet from the end of the path to the top of the rim would involve climbing up the rock face. There were enough burrs and fissures on the face to make climbing possible, but there was nothing underneath to stop a fall if he, or one of the others, lost their footing.

It was silent except for the watery sound of a warm breeze high in the trees and Stewie's labored breathing. Stewie was wheezing with exertion. Mirroring the feeling of dread Joe felt, the sky had taken on a darker patina and the light was fusing into the rock. A bank of dark thunderheads, heavy with rain, was beginning to roll across the sun. The temperature had dropped and there was the feeling of static electricity in the air, which signaled that a summer rainstorm was indeed on its way.

Looping the rope over his head and shoulder to get it out of the way, Joe began to climb. Hand-over-hand, he found holds that would support his weight and he pulled himself up the wall. His biceps and shoulders were screaming with pain by the time he reached the top, but he managed to kick out and swing himself over the edge, where he lay gasping for breath. But he needed to fight through his exhaustion and hurry to bring Stewie and Britney up.

Crawling toward the trunk of a tree, Joe looped the rope around its base and tied it fast. He tested it with his full strength, then crawled back to the edge of the rim. Stewie and Britney stood still, their pale faces tilted up to him. He dropped the rope in a loose coil at their feet.

"Can you climb up the rope or do I need to try and pull you up?" Joe asked, his voice hoarse. "It's tied off on a tree up here."

"Ladies first," Stewie said, then made a mocking face as if realizing what he had said and taking it back. This guy takes nothing seriously, Joe thought.

"I don't think I can climb it," Britney said vacantly.

"Then tie it around your waist and do your best to help me when I pull you up. Use the handholds in the rock to help yourself. If the rope slips, don't panic—it'll pull tight from the tree."

Stewie helped Britney tie a harness, and when it was secure he smiled up at Joe and gave him the thumbs-up signal.

"I hate this," Britney whined.

"Joe hates it even worse," Stewie cackled.

Joe wrapped the rough rope around his forearm and backed away from the rim until the rope was taut.

"Here goes!" he called out, and eased his weight backward. She was heavy, but he was able to pull the first three feet of rope up fairly easily. But then Britney apparently lost her hold on the wall and the rope pulled back, straining against him, cutting through his shirt and skin. He grunted, and braced against the tree, raising Britney another two or three feet. He expected to see her hand reach over the rim at any time, which it did, and he watched through the pain as her hand groped around in the grass, trying to find a root or rock she could use to pull herself over the top.

Then there was a rifle shot and Britney's hand vanished. Her body instantly became dead weight against the rope and Joe was flung forward into the dirt, the rope sizzling through his hands until he was finally able to double it around his wrist. Another shot boomed across the canyon and Joe felt a tug on the rope that was not unlike that of a trout taking his fly.

Suddenly, Joe was being pulled forward, hard, toward the edge of the canyon. The rope burned through his hands, flaying his palms open, before he managed to dally it around his forearm where it held tight. It made no sense that Britney's weight could cause this. Then he realized that

Stewie was climbing the rope, scrambling to get to the top.

"Stewie, I've got to let out the slack!" Joe yelled, letting the rope hiss through his hands until it pulled tight, straining the knot he had tied on the tree.

Another shot ripped through the canyon, but the rope didn't jerk.

"Stewie, are you okay?"

Stewie's terror-filled face and wild hair appeared at ground level above the rim, and Joe held out a bloody rope-burned hand to help him over the edge.

The two of them stumbled back away from the rim and fell into a gaping depression in the dirt made by the upturned root pan of a spruce tree.

"Britney?" Joe asked, still trying to get his breath.

Stewie emphatically shook his head no.

"The son of a bitch practically cut her in half," Stewie spat, enraged. "Then he shot her again to keep her spinning." He reached over and grasped Joe's arm, his eyes wild. "Don't let her hang there and get blown apart."

Joe unsheathed his knife. Reaching through the vee of two gnarled roots, he sawed through the rope, letting Britney's body drop. The pounding of his heart in his ears drowned out the sound of her body hitting the surface of the Middle Fork of the Twelve Sleep River.

"Poor Britney," Stewie seethed. "That poor girl."

As a bullet slammed into the tree trunk, shaking pine needles and pinecones to the ground, Joe realized that cutting Britney loose had pinpointed where they were for Charlie Tibbs.

With his chin in the mud of the depression, Joe peered through the roots to the opposite rim. Thunder rolled across the mountains, reverberating through the canyon.

There was a stand of thick juniper on the other side of the canyon, bordered on both sides by spruce. The juniper would be the only place, Joe thought, for Tibbs to hide. The distance was 150 yards—out of range for Joe to aim accurately. Nevertheless, he fitted the thick barrel of his .357 Magnum through the roots and held the weapon with both hands. He sighted on the top of the juniper bushes, aiming high, hoping to lob bullets across the canyon and into the brush.

Joe fired five shots in rapid succession, squeezing the double action until it clicked twice on empty chambers. The concussions seemed especially loud, and they echoed back and forth against the canyon walls until they dissipated and all Joe heard was a ringing in his ears.

He rolled onto his back, ejected the spent cartridges, and reloaded, keeping one cylinder empty for the firing pin to rest.

"Did you hit him?" Stewie asked.

"I doubt it," Joe said. "But at least he knows we'll fight back."

"You bet we fucking will," Stewie said.

THEY LAY IN THE ROOT PAN depression for what seemed like an hour waiting for more rifle shots that never came. To Joe, the images and sensations of the last two days played back in his mind. He could not believe what he had seen and been through. His entire life had been reduced to one thing: *getting away.*

The first few raindrops smacked into pine boughs above their heads, sounding like gravel on a tarp. Thunder boomed. The sky was close and dark, the bank of thunder-heads pushing out what little blue remained. Any possibility of a rescue by air was now remote.

Joe lay on his back with his .357 Magnum on his chest. The first drops on his face made him flinch. He closed his eyes.

The rain came.

35

YOU KNOW, JOE, I learned a lot during that thirty days I spent crawling across the country after I got blown up by that cow," Stewie said as they walked. "This is bringing it all back—the hunger, the elements, the cloud of absolute terror hanging over us."

They were walking through the night in a steady but thin rain. Joe was soaked through, and rivulets of water streamed down from his hat when he cocked his head. The heavy clouds obscured the moon and stars, but there was enough ambient light for them to see by. Both Stewie and Joe lost their footing from time to time on rain-slick pine needles, and they had tripped over branches hidden in dark low cover. But they kept going; they kept bearing south. They stayed close together, within reach, so they wouldn't run the risk of losing each other in the darkness. Slowly, almost imperceptibly, Joe thought, they were descending the mountain toward the river valley. The terrain on this side of the mountains was easier to cover.

"So what does it bring back? one might ask if one were interested in the question posed," Stewie said sarcastically, since Joe hadn't spoken. "Well, I'll tell you. What it brings back are feelings and theories I got when I was huddled up under a tree for the night or crawling beside a road hoping to find a particular residence I knew about. You see, Joe, I knew where a certain gentleman—one of the biggest contributors to environmental causes in the country—had a second home. I had been there once for a meeting. It had a helipad so the gentleman could get back and forth from San Francisco when he needed to. Anyway, this gentleman owns thousands of acres and a multimillion-dollar gated palace on an old ranch homestead. And I crawled all the way to his land."

Stewie had conducted a series of monologues through the night as they walked. Joe didn't mind, because they kept his mind off of his hunger and exhaustion. He likened it to listening to talk radio while he drove down the highway.

"But you know what happened when I got to his land, Joe?"

"What?"

"The son-of-a-bitch had put up a ten-foot buffalo fence and electrified it. I made the mistake of touching the fence and it just about cooked my ass off. I crawled around it for a day and couldn't find a way in."

Stewie spat angrily. "Here is a guy who gives hundreds of thousands of dollars to groups like One Globe so we can fight the bastards who are ruining the earth, but he buys a huge old ranch in the mountains and puts up an electrified buffalo fence to keep everyone out."

"Isn't that his right?" Joe asked.

"It's his right, but there's nothing right about it," Stewie argued angrily. "It's so fucking elitist and hypocritical. Think about it: He builds a castle where a little ranch house once was, he closes roads that had been open to the local public for years, he puts up 'No Trespassing' signs, he builds a helipad, and he shuts the world out. Tell me how this guy is any better than an oil company that moves into an area and sinks wells? Or a lumber company that comes in and cuts the trees? *And he's one of us!*"

"That is something I've always wondered about," Joe said.

"I can see why," Stewie agreed. "Some of our own behave worse than the ranchers they bought out and, in many cases, the companies who lease and exploit the land. They fight development because they've already got theirs. This kind of selfishness destroys the credibility of the movement."

JOE REALIZED HE was now operating under the assumption that Charlie Tibbs was no longer following them. Joe no longer cared about the sloppiness of the trail they cut, and no longer felt it was necessary to do anything other than head straight south. He couldn't envision Tibbs attempting to cross the canyon the way they had. Leaving his horse and the bulk of his equipment would lessen Tibbs's advantage, and it was inconceivable that he would expose himself against the canyon walls the way Joe, Stewie, and Britney had done.

This assumption caused a lessening of immediate pressure, and Joe realized how hungry he was. His last meal had been breakfast on Saturday. It was now—*what day was it?*—Monday morning.

Joe wondered if it had been possible that one of his shots had actually hit Tibbs. He doubted it. At the range he was firing, the slugs would not have traveled in a true arc. They would have fluttered and tumbled end-over-end. But if Tibbs had been hit, Joe thought, the damage would have been devastating. Tumbling .357 Magnum slugs would make a big hole.

No, Joe decided, Tibbs wouldn't attempt to follow them. He would have turned back. On horseback, it was possible that Tibbs could make it back to his truck before Joe and Stewie hiked down the mountain. Racing around the mountain range to meet Joe and Stewie would be difficult, given the time, but possible. Considering what they'd already seen of Charlie Tibbs—his ruthlessness, his tracking abilities—Joe opted to push through the night.

JOE, TELL ME ABOUT MARYBETH," Stewie said after nearly an hour of silence. "Is she still a babe?"

Joe stopped, and Stewie nearly walked into him.

"I thought we agreed that Marybeth was not a topic of discussion," Joe stated.

"We did, but I was just thinking about how it was that you came to the cabin in the first place," Stewie said in a reasonable tone.

"Think all you want," Joe said, turning to walk again. "Just try to resist the urge to let everything you think about come out of your mouth."

A long roll of thunder rattled across the sky.

"Yup," Joe said, after a long pause. "She's still a babe."

THE RAIN STOPPED and the sky opened up to reveal brilliant swirls of stars that lit the ground and gave shape to the dripping trees and brush. The fluttering sound of wings shedding rain in the shadows ahead signaled to Joe that they had come upon a flock of spruce grouse. The birds were nested in for the night, perched on low branches and downed logs, backlit in romantic blue by the stars and moon.

Spruce grouse were not intelligent birds—they were known as "fool hens" by local hunters. Joe and Stewie exchanged glances and came to an immediate understanding: *Get those birds!*

Picking up a stout branch, Joe bounded into the flock and stepped into his swing like a hitter pulling a fastball, lopping the head off a grouse perched on a log. He stepped back and swung again, connecting with another grouse as it started to rise. Stewie killed one with a well-thrown stone. The rest of the flock, finally realizing the threat, rose clumsily through the trees. The three downed birds flopped and danced in the dark grass.

They found dry pinecones under brush to use for kindling, and started a fire with a plastic butane lighter Stewie had found in his trouser pocket. As the fire grew, they added short lengths of wood. Stewie built the fire up while Joe cleaned and skinned the birds. Their flesh was warm to the touch and their blood smelled musky.

Roasting the grouse on green sapling sticks, Joe found himself trembling. He could not remember ever being as hungry as he was now. The hardest part was waiting for the grouse to be cooked through.

"Are they done yet?" Stewie asked repeatedly. "Jesus, that smells good."

Eventually, Joe pricked one of the grouse breasts with his knife and the juice ran clear. It dripped into the fire and there was a sizzling flare-up.

"Okay," Joe said, his mouth watering so badly that he had

trouble speaking. He lifted the stick to Stewie, who hungrily grabbed the first bird.

The grouse breasts were tender white meat and they tasted faintly of pine nuts. Joe ate one grouse with his hands and split the remaining down the middle, giving half to Stewie. In the firelight, Joe could see Stewie's lips, fingers, and chin shine with grease. Joe sat back and finished off a drumstick.

"This," Stewie declared loudly, each word rising in volume, "is the best fucking meal I've ever had!"

Joe Pickett and Stewie Woods sat across from each other on the damp earth, the fire between them, and grinned goofily at each other like schoolboys who had just pulled off the greatest practical joke in the history of fifth grade.

Joe looked at his watch. It was three-thirty in the morning.

"Let's go," Joe said, scrambling to his feet. "We can't afford any more breaks."

"Even if we find more of those birds?" Stewie asked.

IF I HAD KNOWN THEN what I know now, I never would have structured One Globe the way I did," Stewie was saying. "I formed the organization the traditional way, with me as the president and a board of directors, with bylaws, newsletters, the whole works. I was told I needed to do it that way for effective fund-raising, and we did raise some good money. But I fucked up when I let the board talk me into moving our headquarters to Washington, D.C. I was best at monkey wrenching and public relations, as we all know. But the fund-raisers started taking over. That was the beginning of the end for me and they booted me out.

"One thing that discourages me about One Globe and most of the other environmental groups is that we need crises to raise funds. There've always got to be new demons and new bad guys in order to raise awareness. That means we can never be happy. Even when we win, which is often, we're never really happy about it. I'm inherently a happy guy, so this started to be a drag.

"And when we do win, we're out of business. Headlines are only headlines for a day, and then they're old news. So we constantly need new headlines. That gets pretty old, and it's hard not to get cynical when we start thinking of our cause as a fund-raising business.

"If I had it to do over again, and I still might, I'd organize differently. I'd do it like the Earth Liberation Front and the Animal Liberation Front, with no centralized hierarchy. They can operate cheaply without all the fund-raising crap. They're effective, too. Where do you think the Unabomber, Ted Kaczynski, got his Eco-Fucker Hit List? The future of our movement is in small, mobile, hard-to-find groups like Minnesota's Bolt Weevils, Hawaii's Menehune, Wisconsin's Seeds of Resistance, or Genetix Alert. If we were set up that way it would be harder for a group of bastards like the Stockman's Trust to find us."

"What do you think about that, Joe?" Stewie asked.

"About what?" Joe answered, although he had heard every word.

DEEP INTO THE NIGHT, Stewie declared that much of his life had been wasted. He turned morose, blaming his own egomania for the death of his wife of three days, Britney, and the others.

"When I was crawling across these mountains I had a thought that haunts me still," Stewie said, his voice dropping to a whisper. "I wondered if I would have done more good if I had spent all my time and energy raising money to buy land, then planting trees on it, and turning the whole shiteree over to the Nature Conservancy or some other white-bread outfit. At least then I'd have something to show for my life. What I've got now, is this . . ." He gestured toward the sky and the treetops, but what he meant was *nothing*. "That thought just won't go away."

He told Joe that his new mission in life, though, was to be an avenger. An *ugly* avenger.

"It's a bummer looking like a monster," Stewie lamented.

IT WAS AN HOUR BEFORE DAWN, the coldest time of the day. The ground was spongy from the rain and the long grass was bent double as raindrops still clung to the blade tips. Mist began to rise from the meadows.

Joe pushed through a thick stand of aspen and emerged in an opening. He stopped suddenly and Stewie walked into him.

"Sorry," Stewie apologized.

"Do you see it?" Joe asked, his attention focused on the sight before them. Fifteen miles away, on the dark flats below, a tiny yellow light crossed slowly from right to left.

"It's the highway," Joe said.

36

THE IRRIGATED HAYFIELD had recently undergone its first cutting of the season and it still smelled sharply of alfalfa. Mist rose from the still-wet ground and blunted the outline of the cottonwood trees in the dawn horizon. Joe and Stewie slogged through the wet field, their boots making slurping sounds in the mud.

Joe felt giddy with happiness. The barbed-wire fence they had crossed a half hour before was one of the most beautiful things he had ever seen. Stewie had reluctantly agreed. Struggling across the cut, flat hayfield seemed easy compared to the rugged country they had been through. Cottonwoods were a welcome sight, because cottonwoods grew where there was water. Therefore ranch houses and buildings were more likely located near groves of cottonwood. In the rural west of the Northern Rockies, cottonwood trees meant that people would be somewhere nearby. Stewie picked up a crumpled Coors beer can in the stubby grass and held it aloft.

"This," he declared, "is a sure sign of civilization."

Joe marveled at Stewie's strength, and wondered how it was possible that Stewie seemed stronger now than when they had begun their trek. Stewie also seemed strangely wistful, and content. He was no longer thundering on about environmental politics or revenge. Stewie Woods was certainly a puzzle, Joe thought.

They crossed another barbed-wire fence and entered a herd of black baldy cattle. The cows shuffled, then mindlessly parted so Joe and Stewie could walk through the herd. Joe noticed the brand on the cows—it was the Vee Bar U.

"Damn!" Joe spat. "Of all of the places to end up. This is Jim Finotta's ranch."

"Jim Finotta?"

"Long story," Joe said.

· · ·

As THEY APPROACHED the thick cottonwoods in the mist, the sharp angles of the gabled roof of the magnificent stone ranch house emerged, as well as the sprawling outbuildings. Between where they were in the mud and the ranch buildings were a series of corrals filled with milling cattle, separated by age and weight. They heard heifers bawling, splitting the silence of the early morning. They climbed over several wood-slat fences, which reminded Joe of how sore and bruised he was. The cattle let them pass. The smell of fresh manure was ripe in the air and hung low in the mist.

After the last fence, Joe walked across the gravel ranch yard toward Finotta's house. He skirted a massive steel barn building on his left. As they passed the windows of the building, Joe glanced in and saw a parked vehicle. He had already taken several steps past the window before what he had seen connected: it was a new model black Ford pickup.

Joe grabbed Stewie, pulling him against the building and out of sight of the ranch house. Silently, Joe pointed at the pickup through the window.

"That looks like the pickup Charlie Tibbs was driving," he whispered. Stewie's eyes widened and he mouthed the words, *"Holy fuck!"*

They backtracked along the building, going from door to door, finding each one locked. Around the corner was the big garage door. A set of muddy tire tracks crossed the cement threshold pad into the building. Joe leaned against the garage door and tried it. It raised a few inches.

"It's unlocked," Joe whispered to Stewie.

Stewie arched his eyebrows in a *let's see what's*

inside expression.

Joe paused, and looked back at Stewie, who was inches away.

"I don't know what to do now," Joe confessed.

"You mean, do we go in?"

Joe nodded yes.

"Or do we leave things be and go to the ranch house and ask to use the phone?"

Joe nodded again. This didn't make sense to him. Could this possibly be Charlie Tibbs's pickup truck?

He decided that he had to find out. Opening the door slowly to make the least possible noise, Joe raised it two feet. If Charlie Tibbs was in the truck or somewhere in the garage, Joe didn't want to startle him. He dropped to his belly and crawled inside the garage and Stewie followed.

Inside, the floor was cold, polished concrete. The room was large. They shut the garage door and stood up. A muddy tractor and the four-wheeler Joe had seen Finotta's ranch hand, Buster, drive were parked under a high ceiling. There was enough room in the building for several more vehicles. The corners of the big room were dark, and the only light came from three small, dirty windows along the outer wall. The black Ford was parked and partially hidden behind the tractor, its muddy tracks still moist on the floor. There was a dull glow in the dark coming from where the black Ford was.

Stewie tapped Joe's shoulder, and Joe turned. Stewie had located a light switch. Joe withdrew his revolver and nodded to Stewie, who flipped on the overhead lights.

To their left, along the wall, was ranch equipment: welding machines, drill presses, benches scattered with hand tools, rolls of fencing, and stacks of posts. There was also a set of wooden steps that led to a second level in the building and a closed door.

They approached the pickup from the back. It no longer had a horse trailer attached. A large metal toolbox was in the bed of the pickup. Joe noticed the mounts inside the bed for a telescope—or a mounted sniper's rifle. It was parked at an awkward angle and the front door was open, the dome light on. That was what had made the glow.

Inside the cab there was blood on the floor and seat, and spatters of it leading from the open pickup door toward the wooden stairs.

"He's hurt," Stewie said, amazed. "Maybe you hit him after all. Damn!"

Joe was astounded, both sickened and a little proud. While Joe inspected the inside of the cab, Stewie rooted through the toolbox in the back.

"Son of a bitch!" Stewie whispered. "Look at this."

Stewie held a brick-sized package of C4 explosive in one hand and a blue nylon harness in the other. "These are the tools you need to blow up a cow by remote control." Stewie whistled. "Isn't this just a hoot?"

"Do you see a phone anywhere?" Joe asked.

"Nope," Stewie answered, pointing toward the stairs and the closed door. "But if there is one, I bet it's up there. That looks like where the ranch hands live and where our friend Charlie Tibbs went.

"So the question is," Stewie continued, "Do we follow the blood or get the hell out of here?"

Joe paused a beat. He thought of Lizzie and all that he and Stewie had been through. "Follow the blood. That son-of-a-bitch is hurt."

"What if there are more bad guys up there?" Stewie asked.

Joe shook his head. "Finotta only has one ranch hand that I know of."

Stewie grinned maniacally.

JOE CREPT UP the wooden stairs—they were handmade of rough-cut two-by-fours but slick on the surface from years of use—as quietly as he could. Stewie was behind him. Joe's eyes were wide and his breath was shallow; he was scared of what might await him on the other side of the door. On the landing he paused with his rope-burned hand on the doorknob. It did not open quietly, but with a moan, and he pushed the door open and dropped into a shooter's stance with his revolver pointed ahead of him. A dark hallway led to the right. Nothing moved.

Removing his hat, Joe cautiously peered around the doorway. There were four other closed doors along the hallway, two on each side. At the end of the hallway, there was an L of gray light from a door that was slightly ajar. Staying low and trying to be ready to react if a door opened, Joe moved down the hallway toward the L of light. Stewie stayed back at the landing.

Joe stood with his back to the slightly open door, then swung around, kicking it open and stepping inside. There was a surge of red-hot panic in his throat when he realized that the man he had seen damaging the Mercedes near the mountain road—Charlie Tibbs—was splayed out on an old brass bed just a few feet away.

Charlie Tibbs lay on his back, fully clothed, on top of a

faded, worn quilt. He had not removed his boots; Joe could see their muddy soles cocked in a V before him. Charlie's head, still wearing his Stetson, was turned to the side on a pillow, and his face was the color of mottled cream. His mouth was slightly open, and Joe could see the tip of Tibbs's dry, maroon tongue. His brilliant blue eyes, once piercing, were open, but filmed over and dull. Above the breast pocket of Tibbs's shirt was a pronounced dent and in the middle of the dent was a black hole. A spider's web of blood had soaked through the fabric of his shirt and dried.

With his heart thumping, Joe cautiously lowered his weapon and stood next to Charlie Tibbs. Tibbs was a big man constructed of hard edges and sharp angles. Both of Tibbs's large hands were open beside his thighs, palms up. Joe held the back of his hand to Tibbs's mouth and nose: no breath. He touched his fingertips to Tibbs's neck: it was clammy, but not yet cold or stiff. Charlie Tibbs had died within the hour.

Joe reached down and turned Tibbs over slightly. The quilt beneath him was soaked through with dark blood from his back, where the bullet had exited. The exit wound was ragged and massive. The smell of blood in the room was overwhelming, and it reminded Joe of the stench of the badly hit or badly dressed big game carcasses he saw during hunting season. Joe thought it astounding that Tibbs had been able to ride back to his truck, unhitch the horse trailer, and drive all the way to the Finotta ranch to die.

What a lucky shot, Joe thought.

"You shot my horse, you son-of-a-bitch," Joe whispered. "If you ever see her where you both are now, I hope she kicks the hell out of you."

Then to Stewie out in the hallway: "He's here and he's dead!"

"Charlie Tibbs?"

"The same," Joe said, sliding his revolver into his holster. Suddenly, Joe felt very weak and sick to his stomach. He stared at Tibbs's face, trying to find something in it that indicated thoughtfulness, or gentleness, or humility. Something redeeming. But Joe could only see a face set by years of bitter resolve.

"Okay," Stewie said from the doorway after studying the scene, "Charlie Tibbs is dead. But why is he here?"

Joe looked up. He had no idea, although one was forming.

JOE REMEMBERED PASSING under a telephone in the dark hallway. It was an old-fashioned, wall-mounted rotary-dial telephone, probably installed there years before, for the use of ranch hands, who were no longer needed on Finotta's hobby ranch.

As he and Stewie had descended the mountain, Joe had practiced over and over the first words he would say to Marybeth. He would tell her how much he loved her, how much he missed her, how much he loved their girls. How he would never again approach a suspect's location without proper backup. Joe didn't even care if Stewie was standing next to him to overhear; his emotions were heartfelt and boiling within him.

He picked up the receiver and was about to dial when he realized there were voices on the line. It was a party line, presumably connected to the ranch house.

"Who is that?" someone asked. "Did somebody just pick

up a phone?"

"I didn't hear it," another voice said.

"I heard a click," another, deeper voice intoned.

"Don't worry, gentlemen." Joe recognized this voice as belonging to Jim Finotta. It was louder and more clear than the others, due to Finotta's proximity. "I'm the only one here, so it's not on my end. These lines are old."

No doubt Finotta had long forgotten about the unused phone in the outbuilding.

Stewie was now leaning against Joe, his face in Joe's face so they could both hear. Joe cupped his hand over the mouthpiece and listened. It was a conference call and there were at least six men on the line. There was a meeting going on, and Jim Finotta seemed to be presiding. One of the voices called Finotta "chairman."

"You know what this is?" Stewie hissed, his eyes bulging, "You know *what this is?*"

Joe shot Stewie a cautionary glance and gripped the mouthpiece harder so they wouldn't be heard.

"This," Stewie said through clenched teeth, "is an emergency meeting of the *Stockman's Trust!*"

THE DISCUSSION WAS rushed at times, and participants talked over one another. The only voice Joe could clearly discern was Jim Finotta's, who was five hundred feet away in the ranch house.

What Joe heard was fascinating, disturbing, and disgusting. He wished he had his small pocket tape recorder with him so he could tape the conversation and use it later as evidence at the murder trial.

Finotta: "He's dead in my bunkhouse right now. I don't

know what in the hell to do with him. Does anyone want him?"

Laughter.

Gruff voice: "What happened to John Coble? Did he say?"

Finotta: "He said Coble turned tail and tried to inform Stewie Woods. Charlie caught him at the cabin and put him down. Coble's remains burned up in the cabin when Charlie torched it."

Gruff voice: "Thank God for that."

Fast voice: "I'm surprised at Coble. I thought he was more solid than that."

Finotta: "You just never know what a guy is going to do under pressure. But we have another matter at hand."

Texas twang: "Soooo, you have a body and you don't know what to do with it. Do you have any hogs, Jim? They'll eat just about anything."

Finotta: "No, this is a cattle ranch."

New voice: "Jim, you've got to come clean with us about this game warden deal. It really disturbs me that a game warden somehow got involved. He had absolutely nothing to do with our effort."

Gruff voice: "I sure as hell agree with that."

Finotta: "Charlie Tibbs said the game warden was at the cabin when he got there. He called me about it and explained the situation, and I told him to proceed. It was just a bad coincidence that the game warden was in the middle of everything when Charlie took action. Besides, I knew the guy. He's the local game warden. Name is Pickett, Joe Pickett. He's been a pain in my side recently."

Silence.

New voice: "I still think Charlie went way over the line. You should have let us know about this, Jim."

Gruff voice: "Before now, we mean. Now it's too late."

New voice: "That's why we have an executive board—to agree on these things. No one has the authority to just willy-nilly decide who lives and who dies. Not even you. That's why we made that list in the first place—to clearly define all of the targets."

Finotta: "Can't we discuss this later? I've got Charlie Tibbs in my bunkhouse and we don't know where in the hell Stewie Woods and the game warden are."

Gruff voice: "Probably dead of exposure. You say the local sheriff sent out a helicopter to look for them?"

Finotta: "Yes, but the weather got bad and the helicopter was grounded. But the pilot and spotter never saw anybody."

Gruff voice: "Yup, those two saps are worm food by now."

Texas twang: "But Charlie got that lawyer and that wolf woman, that's what I'm hearing?"

Finotta: "That's what Charlie said."

Gruff voice: "So he cleared the entire list, huh?"

Texas twang: "That Charlie was something, wasn't he?"

Joe despised these people. He held the phone away from him, stunned. Stewie had been so close as they listened that Joe felt uncomfortable. Stewie had been practically on top of him, pressing closer to hear. They both smelled bad after their time in the mountains, but in Joe's opinion, Stewie smelled worse. Joe felt a tug on his belt. Then Stewie suddenly wrenched the telephone from Joe's hand, and held the receiver to his mouth.

"You were wondering about Stewie Woods?" Stewie cut in. "Guess what? *It's your lucky day, you assholes!*"

"Who the hell was *that,* Jim?" Joe heard the Gruff Voice say before Stewie slammed down the phone.

When Joe reached to retrieve the telephone, Stewie pointed something so close to Joe's eyes that Joe couldn't focus on what it was.

The blast from his own canister of pepper spray hit Joe full in the face and eyes and he went down as if his feet had been kicked out from under him.

"Sorry, buddy," he heard from somewhere above him. Joe was thrashing, his arms and legs jerking involuntarily, his lungs burning. He tried to speak but his voice only made a hoarse, bleating sound he couldn't recognize. A jet turbine roared in his ears. His head was on fire and his eyes felt like they were being burned from their sockets by a blowtorch. He was literally paralyzed, and excruciatingly painful muscle spasms shot through his body. Coughing and gasping for breath, he felt himself being pulled across the floor. His hands were wrenched together. Through the howl of the jet engine in his ears, he heard the phone being ripped from the wall and felt the phone cord looping around his wrists and being knotted tightly. Then he heard the unsnapping of his holster.

37

IT TOOK TWENTY MINUTES for Joe Pickett to recover enough from the pepper spray to stand up. His eyes and throat still burned, and it seemed as though most of the liquid in his body had drained out of him in bitter streams through his nose, mouth, and eyes. He leaned against the wall in the hallway, next to the telephone that Stewie had ripped from the wall as he left, and tried to shake the fog from his head.

Slowly at first, he regained control of his legs and moved down the hall, clomping unsteadily like Frankenstein's monster. He kept his left shoulder against the plaster for balance until he reached the door to the stairway. He descended the stairs one deliberate step at a time and held the rail with both tied hands. The building was empty; the black Ford truck still parked with both doors—and the toolbox—open.

Joe shouldered the overhead door open and stood outside, gasping damp fresh air and blinking back tears from the sting of the pepper spray. He turned toward the ranch house, where he presumed Stewie Woods had gone.

The front gate was open and so was the massive front door. Joe entered, stopped, tried to see in the gloom. On the floor was the writhing body of Buster the ranch hand. Buster's hands were covering his face, and he was rolling from side to side, whimpering. Pepper spray, Joe thought. Probably a shot of it from Stewie on the way in and a second shot of it a few minutes ago, judging by the whiff of the spray still hanging in the air.

"If I were a snake I could have *bitten you*." Her voice startled Joe, as it had the first time. She was in her chair, its back pushed up against the wall. Her face was cocked to the side and thrust forward at Joe, twisted as if she were confronting him.

"Did a crazy-looking man just come in here?" Joe asked, his voice still thick with mucus.

Ginger Finotta raised her thin arm, pointing a gnarled finger past Joe's ear.

"They went outside together," she said, her voice high and grating. "Tom Horn is in our bunkhouse!"

Joe stopped. *Tom Horn?*

"You mean Charlie Tibbs."

"He's in our bunkhouse!" she repeated. "Someone shot him!"

Joe tried to focus on her face, but couldn't. Her face swam in his vision. "That was me," Joe coughed. "I shot him."

He wished he could see her face to gauge her reaction. But he heard it.

"Bravo, young man," she squawked. "Hanging a man like Tom Horn would have been a waste of good rope."

BACK IN THE RANCH yard, Joe heard a shout from a distance.

"Hey Joe!" It was Stewie. Joe turned toward the voice. It came from beyond the corrals, over the tops of milling cattle. "I'm glad you're okay, buddy!"

Joe walked toward the voice. His vision was still blurry. The cord bit into his wrists, but he didn't want to take the time to try and unknot it. As he climbed the first fence he saw Stewie standing in the pasture beyond the corrals. Stewie and a lone cow.

"Don't come any closer, Joe!" Stewie cautioned.

Joe ignored him, and pushed his way through the cattle. When he climbed the back fence he stopped, focused, and felt his eyes widen and his jaw drop.

At first, he thought that Jim Finotta was slumped over the back of the cow in the pasture next to Stewie. Then he realized that Finotta was strapped on, his hands tied under the

275

cow's belly, with another rope around the hips of his stretch Wranglers, securing him to the cow. Finotta's face was pressed against the shoulders of the animal, looking out at Joe. Blue nylon webbing, loaded with full charges of C4 explosive from the toolbox in the black Ford, was lashed between Finotta and the cow. A single, spring-mounted antenna bobbed from one of the charges.

Stewie stood near the animal's haunches holding a remote-control transmitter in one hand and Joe's .357 Magnum in the other.

"Don't come any closer, or the lawyer gets it!" Stewie hollered cheerfully. Then Stewie's voice took on a more determined tone. "I'm serious, Joe. I'm sorry I sprayed you with pepper spray back there, but I knew you wouldn't help me do what I needed to do."

"Oh, Stewie," Joe croaked.

"We were just having a chat," Stewie explained. "Mister Jim was about to tell me the names of the executive board of the Stockman's Trust, and why they voted to wipe out me and so many of my colleagues."

Joe swung his other leg over the fence and now sat on top of it. The scene in the pasture was beyond comprehension. Stewie had maced Joe, gathered up the nylon webbing and the explosives from the truck, selected a cow from the corral, charged the house, maced Buster, marched Finotta at gunpoint to the pasture, and tied him and the explosives to the cow.

"Please help me," Finotta called to Joe. "You are an officer of the law. Despite our earlier disagreements, you have a duty to protect me. Please . . . I'm friends with the governor . . . I can be of great influence on your behalf."

Stewie snorted. "Up until that last bit, he was kind of convincing." Stewie stepped forward so Finotta could see him, then raised the transmitter and took several steps backward. Finotta shrieked and buried his face in the hide of the cow. The cow continued to graze, and Stewie lowered the remote control, and winked at Joe.

"You've given him a scare," Joe said, his voice as steady and flat as he could make it, given the circumstances and his condition. "You've scared the hell out of him. Now let's untie him and go have some lunch. Think about it, Stewie: Does Finotta seem like the kind of guy who wouldn't rat out his buddies in a plea bargain? We'll find out who the Stockman's Trust is and we'll put them all into prison. If Finotta ordered the killings, he may get the death sentence."

Stewie listened, thought about it while he rubbed his chin and studied Finotta, then laughed.

"Like I believe that a great lawyer and butt-buddy with the governor will ever see the inside of a prison in this state," Stewie said sarcastically.

Then Stewie turned to Finotta, waving the remote control in front of him like a wand. "Let me remind you, Jim Finotta, of some names," he said. "These names are only names on a list to you. But to me they are real people—friends, lovers, colleagues."

"Annabel Bellotti. Hayden Powell. Peter Sollito." Stewie shouted each name. And with each, his face got redder, and he got angrier. "Emily Betts. Tod Marchand. Britney Earthshare. Even John Coble and Charlie Tibbs!"

Stewie was so enraged that Joe, even from a distance, could see Stewie shaking.

"You started the first fucking range war of the twenty-first century!" Stewie bellowed. "You waged that war in a vicious, cowardly way! And now you're going to find out what it is like to be on the receiving end!"

Stewie backed away further from Finotta and the cow. There was now about one hundred feet between them. He again raised the remote control.

"The headlines about the environmental activist getting blown up were good ones, Jim. I bet they made you chuckle. But the headlines about the president of the Stockman's Trust getting blown up *by his own cow* are *even better!*"

IN HIS PERIPHERAL VISION, Joe saw a stream of vehicles with flashing lights emerge from the cottonwoods on the ranch road from the highway. Joe turned. Sheriff Barnum's Blazer was leading two other sheriff's trucks. Trey Crump's green Game and Fish pickup, lights flashing, followed. The vehicles drove straight across the ranch yard and braked at the first fence. Doors opened and officers poured out with rifles and shotguns. Joe saw Barnum, Trey Crump, Deputy McLanahan, and Robey Hersig. Marybeth jumped down from the passenger door of Trey Crump's pickup. Joe didn't recognize the armed deputies who spread out along the corral fence.

"Is that you, Mary?" Stewie called, working his way behind the cow in the distance so that Finotta and the cow were between him and the deputies. Joe heard the racketing pumps of the shotguns and the bolts being thrown on the rifles.

"It's me, Stewie," Marybeth answered. Her voice was strong. "Please don't hurt anyone, and don't hurt yourself."

Joe felt a strange pang hearing the familiarity with which she addressed Stewie and he addressed her. For a moment he was buffeted with several emotions; jealousy, confusion, anger, and deep sadness.

Mary?

"Joe," she cried, "you need to get back here with me."

"You are still a beauty, Mary," Stewie said, both admiring and wistful. "Joe is a lucky man. And Mary—Joe Pickett is a good man. That's a very rare thing out in this cow pasture."

Finotta swung his face toward the line of officers behind the corral fences. "Barnum, you need to take him out! *Now!*"

Joe heard Barnum hiss at his deputies not to fire.

Deputy McLanahan, farthest away from Barnum in the line, used the post of the fence for a rest, fitted the top half of Stewie Woods into the notch of his rear open sight, and squeezed the trigger of his rifle. The high crack of the shot snapped through the air.

Stewie jerked and sat back heavily in the wet grass. Marybeth screamed, and Barnum let loose a firecracker string of curses toward McLanahan.

Jim Finotta raised his head, saw Stewie sitting on the ground with the remote control and revolver in his lap, and yelled, "Hit him again! He's still moving! *Take him out!*"

Joe slipped down from the fence into the pasture and took a few tentative steps. He locked eyes with Stewie across the field. Pain gripped Stewie's face, making the edges of his mouth tug up in an inappropriate smile. *How alone he is,* Joe thought, feeling gut-wrenching pity. *Practically everyone he cares about is gone.* Joe thought about rushing Stewie and wrenching the transmitter away, but the look in Stewie's eyes warned him not to. With a wistful shrug, Stewie pushed the button on his transmitter.

The force of the explosion hurled Joe back toward the corrals, where he smashed full force against the fence.

Through slitted eyes and with the dead silence of instant deafness, Joe watched as pieces of Jim Finotta, the cow, Stewie Woods, and bromegrass turf rained from the sky for what seemed like hours.

38

THE DREAMS JOE HAD in the hospital were not good dreams. In one, they were once again climbing out of Savage Run Canyon with Charlie Tibbs and his long-range rifle on the opposite rim. Only, this time, Stewie was the target. One shot ripped Stewie's left arm off at the socket, but he kept climbing one-handed. Stewie kept making jokes, saying he was happy he still had his right hand because without that he would have no dates anymore. Joe was scrambling to the top, ahead of Stewie, his muscles shrieking, contracting, in terrible pain. Another shot hit Stewie in the thigh, breaking the bone, leaving his right leg useless. A third hit Stewie square in the back and exited out the front, his entrails now blooming from a hole in his stomach like a sea anemone. But he just kept climbing behind Joe, joking that he no longer had the guts for this sort of thing.

JOE'S PROBLEM WAS that a large piece of the cow—either the head or a meaty front shoulder—had hit him hard enough in the chest to crack his sternum and break his collarbone. He couldn't remember actually being hit. Marybeth told him that when she had reached him near the fence, he had been vomiting blood. The EMTs had suspected a much more serious injury at first as well, because he was spattered by gouts of blood and it was difficult to discern if the source was internal or external. Marybeth rode with him in the Twelve Sleep County ambulance, holding his hand, wiping his face clean.

Although neither injury required a cast, his doctor decided to keep him for rest and observation at Twelve Sleep County Hospital for three days. He had lost fifteen pounds since Sunday, and was dehydrated enough to require an IV.

Outside the hospital window, cottonwood leaves rattled in the summer wind. Daylight was lengthening. Joe could smell and feel a long summer coming.

WHILE HE WAS IN THE HOSPITAL, Joe was interviewed by the Wyoming Department of Criminal Investigation (DCI), the FBI, the Game and Fish Department, and an officer from the Washington, D.C., Police Department who was in charge of the investigation into the death of Rep. Peter Sollito. He told them all the same story, the truth. When they asked him questions about the motivation behind the Stockman's Trust or Stewie Woods, Joe said he wasn't the person to ask and that he wouldn't speculate. Trey Crump came and Joe went into great detail about the long march through the Bighorns, about Savage Run. In turn, Joe asked about the events of the day when Trey Crump discovered his disabled pickup and the black Ford.

NEWS OF THE STOCKMAN'S TRUST and what they had done

was strangely muted. It was a scandal few really cared about, because it was too murky and too complicated to grasp. No one knew, or was willing to admit, who the executive board members were. Inquiries went nowhere, because a search of Finotta's home and office revealed no list of membership, no past meeting minutes, no record of incorporation. A run of Finotta's phone records showed that all of the participants in the conference call had apparently called him, so there were no clues in Finotta's outgoing calls. The Stockman's Trust, apparently, had long ago reorganized without a centralized hierarchy—a perfect model of the nonstructural organization Stewie had wanted to emulate. Although he tried, Joe was unable to positively identify the voices that were on the telephone, even when the FBI asked him to listen to tapes of various nationwide wiretaps. As far as the various law enforcement agencies were concerned, Jim Finotta was the president of the board of executives and Jim Finotta had been blown to vapor by an exploding cow. Further investigation, as far as Joe knew, would go nowhere.

Just as the Stockman's Trust had gone into dormancy after the hanging of Tom Horn at the turn of the last century, the new Stockman's Trust had seemed to recede into silence once again, at the turn of this century. The Stockman's Trust had arisen, won their brief war, and had vanished.

SHERIFF BARNUM HAD come, hat in hand, to see Joe the day before he was released. They exchanged pleasantries while Joe eyed the sheriff warily. Barnum stared at the tops of his own boots and mumbled that it was unfortunate he had been out of town when Joe rode up to the cabin.

"According to Trey Crump, you were with him the day he found my pickup and the burned-up cabin," Joe said gently. Barnum nodded, looking up above the dark bags under his eyes.

"You volunteered to stay there while Trey circled around the mountain in the helicopter."

Barnum nodded again.

"So how did Charlie Tibbs ride back, get in his truck, unhook his horse trailer, and drive to Jim Finotta's place without you seeing him?"

Joe watched Barnum think, watched the tiny veins in his temples pulse. Barnum had lowered his eyes again, and stood still. Joe could hear Barnum's nicotine-encased lungs weakly suck breath in and push it back out.

"You saw Charlie Tibbs ride back out of the mountains, didn't you?" Joe asked, nearly whispering. "He was badly wounded, but you saw him coming back toward his truck, didn't you? And when you called Jim Finotta, you both agreed that you ought to get away fast, so you would have no contact with Tibbs and plenty of deniability."

Barnum coughed, looked around the room at everything except Joe.

"I can't prove it, and you know that," Joe said. "Just like I can't prove you're a member of the Stockman's Trust, unless you admit it to me."

Barnum shuffled his boots on the hard linoleum floor, then briefly raised his eyes to Joe. Joe detected an almost imperceptible quiver of Barnum's lower lip. Then the sheriff clamped on his hat, turned, and reached for the knob on the door.

"Sheriff?" Joe said from the bed. "I know now that you're a man who will look the other way."

Joe lowered his voice and spoke calmly, but with a hint of malice: "Someday, we need to have a conversation."

Barnum hesitated, his back to Joe, then let himself out of the room.

THE BIGGEST FOCUS of attention was on Stewie Woods. Old-line environmental activists now had themselves a mythic, noble, butt-kicking martyr. One Globe exceeded all of its records for fund-raising. A photo of Stewie's pre-explosion face was now used on their stationery, envelopes, business cards, website, and on the cover of their magazine. He was being touted as the "Environmental Movement's Ché Guevara." A move was afoot to rename Savage Run the "Stewie Woods/Savage Run National Wilderness Area." It was a losing effort, using Stewie's name, but it gave the group a new cause to rally around. Politicians and others who objected were called "environmental racists" and targeted for future vitriol. Joe smiled bitterly when he read about it, knowing that in his last days on earth, Stewie considered himself an outcast from the organization he had founded, promoted, and lived for. Now One Globe had taken Stewie back. He was good for business.

39

AT HOME, JOE placed the battered Cheyenne doll on top of the bookcase. Both April and Lucy said they wanted to play with it, and Joe let them after they promised to be gentle. But they preferred their Barbies, choosing nice clothes, long hair, and massive breasts over featureless leather, and

Joe later found the doll on the floor and put it back on the bookcase.

After a fried chicken dinner, Joe's welcome-home request, he and Marybeth cleared the dishes and the girls went out to play.

Marybeth told Joe that she had received another call from a reporter looking for a comment. According to the reporter, the rumor was floating through the environmental community that Stewie's body had not been positively identified. Joe scoffed, saying that the damage had been so great that it was unlikely that Stewie, Finotta, or the cow could have been positively identified. So it was a good thing there was no need for medical testing, since seven law enforcement officers and Marybeth had witnessed the entire incident.

"I couldn't tell the reporter with any assurance that I actually saw Stewie's body," Marybeth said. "There was so much smoke and stuff falling from the sky that we all covered our heads and eyes. When we finally recovered from the shock of the explosion, you were the only person I looked for."

Joe liked hearing that. Marybeth asked if he still felt jealous. Joe said yes, a little. But he said that it was hard not to like Stewie. And he told her that he had punched him in the nose.

"Somehow, I like it better that no one is sure about Stewie," Marybeth said. "This is what he would have wanted. It's right up his alley."

Joe smiled.

SITTING ON A BALE of hay in the last light of the evening,

Joe watched Marybeth work Toby in the round pen. Sheridan sat beside him, reading a Harry Potter book. Lucy and April played in the backyard. It was a perfect, still, warm summer evening. Joe wished he could drink it in. Instead, he settled for a tumbler of bourbon and water.

"Are we going to get another horse?" Sheridan asked, while Toby's hooves thundered in the soft dirt.

"Eventually," Joe said. He still didn't like thinking or talking about Lizzie.

"Dad, I'm trying to figure out what happened between the environmentalists and the ranchers, how it got so bad."

"First, Sheridan, it isn't '*the ranchers.*' Most ranchers take their role as stewards of the land seriously. This was a particular group of people who went too far."

"But how did it happen?"

"I'm not sure what it was that set it off," Joe said, putting the drink down. "I think it had been building for the last ten years, maybe more. On this end of the scale," Joe started to gesture with his hands, felt a sharp pain from his right arm, which was in a sling, and settled for gesturing with his left hand, "you've got the environmental terrorists, the most extreme of the extreme. Stewie Woods was one of those guys, at least at first.

"Over here," Joe straightened his fingers from the fold of the sling in lieu of sweeping with his arm, "you've got the other end of the scale, which is the Stockman's Trust group of hard-core, violent men. What this war did was cut back just a little on both sides of the scale."

"Where do we fit on the scale?"

Joe chuckled. "Somewhere near the middle. Like most folks."

"I hope it doesn't happen again."

Joe nodded. "Me, too. But I'm not as optimistic as I'd like to be. This wasn't the first range war. There will be others, I'm afraid."

Sheridan turned and looked hard at him. They had had a conversation like this before.

"I love you, Dad," she said. "I'm glad you're back."

Joe felt his face flush. He leaned forward and buried his head in her hair. "I love you too, honey. And it's good to be back."

SLICKED OUT AND SWEATING, Toby pounded the packed earth in the round pen. Marybeth turned him and asked him to lope in the other direction. She was working him hard, very hard. As if she were exorcising something out of him. Or herself. Joe was intrigued by the fact that he was still learning about the woman who was his wife.

Joe's eyes wandered away from the horse, over the corral to the humpbacked Bighorn Mountains. There was no conceivable way that Stewie could have survived the explosion. No possible way.

No possible way.

Center Point Publishing
600 Brooks Road • PO Box 1
Thorndike ME 04986-0001 USA

(207) 568-3717

US & Canada:
1 800 929-9108

HICKMANS